LAURENCE HALLEY

ABIDING CITY

Let us go forth therefore unto him
without the camp, bearing his reproach.
For here have we no abiding city,
but we seek one to come.

St Paul: Epistle to the Hebrews
Chapter 13 vv 13 and 14

(The second verse was the text of St Thomas Becket's
last sermon at Canterbury: 22 December 1170)

THE BODLEY HEAD
LONDON

For Elaine Markson
who kept the faith when the author had none

British Library Cataloguing
in Publication Data
Halley, Laurence
Abiding city.
I. Title
823'.914[F]   PR6058.A534
ISBN 0-370-30730-5

© Laurence Halley 1986
Printed in Great Britain for
The Bodley Head Ltd
30 Bedford Square, London WC1B 3RP
by Redwood Burn Limited, Trowbridge, Wiltshire
First published 1986

- INTROIT -

All was in order. Everything had been prepared. Nothing, it seemed, could go wrong. This was Canterbury, mother church of the Anglican communion, bred to ceremony over fourteen hundred years.

The first note, struck low in the register, throbbed almost inaudibly. Then, swelling like distant thunder, it caused the multicoloured glass to quake: in the great west window, a glowing Adam delving the earth, grieving for the lost Paradise; a throned Methuselah in the south-west transept; Noah leaning from his Ark to welcome the returning dove; Jonah disgorged by the whale; the pillar of salt and the dream of the Magi. The English kings: the innocent Edward the Confessor; the guilty Edward the Fourth, kneeling before Elizabeth Woodville, his Queen, and their brood of girls. The three knights banging at the cathedral door, about to create the English martyr so long buried in this place.

The note thus hung on the air for a moment before the choristers took up the antiphon, a Jacobean setting of the ancient Latin in honour of both the guest and the host.

> 'Asperges me, domine, hyssopo et mundabor:
> Lavabis me et super nivem dealabor. . . .'

The congregation rose the whole length of the cathedral to the scraping of a thousand chairs. The procession was beginning to enter through the western doors. Cameras, perched high in the temporary scaffolding, recorded the order: the Canons Residentiary in Anglican surplice and cassock; the red-gowned bearer of the wand of office; a coped figure bearing the reversed crucifix.

5

The Pope: successor to Peter, the Fisher of Men; Servant of the Servants of God; Pontifex Maximus; Bishop of Rome. Boniface X, supported by the Archbishop of Canterbury and the Cardinal from Westminster, all three enmitred, all three carrying gold croziers sparking under the lights.

The Dean displaying a ruffled neckband under his cloak. The Nuncio resplendent in cardinal red. The two domestic chaplains, pious-eyed, in lawn.

The Pontiff's vast age made the pace slow but easy. These were men used to the encumbrance of chasuble and cope; the bonds of the suffering Christ around the waist, the collar and the forearm; his image lying flat against the pectoral bone.

The cameras measured their progress down Yvele's honey-gold nave. Past the heavy pillars of the narthex; the Laudian font; the memorial to Gibbons, composer of the antiphon still swelling through the vault; the gilded pulpit. The shallow steps and then the steep steps under Bell Harry.

At the screen, the Archbishop and the Cardinal stood aside. The Pope crossed to the left and fell to his knees, eyes squinched in prayer. The cameras coming in at right angles adjusted to take in the longer focus. In the well to the side of the kneeling profile was the place of martyrdom and, on the wall above, the inscription:

Thomas Becket
Archbishop † Saint † Martyr
Died Here
Tuesday † 29th December
1170

The cameras in the triforium took up the story when the procession debouched between the choir stalls on the inner side of the screen. As if rehearsed, the Pope emerged when the climax was reached:

'Gloria Patri, et Filii, et Spiritu Sancti
Sicut erat in principio et nunc et semper
Et in saecula saeculorum.'

He reached the two shallow steps between the lectern and the throne as the choristers rallied round the major chord of the Amen. He climbed the steep carpeted steps with painful effort and finally the two steps to the altar. He turned to face the immense multi-plumed congregation below him in the presbytery and the choir. He intoned:

> *'Show us O Lord thy mercy.'*

The vast crowd joined the choristers in the response:

> *'And grant us thy salvation.'*

It was time to begin.

And yet it was at this moment that a mischievous cameraman essaying some crowd effects took a fancy to picking out close-ups of the group gathered to the left of the altar in front of the Bourchier tomb. In due course he alighted upon Benton in his morning dress, every inch the tall tight-jawed Englishman of legend, the cross of the Victorian Order suspended one inch below the knot of his tie as prescribed in the regulations.

For an instant, the millions looked on the ruins of Benton, his lean head neatly brushed, his fingernails impeccably clipped. And his mind, had they known it, racing.

For Benton had just spotted Welch in the crowd over by the throne. He had half expected it. It was like fingering a piece of wood and coming across a knot, a burr, the head of a nail. Over the rapt heads he had caught the glitter of fanatic eyes, a clenched white face. A giant of a man in surplice over cassock, a tower of protest.

Welch, though Benton did not know the name.

- GRAND STAIRCASE -

'Blow me,' Willett said, 'it's Benton. What on earth is he doing there? I thought this was a Canterbury do. No?'

'He had to be invited,' explained the Assistant, his eyes intent upon the screen. 'Lambeth were on to him twenty-four hours a day before Christmas, it seems. They were having a devil of a job with the protocol. They didn't like it, but they simply had to call for reinforcements from Church House, which means our friend Benton. He may be an old stick, but there's no one in the business who knows more about who-goes-where on these occasions. So Lambeth swallowed its pride and called him in.'

'Good God, old Gareth Benton. Who'd have thunk it? Haven't seen him for ages.' Willett, Head of News Department, had gathered his people round the television set. It was the empty week between Christmas and the New Year, more than usually slack this year when all eyes were on the unfolding drama at Canterbury. Even the door of No. 10 opposite had remained obstinately shut all morning, with none of the usual comings and goings.

'You've got to admit he looks the part,' Willett said. 'Gareth's everyone's idea of Protocol. He could make a fortune modelling aftershave.' Willett wore baggy suits, rarely pressed, and flamboyant ties. He had a mane of red hair and a loose tongue. Gossip was his life, the source of his popularity. He was ideal for the job. 'He was pretty able, I remember, when we were in Berlin together. A good officer. Much senior to me, of course.'

8

'A proper sadist,' a young desk officer volunteered. 'Or so they say.'

'No, not any more,' the Assistant Head objected. 'I see him around Westminster now and again. He's gone very old-womanish. You can practically hear the stays creak.'

Willett noticed the others were growing restive as the scene shifted again to the High Altar.

'Count your blessings,' he concluded. 'You'll never have to work under him. Left here ages ago when he realized there was no future for him. And gossip has it he's retiring from Church House in the summer. To Marrakesh, it seems.'

*

'Looking forward to retirement, Gareth? Found somewhere decent to live?'

His contemporary, Charles Napier, on the Grand Staircase in the week before Christmas, a week Benton had spent almost entirely in the Foreign Office tying up Church and State protocol. They had met under the magnificent chandeliers, their voices automatically modulating to the cavernous echo above the gesticulating statuary. Napier was coming down, evidently from the Private Office, antechamber to the Foreign Secretary's room. He was half smiling to himself, the smile of the secretly gratified. Benton felt the familiar stab of pain.

'I still have some time to go,' he replied stiffly. 'But yes, I have found a little place. Marrakesh, actually.'

'Ah,' Napier said. 'Lucky you. You can really put the shutters up in a place like Marrakesh. I wish I were in your shoes, lucky dog.'

No you don't, Benton thought, oh, no you don't. And what did he mean by dog? He tried to quell the rictus of envy clutching his lower jaw. But Napier was a friend, a contemporary, someone with whom it was not proper to quarrel. He snatched at a subject.

'How's Anne?'

'Not precisely complaining. No one would believe her if she did. All those flattering Italians smarming about.'

Benton suppressed visions of golden hair, the delicious tilt of nostrils, a swaying waist, the sleek assurance bred of a lifetime of admirers.

9

'The money's rather tight, though. Hard to keep up.'

'And the Villa? As beautiful as ever?'

'We try to keep it so, especially the garden. Frightfully expensive, though, with the servants. We've had a little flat made upstairs for the times when there are just the two of us. Hardly ever happens, of course, in Rome. But it helps with the bills, and it gives Anne a chance to be the little hausfrau. Good training for retirement, what?'

Despite himself, Napier was glancing from time to time up to the great polished door at the head of the stairs.

'Anyway,' he said, 'retirement's not for us, I think, not for a while yet. There seems to be something brewing.'

'Congratulations.'

'It's not certain yet. But thank you anyway, Gareth. It's time for a change. Four years is long enough, even for Rome.'

There was an awkward pause as the small gush of human sympathy dried up between them. Napier, fat little Napier, with his knighthood and the Villa Bolkonsky, soon to be exchanged for the Faubourg or Massachusetts Avenue. Fat little Napier with his gleaming glasses and his tranquil confidence and his radiant Anne only now beginning to fade. Really, there was nothing else to say.

'Well, look after yourself, Gareth.'

'Thank you.'

'And good luck for your retirement, lucky fellow.'

'Yes. Well. Good luck to you too. Love to Anne.'

'I'll tell her I've seen you. She'll be pleased.'

They did not shake hands. Benton hurried up the staircase, twitching. Damn, damn, damn, he thought. Damn. In the corridor between the high doors a young secretary watched him pass, wondering. She did not know who he was, of course, and was not aware of his fearsome reputation. But even so she was shaken by the cold blaze in his eyes as they passed over her, apparently unseeing.

And Benton did not in fact see her. He was remembering fine summer evenings in Berlin years ago, before the children. The time when. . . .

*

The time when. Soft Berlin evenings before Charles had put on weight, when as two slim First Secretaries they had served as advisers to the British Commander-in-Chief. Looking impossibly secure and glamorous, the Napiers would cast off, letting the yacht drift gently into the still lake. The wives would trail their fingers in the dark water and the two men would take turns at the helm. It was the time and the place for confidences.

'Gareth?'

'Mmm?'

'Had a frightful run-in with you-know-who today.' Charles nodded over to the lights of the Villa Lem, official home of the Commander-in-Chief. 'Who'd ever work for a general? That makes three times this week alone. Can't stand the fellow.'

'We seem to get on all right. His bark's worse than his bite. Just throw in a few "sirs" and stand up straight. He thinks we civilians are awfully sloppy.'

'Well, what I told him was that if that was the way he feels he should ask for my recall. Seems he's going to do it too, the frightful shit.'

'Isn't that a bit risky, Charles? The Office might take um—'

'Oh, stuff the Office. If they don't like it I could always ask Anne's papa for a job in the Bank.'

'Patience could have a word with Lady MacNeil.'

'What? Mrs General? I know they're thick as thieves. No. Best leave the women out of this. Anne? Stop hogging the champagne.'

*

Napier had been recalled, but it scarcely seemed to matter. He had moved on and up through the Service, Anne always at his side, until it was time for the splendid Villa and the petty economies. Rome with something even better to come. Napier scarcely looked any older despite his weight. There was a touch of grey perhaps at the temples but the same serene self-confidence shone through his glasses from eyes as bright as when he was thirty. Damn, damn, damn.

Charles watched his old acquaintance Gareth hurry away with genuine sadness. All so simple, this business of life, he thought, provided one didn't get in over one's head, let the women get out of hand, that sort of thing. Such a pity, old Gareth's problem all those years ago. Ruin of a good career. Such an unlikely thing to happen. But of course the Office was right, absolutely right. There was nothing else they could have done, given the fool he'd made of himself. .... Still, it was an awful pity. Disappointment did nothing for a chap really, simply made him lash out. So unfortunate.

He turned again and went soft-footed down to the ground floor. The agency terminals under the stairs were chattering out the stories. In News Department opposite, some careful briefing was in progress on the British attitude to some event or another. The life of the Office went on, Napier reflected, as if by a momentum of its own, almost indifferent to the human element.

He paused at the tapes pinned in long sheets to a board in the vestibule outside the News Room. The main story, carried at enormous length, was of the preparations under way to receive the Pope. Visit to include High Mass at Canterbury, the first since the Reformation. December 29, the feast of St Thomas of Canterbury, Bishop and Martyr, murdered in the cathedral December 29, 1170. Service for Christian Unity, blah-blah-blah.

A short biography of the Pope, Boniface X, formerly Patriarch of Venice. Another Italian chosen to succeed the Polish Pope, the dangerous one, the one who made waves. Formerly Nuncio at the Court of St James's returning to England after twenty-five years. Good English. He would say, and sing, the Mass in English.

There was a long piece from Rome: *Osservatore Romano* quoting Vatican sources, doubtless Boniface himself. High Mass at Canterbury, an ambition conceived when he visited the cathedral twenty-odd years ago as Nuncio. For all Christians, etc., etc. Boniface's hope that common worship would point the way forward for churchmen everywhere....

How odd, Charles thought, all the fuss. You'd think they'd all agree to differ since there was no settling the arguments rationally. On his way down the long corridor to the Main Entrance he brightened at the thought that the whole affair would not be for him but for his colleague at the Vatican whom he detested. He, Charles, was not given to religious fervour and church services gave him a headache.

He wondered whether he should telephone Anne now or

12

whether to wait until she met him at Fiumicino to give her the good news.

On the steps he glanced round the splendid courtyard contemplating the pale blue winter sky. Yes, on the whole, he thought he should telephone, hang the expense. After all, it was Paris he was being offered. She *would* be pleased.

-PUBLIC CONFESSION-

It was as if a great marine bird were settling, missing the foothold, resettling in a heavy beating of wings.

From his position, Benton watched the rustle spreading in both directions: up the pilgrim-worn steps to St Augustine's Chair and the Trinity Chapel beyond; down through the presbytery to the incomparable choir. A vast congregation, in a blaze of colour, settling to its knees.

In the deepening silence the Pope began the introductory rites. Cameramen in the triforium adjusted their focus rings for the close-up. Millions throughout Europe and the Americas saw his lips purse to form the words:

> *'In the name of the Father,*
> *and of the Son, and of the Holy Spirit.*
> *Amen.*
> *The Grace of our Lord Jesus Christ . . .'*

His English was unaccented, or nearly so, but liquid, latinate. The Supreme Pontiff, and looking every inch the part.

A great tropical bird, Benton thought, the feathers dazzling. And red, predominantly red, the red of martyrs. As agreed, the Anglicans and the Romans had intermingled, joined by bearded old Greeks and Serbs and Russians, robed in the cruder colours of the Byzantine rite. Even the nonconformists, Congregationalists, Methodists, Unitarians, in sober black and white, were there, dark flecks in the multicoloured plumage setting off the brilliance of the rest.

'I confess to Almighty God . . .
That I have sinned exceedingly
in thought, word, and deed
Through my fault, through my fault,
through my most grievous fault. . . .'

Boniface genuflected, assisted by the Archbishop on his right, the Cardinal on his left. Benton was near enough, the quiet deep enough, to hear the creak of arthritis, the heavy bump of knee on carpet. For a moment all was still, in suspense. A chair scraped on stone. Someone, somewhere, coughed, the hollow sound echoing from wall to wall.

All heads lowered—all, that is, but one.

At length the Pope rose for the absolution:

'May almighty God have mercy on us, forgive
us our sins, and bring us to life everlasting.'

All eyes came up, waves of adoration, almost palpable, washing the altar steps.

And still there was Welch, over against the throne, his white face haggard under brooding eyebrows. Benton watched out over the crowd until their eyes crossed.

They both understood what was to happen and why. They had never spoken, never met. But each knew his own part and the role of the other.

OUTWARD BOUND

-LIFE-

All so simple, the business of life. There was a time when Benton too had thought so.

His headmaster, an elderly cleric, had tried to put him right but it had not been easy. Indeed, the headmaster ruefully reflected afterwards, it had been a total failure. The boy was impenetrable. Clever, deuced clever. Too bad he was no good at games. But good-looking, no difficulties on that score. A splendid father, decent background, that sort of thing. A pity there was no mother, but then there were many boys without mothers. It all looked all right, but there was no escaping it. There was something wrong with the boy, indeed there was. And, somehow, when he came to explain it, the words had not been right. The headmaster had tried but had not found the words. That wasn't the boy's fault. Quite mystifying, really. It wasn't that he was unused to boys. He had been working with them for almost forty years.

He had chosen his moment, a misty November evening when the lights in the quadrangle had been put on early. Benton pushed open the heavy door to the great ribbed study where the silence was palpable after the hugger-mugger of the schoolrooms. The headmaster looked up over his half-rimmed reading glasses and flapped an arm in the direction of the chair on the other side of the desk.

'Ah, Gareth. Come in. Come in.'

'You wanted to see me, sir?'

The headmaster paused a moment to light his pipe. The match flared and he spoke between puffs.

'Yes . . . as a matter of fact . . . I thought it was time for . . . a little . . . chat, don't you know. . . . The future . . . that kind of thing.'

'Ah,' Gareth said smoothly, 'the future.' He had had premonitions that something embarrassing was about to take place and he evidently had not been wrong. He detested tobacco, something inherited from his father, the eminent surgeon who had seen the victims. 'Not really a lot to say, is there, sir?' he suggested hopefully but knowing they would have to go through with it.

A billow of smoke went up between them. Gareth's eyes started to sting as the headmaster sat back sideways on, legs crossed, to observe him quizzically.

'Thought what you're going to do? When you leave here?'

'Yes, sir, as a matter of fact. I hoped I might go to Cambridge.'

'Well, yes, of course,' the headmaster said, a trifle irritably. 'I meant what you're going to *do*. Afterwards. You know—life?' Good heavens, if only the boy wouldn't look so smug, as if he had everything worked out. The headmaster's smile grew broader, more encouraging, but he could feel the tension mounting, as it always did with Benton.

'My father wants me to read Natural Sciences and follow him into Medicine. But then, of course, he would.'

'I take it that's an impossibility?'

'He understands.'

There was a pause while the headmaster regrouped his forces in the face of this maddening self-possession. He fiddled with his pipe, tamping the tobacco down and lighting up again. This time the pipe drew well, releasing altogether smaller quantities of smoke into the stale air.

'Thought about the Church? You'd do well in the Church.'

This too was expected. The headmaster advised everyone to try the Church. Some were fool enough to agree. Gareth had his answer prepared.

'Well, I thought I'd try the Foreign Office, sir, if you don't mind.'

'Mind? Why should I mind? It's just that the Church needs people like you. If you have the vocation, that is. You do understand?'

'Oh, yes, sir. It's just that I believe I stand a better chance in the Foreign Office.'

'Better chance? Better chance of what? Getting in?' The headmaster tried not to sound incredulous, but his voice had risen perceptibly.

'Oh, no, sir. Of service. To the community. The country.'

The headmaster looked at him sharply, as if he suspected some sort of leg-pull. But no, Benton's brow was serene, his look untroubled. And gosh, yes, he was handsome, really a great credit to the school: a little awkward of movement admittedly, but then so many of them were. The headmaster softened a little.

'Cambridge then, eh? Jude's, like your father?'

'Yes, sir.'

'I was at Jude's, y'know. Good college. A bit before your father's time, of course. He did rather well, didn't he?'

'I believe so, sir.'

'Well, he might just drop the Master a line. It does no harm. I'll do the same myself.'

'He's already had a word, sir. Last summer when he was elected an honorary Fellow.'

'Ah. Well. Yes, quite.'

The headmaster tapped his pipe, rather too loudly, on the ashtray. He made a great business of blowing his nose before folding his handkerchief carefully and returning it to his pocket. Gareth looked at him courteously, in no doubt at all about his future.

'I thought I should read History. Do you think it's a good idea, sir?'

'Can't do much harm,' the headmaster said, having lost track for a moment. 'Theology's a lot better, though. Frightfully good intellectual discipline, even if in the end you don't have a—well, a vocation.'

'For the Foreign Office,' Gareth reminded him gently, 'I thought History would give me a better chance of acceptance.'

The headmaster understood. Like so many boys, Benton was already lost to the faith, one of those smug blighters who thought religion was a lot of rot. They wouldn't have in the war, he thought, the real war, '14 to '18, in the trenches. An awful lot of praying went on there, he remembered, along with the cursing and the obscenities. He sighed inwardly but Anglican good manners forbade any further discussion of it with Benton.

'You'll need languages. I don't suggest you should read languages for the Tripos. But you'll need languages for the Foreign Office.'

'I speak a little French, sir. On holidays and so forth. Father always insisted.'

'You'll need another. Try German. Spanish is more useful, but anyone with Latin can pick up Spanish later. Italian too, if it comes to that.'

'Thank you, sir. I've already arranged to go to Bremen after the Cambridge entrance examinations.'

'Good. Very good. You might do well. Yes, I think you might even do very well.'

Gareth smirked. Of course he would do well. The Master of St Jude's had already told his father that great things were expected of him. Simple, really. The History Tripos. A couple of languages. The Foreign Office examinations, tricky but possible.

Nothing to it, life.

'I say, would you like a glass of sherry? I think we've time before supper.' The headmaster was feeling he had been wrong-footed, a novel experience when dealing with boys. He felt like trying a safer subject than the Future. 'How are you getting on with Lucretius? A bit of a slog after Virgil, what?'

'Much more rewarding, though, don't you think, sir?'

By this time the headmaster was buried deep in the drinks cupboard, normally reserved for parents. He brought out two small Waterford glasses and poured little nips from a Waterford decanter.

They stood at the window looking down on the ancient quadrangle, the model for lesser, more recent, schools. Despite everything Gareth loved the school, its air of rightness, as if it had always been there, which in a sense was the case. The buildings loomed blackly in the night air, with small touches of Gothic grey under the lights. The place looked deserted but only because, as they both knew, all heads were bent over books in this hour before supper. They talked of the Latin poets, which was safe enough. The boy was clever, and the older man was clever enough to know it.

The headmaster, feeling he had somehow failed, took the two empty glasses over to the desk before making a final attempt. 'That's settled, then?' he said. 'Good. Off you go to supper then.'

'Good night, sir. Thank you for the sherry.'

'Good night,' the headmaster replied, turning round to face Benton squarely. 'Oh. And, I say, Gareth?'

'Yes, sir?'

'Just one word of advice. You don't have to take it if you don't want. Just a friendly piece of advice from someone a bit older than you. Might come in useful.'

'Yes, sir?'

The headmaster could see it was pointless, from the very way the boy held his head, standing tall, puzzled, impenetrable.

'Try listening a little more,' he said slowly. 'You must make room for a little humanity, a little understanding. Life isn't all examinations and career. There are lots of knocks.'

'Oh, yes, sir, I know that,' Gareth said in some surprise. 'Everyone knows that.' He thought of his mother's death when he was a small boy: a policeman's shadow against the frosted glass; the lowered voices in the next room before he himself was brought in to be told. And then, afterwards, the total absence, the pain of loss. A lot of knocks.

'Yes, I dare say they do.' The headmaster tried a little reassuring twinkle which often worked with adolescent boys. 'You'll only be able to take them if you've given something of yourself to others. Learn a little about vulnerability. Everyone's vulnerability. Yours. Mine. Everyone's. You do see that?'

'Oh, yes, sir,' Gareth said patiently, wondering what the old fool was driving at. 'I do see that. I do indeed.'

'Do you? Do you really? I am delighted,' said the headmaster, finally admitting defeat. Really, the boy was impossible. It was as if he were armour-plated.

'Good night, sir.'

'Good night.'

From the window the headmaster watched Gareth cross the quadrangle, as awkwardly articulated as ever but unruffled, as if nothing had been said. He entered the arch leading to Hall. The headmaster felt a foreboding beyond his powers of analysis.

23

St Jude's awarded Gareth one of its minor scholarships but only because, as the Master explained to his father, the Governing Body these days had reserved the major awards to young men of more modest backgrounds. Gareth was content: a minor scholarship was enough for his purposes.

And Cambridge: grey, fleeting-white Cambridge held few surprises. He first went up, as his father before him, by train from King's Cross. He had been offered a lift by another parent but the train was more traditional, more in keeping. The town was already familiar from earlier visits when his father, impressively, had taken a slot in the Master's car park before letting him loose for an hour or two while Sir Robin himself went to demonstrate at the Addenbrooke. Thus Gareth knew roughly which college succeeded which in the long walk up from Magdalene to Peterhouse. The finer details would come later, as the months passed. That was the way things were. So very simple, life.

As the son of an honorary Fellow he was shown a certain consideration. From the first day the Head Porter and the Steward knew who he was and spoke to him in the subtle confiding way they normally reserved for the third-year undergraduates. And he found himself allotted rooms in one of the ancient courts, not having to share a set with some pimply northerner in the New Buildings. The view from the windows was breathtaking, the jumbled mass of leaded roofs under the pale East Anglian sky leaving space enough for the crockets and pinnacles of the chapel at King's. A thin gleam of satisfaction warmed his heart every time he went over to the window that first term. Afterwards he scarcely noticed it.

But he loved the college as he had loved his school. Or rather the idea of the college, its ancient corporate existence rather than its moderately interesting Tudor brickwork or his fellow undergraduates in their unsettling diversity. There was something clumsy, coarse-grained in their mutual tolerance, their rough jostling into Hall before settling for Grace, the beer and cigarettes that seemed an indispensable part of their lives. There were no standards, he felt, not as his father understood standards.

Early in the term he was invited to sherry by the Master along with the sons of other old members. Afterwards, at supper, his name had come up.

'Funny chap, that Gareth whatsit, Robin Benton's boy,' the Master said half to himself as the steward bent over him with the *sole véronique*. 'Only nineteen and already the oldest member of the college.'

'Don't be uncharitable, Humphrey,' his wife said crisply between forkfuls. 'Many of your young men act like that until they grow up. They soon learn to be as frivolous as the rest of you.'

'Oh, I do hope so,' the Master sighed. 'But until then such assurance, such weightiness. It's quite unnerving.'

'Rather like his father, wouldn't you say, Master?' said the Steward in his complicit man-to-man way which the Master had long since reconciled himself to. 'His father was much the same at his age, as I recall.'

'Of course. You must have known Sir Robin in those days,' the Master cried. 'Which staircase was it now?'

'Main Court VII, Master, 1920–1923. Natural History Tripos before he went off to London to that teaching hospital of his. You were on the ground floor. Mr Benton had the set above.'

'I remember,' said the Master, brightening. 'Yes, I do remember. Of course. Well, his father didn't come to any harm now, did he?'

'A clever man, they do say,' the Steward said evasively. 'Always was. But look at him now, President of the Royal College and all,' he added, pouring the Sancerre. 'Arthritis is his speciality, he was telling me.'

'When was that?' enquired the Master, impressed.

'Last time he came to stay. Last October it was, when he came up to introduce his boy to us all. Before the entrance examinations, you'll remember.'

'Ah,' said the Master, exchanging glances with his wife. 'Then.'

'You were so busy sparking off Robin,' his wife added, 'that you hardly noticed the boy. I thought then he had a nice smile. When he did smile, that is. Seemed rather in awe of his father, I thought.'

'Poor chap. Living with Robin can't be all that easy.'

25

'That's what his wife thought. Poor Gwen.'

'A rare spirit.' The Master sighed again. 'A great loss.'

Gareth knew from the beginning what was important and what was not. He could have rowed but preferred cross-country, elegantly unfashionable and sufficiently eccentric for the Foreign Office Selection Board. The cadet corps would have been hopeless, the Boy Scouts worse—suitable only for owl-like figures with ambitions to become social workers or prep school masters. He went on field trips with the University Ornithological Society and afterwards courteously drank a half pint of beer with its bespectacled members in country pubs. They found him intimidating, not like anyone else. Some of the friendships, if that is what they were, made with the ornithologists endured long after his Cambridge days, and there were godchildren among the next generation.

He avoided the political societies but particularly the religious ones. To go, even out of curiosity, would, he thought, be looked on as most unsound. He contemplated making an exception of the Fisher Society where there were a number of agreeable scions of the old Roman Catholic families but these he could meet anyway in a less confessional atmosphere.

Instead he joined the University Historical Society with the aim of becoming President, potentially therefore a leader of men. He was not popular there, or indeed anywhere, but his abilities were eventually recognized and he was elected Treasurer in his third year. He went to the indispensable lectures, avoided the rest. Above all he worked, regularly and with application, at his books. He was glad he was so bad at ball games, particularly cricket, which entailed wasting time on a heroic scale all summer. There was no tempting him with anything aesthetic. Music could not and, except for a few short weeks of his life, never would enter his soul.

'I don't know, Humphrey,' the Master's wife said. 'Perhaps after all you were right. Gareth Benton is not someone you can warm to after a while. He's somehow unreal, a robot.'

'His tutors think well of him,' the Master objected. 'He looks set for the Chancellor's Essay prize. We might have to think of upping his award and make him a full Scholar.'

The Master's wife shivered. 'Oh, don't do that,' she said. 'He's insufferable enough already. You don't want to start ruining his character further.'

'That's all very well,' the Master said with a sigh, 'but I'd have difficulty persuading the Governing Body to ignore such ability.'

'The boy should have had a mother.'

'I know,' the Master said. 'Poor Gwen.'

His only mistake was to share rooms out of college in his second year with Archer, an old school friend, a premedical student whose interests took a different turn.

'Gareth? I say, Gareth?'

'Mmmm,' he said from behind his book. 'Yes, what is it?'

'Do you mind pushing off for a bit this afternoon? Till six thirty, say?'

'All right. I'll change in college after cross-country.'

'Thanks. Jeannie will be pleased.'

'Which one is Jeannie?'

'The new girl in Heffers. Paperback Department. Sales have soared since she made her appearance behind the cash register. Don't tell me you haven't noticed her?'

'I have an account.'

'You must be the only man round here who hasn't. A real prize, let me tell you. Took a bit of doing with all those virile rugger blues about. One or two have even been known to buy a book. Imagine.'

'How can you tell your women apart? In the dark, I mean?'

'Easy. They've all got different styles, like tennis players. Does wonders for your own style. It's more exercise than cross-country and a lot more fun.'

Inwardly Gareth was repelled by images of Archer and Jeannie, or whoever, in bed, legs intertwined in a fug of bodily juices and tobacco smoke. He had read a manual or two but could not imagine what, exactly, went on between them or what it could possibly feel like before, during, or after. Did they undress together? He shut out disturbing images.

He could not even conceive how you approached a girl with *that* on your mind.

27

'Easy. They can smell me out at a hundred paces. I just have to open the door and wait for the rush.'

'Good God, Jonathan, when did you last read a book?'

'Plenty of time for that, old boy, when I'm in practice. When the patients are milling around outside in the waiting room and the little woman's next door playing the harp. But until then no girl's safe, let me tell you.'

Gareth was not without feelings altogether. He had felt some stirrings the previous summer at the sight of women dressed in crisp linen, winsome under straw hats, when they had come up for May Week and the boat races. On the college barge a white-gloved hand had taken his arm, provocative as a whisper in all the excitement, as St Jude's finally caught Trinity and rowed Head. The same hand had squeezed his with the slow beat of the band at the May Ball that followed. He was a wretched dancer with no sense of rhythm and she soon gave up. She was gowned in tulle or silk or something, and he remembered he had had some feelings for her, if only as an aesthetic object. She had been hectic, edgy, every inch a thoroughbred. So unlike Archer's women, who gazed on the world with knowing, sensual eyes.

The summer, the real summer, came to Cambridge in that second year. The heat lay inert, heavy as fog, over the Backs in May. The examination rooms teemed with candidates wiping their palms with crumpled handkerchiefs. Jeannie had come looking for Archer but found only Benton going over his notes.

'Hello. No Jonnikins then?'

'No. No Jonnikins. He's got practicals over at the lab.'

'Sorr-ee. . . . Busy then, are you?'

She had a mischievous look and there were traces of a soft West Country burr in her voice. She moistened her lower lip, bit it slightly between sentences.

'Yes. Very busy. Examinations all day tomorrow.'

'Oh. That's all right then.'

She was still as a cat waiting to be stroked. She was really very pretty in her wide-eyed country way and the white collar of her bookshop uniform brought out the bloom of her young skin. Her hair was so black it shone a deep copper.

'Look, Jeannie. Come back at six. He's bound to be here then.'

'Seems we have some time then. Before he gets back.'

'You may have. *I* have examinations tomorrow.'

'Bet you know it all already. I bet.'

There was a long pause. Benton pretended to be lost in his notes. Jeannie ran her hand along the mantelpiece, inspected her fingertips for dust. She held them up before her full lips and blew slightly in his direction. Some undergraduates passed under the open window talking loudly. Benton could feel his pulse racing.

She looked up suddenly over her finger ends. Her eyes were hazel, the whites so young, so pure, as to be almost blue.

'No time for a cup of tea even?'

'No. No time. I really must ask you to come back. Please.'

She shrugged her shoulders barely perceptibly. He had a vision of her weight, the sturdiness of her thighs, her nipples pointing.

'All right. Suit yourself. Perhaps you'll have more time later. After the exams, say?'

'Perhaps.'

She hesitated again but thought better of it. From the door she blew him a kiss, winked wickedly, and was gone.

For a while he was unable to see his notes. It was like being stunned by an electric charge. He turned the pages, fretful.

'Jeannie been in?'

'Yes. I told her you'd be back about now.'

'Oh, Lor'. I've been playing footsie all afternoon with one of the lab assistants. She's twenty-five, one of the older types, plenty of experience. She's coming round in a minute to pick me up. Pub supper out in country. Love under a hedge, the best.'

'I'll tell Jeannie you're with your tutor, if you like.'

'Thanks, Gareth. You're a Christian.'

At the door Archer looked back. 'I say, Gareth,' he said, 'why don't you take Jeannie? She fancies you. She was telling me.'

Gareth tried to look stiff-necked but Archer was not deceived.

'Don't look so po-faced. She won't bite. At least nowhere noticeable.'

From the open window Gareth watched Archer getting into a small black Austin. A woman's elbow, already golden with summer, rested on the window ledge on the driver's side. There was a flash of hair, corn yellow, before the car bumped off over the cobbles of the narrow lane. It paused at the corner and then turned left. Archer, glancing back, saw him at the window and gave him a broad grin and a wave.

Gareth absorbed the faint petrol smell gusting up from the hot street. He waited at the window until dusk glowered in the lane, until it was dark enough for the street lamps to come on. Jeannie did not come. It was a relief in a way.

The following day he took shelter in the examination rooms, finding comfort in the routine, the return of the familiar. He could have sought her out, he knew this. Heffers: paperback department: the cash register. But he knew he would not, even though once he caught himself with one foot already on the stairs. Plenty of time for that sort of thing when he had done what he had set out to do.

The last day of term he had to tell Archer. He tried keeping the tone as neutral, as cool as possible. To make it easier to say, he had poured sherry the way his headmaster used to do.

'Jonathan? I'm moving back into college next year. I hope you won't mind.'

'Just as you like, old friend,' Jonathan replied imperturbably. 'I expect you've missed being behind bars. You'll be happier, I'm sure.'

Benton, despite his resolution, felt himself bristling. 'I have had an offer of my father's old rooms in Main Court,' he said coldly, his lips whitening. 'I can't refuse.'

'Oh, I do see that,' Archer replied unabashed. 'The F.O. awaits. A good career, they do say. Worth getting house-trained for, I expect.'

Gareth had the impression of something tearing inside, a parting as of frayed rope. His tone grew icier, the words bitten off one by one through clenched teeth. 'It's filthy enough,' he said, 'having to share for one whole year with a dirty-minded, immature sex maniac. Insolence only makes matters worse.'

Archer looked stunned, unable to believe his ears. 'Steady

on, old boy,' he said. 'It was only a joke.' He sat, sherry glass in hand, blinking, already half penitent.

'I don't see that someone planning to be a second-rate general practitioner in the provinces is in much of a position to mock.'

'I say,' Archer said, 'I have upset you. Do forgive, it's just that I let my tongue get the better of me from time to time. Come on, Gareth,' he coaxed, 'it's the end of term.'

'That's all right,' Gareth said stiffly. His eyes still danced but he felt faintly ridiculous, wrong-footed, having revealed too much. He poured more sherry.

'Father's rooms, eh?' Archer said, gazing into the glass. 'A bit of a compliment, what?'

'They mean it as such.'

'I expect the college were pretty pleased with your First. Congratulations. I saw it in the lists on the board this morning. I forgot to say.'

Gareth felt himself subsiding through all this. Here was more familiar, more reassuring ground. Archer was not a bad fellow after all, he thought; he could afford to be generous. They had somehow survived the year together despite the strains.

'Thank you. I expect they are rather pleased. What will you do? Share again?'

'Certainly.'

'Jeannie?'

'I don't know yet. I'm still working on it.'

Gareth tried to black out disturbing images. She had stood here, here in this very room, her lips pursed to blow imagined dust at him from her finger ends. Here he had sensed her weight, her breasts' sweet cups, nipples bristling.

'Time for Hall,' he said. 'Are you coming? It's the last of the year.'

'No,' Archer answered. 'Fond farewells tonight. My lab assistant.' His tone was uncertain, apologetic, with none of the old swagger. Gareth had wounded him more than he at first realized. It was time they parted. 'I'm off early in the morning,' he said, 'so I'll say goodbye now.'

'Goodbye,' Gareth said. 'Have a good summer.'

'You too, old friend.'

Unexpectedly they found themselves shaking hands. For a

moment Gareth felt the warm glow of good fellowship and half wished it could always be so.

He saw little of Archer in their third year except occasionally in Hall. They would drift together over after-dinner coffee in the combination room if they happened to be there at the same time. An element of mutual respect grew up between them, as between any who have revealed too much of themselves, but neither risked a renewed intimacy. Archer must have pulled himself together and decided to work, for he obtained a decent Upper Second in the end, enough to take him to his London teaching hospital without difficulty.

Benton, sallying from his father's old rooms to the examination halls, got his double first in the History Tripos. Anything else would have been unthinkable. The Master had him to lunch to celebrate.

'To think that man went through this college without making a single real friend,' he said to his wife afterwards. 'That wasn't true of Robin too, was it?' They were in the rose garden at the high point of the year.

'I expect so, dear,' she replied complacently, snipping off another perfect bloom. 'I can't remember anyone actually liking Robin, can you? Oh, you all respect him, I can see that. But he isn't exactly likeable, is he?'

'No,' the Master admitted ruefully. 'The pride, the pride. He can only see the rest of us as clinical material. We're nothing but patients in the making, don't you see? He's a great success, President of the Royal College and all that. But no one wants to get near. Funny, really.'

'I expect that's what's wrong with the boy, don't you? He can't help being near; after all, he is the only child. Besides, what success? Passing examinations? You all do that.'

She had gathered enough.

'There,' she said, 'I do believe it's time for tea. Poor boy, you know I feel sorry for him. Funny, isn't it? And such a good career so far. I expect the Foreign Office will take him, don't you?'

'Oh, yes,' the Master said with resignation. 'There's an examination.'

Benton spent the autumn, once again, in Bremen to perfect his German. His good landlady, who bore the heroic name of Frau Blücher, tried without success to fatten him up. Her two buxom nieces, whom he could scarcely remember from his earlier stay, took to calling, which the indulgent aunt thought no bad thing. Over the strudel and the cookies, Benton listened with unfailing courtesy and attention as they practised their English on him. Immune to gentle sighs, to fluttering eyelashes, he would unsmilingly correct their small grammatical errors, leaving them to conclude that Englishmen were just not like everyone else.

He spent the spring in France with *la famille Hérault* in Le Mans. There were two small children, Pascal and Isabelle, who looked up at him with wondering eyes, this tall grave Englishman who could not be distracted.

-EXAMINATIONS-

The horseshoe table was of mahogany, polished deep enough to suggest the antique. Some of the figures round it also seemed to belong to another, better-mannered age, even though their questions were unexpectedly sharp, almost querulous. They were all men, all in their late fifties or early sixties, mostly spare-framed, lean-headed Anglo-Saxons like the candidate. The Foreign Office Selection Board was in session.

It was the turn of the figure to the right of the Chairman, white-haired, hunched, ruthless. The voice was a fading treble, clear and cold, the voice of Bloomsbury in the twenties. His place indicated he was the senior of all those present, the one who had risen highest. Benton took him for the hard man, put in to balance the Chairman.

'Would you say, Mr Benton, that up to June or so last year the Americans had several choices over Aswan? And that Mr Dulles failed to understand what was at stake for the rest of us?'

Benton had been expecting questions on the Suez crisis, only then beginning to recede from the world headlines. He hesitated a second between the various answers he had prepared before choosing the bold line.

'Yes, sir. That is precisely what I do think.'

'You have no doubts, I see. Rather odd, isn't it, for one of your generation? You're not tempted by the view that the former Prime Minister might have been living in the past, misunderstanding present-day realities?'

'But the question, sir, was about American choices, not Sir Anthony Eden's.'

'Ah, just so. And Sir Anthony? How do you imagine history will judge him?'

Behind the studied casualness there was a perceptible stiffening round the table while the board waited for his reply. In the brief millisecond Benton caught the whiff of dissension, divided opinions. It was the most loaded question of all, offering the choice between success and failure in those tense post-Suez days.

'It's difficult to tell, I believe. So much seems to depend on what Nasser now does and how successful that turns out to be. The trouble is that Nasser has been—how shall I put it?—so unpredictable in the past.'

'Thank you, Mr Benton. You're right. Absolutely right.'

The tension visibly relaxed; eye contact was resumed. It was as though everyone had been unconsciously holding his breath. Benton felt a small glow of satisfaction. One thrust parried, he thought, turning courteously to the next questioner on the far right. From his lowly position it could be deduced that he was of no consequence, someone included for form's sake. The psychologist?

'I see your French is pretty good. Not too much trouble with the German either, although one of the passages into English caused problems. Any explanation?'

'I'm not happy with the sentimental.'

The questioner, obviously the language examiner, looked aggrieved. Benton realized, with a start, that this was the author of the German paper. But it was too late to retreat.

'It was one of Rilke's letters.'

'One might have guessed.'

There was a schoolboy snigger round the table. Clearly the questioner was not popular.

'But you do like languages, I take it?'

'Not especially, sir. They're tools, aren't they? Rather than ends in themselves. For me, that is; I'm not speaking for others. I prefer the more abstract.'

'Such as? What on earth is more abstract than languages?'

Realizing he had drawn blood, Benton went for the kill.

'Speculation. The clash of principles, cultures. Temperament. Ideology. National mythologies. Nasser as Pharaoh. Dulles as—'

'As what, Mr Benton?'

The Chairman had interrupted, evidently interested in this turn of the conversation. He gave Benton a smile of encouragement.

'I can't make up my mind, sir. President of a small Bible College in the Middle West, perhaps. If I may say so without offence.'

'You may certainly not; Mr Dulles would be most offended. Despite all appearances he is a distinguished corporate lawyer and a graduate of Princeton. But I do see what you're driving at when you talk of national mythologies. An interesting thought.'

The Chairman nodded slightly as if to indicate that the verdict was clear. The linguist looked sulky but his turn was over. Benton felt a surge of confidence which he hoped would see him through the rest. There was time before the next question to glance over the lovely room with its great sash windows hanging over the Burlington Arcade. Papers were shuffled before there was a dry cough halfway up on the left. This time the voice was clipped, the voice of Sandhurst and Camberley and the *Daily Telegraph* refolded each morning on a platform at Waterloo.

'Military service next, what? Any idea what you're going to do? I see you weren't in the OTC at school. Didn't take much interest at Cambridge either, it seems.'

Benton realized he had miscalculated. He had not expected the services to be represented. The general, if he was a general, was in civilian dress but the Montgomery moustache was unmistakable.

'I hope to make up for it over the next two years, sir.'

'Disagreeable necessity, would you say? Or would you, like most of the young these days, consider it a complete waste of time?'

'Not at all, sir. A necessity, but how agreeable or disagreeable only time will tell. But we all have our debt to society to pay.'

'You make it sound like capital punishment.'

'Unlike hanging, sir, I expect it to be good for my character.'

The pause lasted a split second before there was a guffaw all round the table in which the general, and even the linguist, joined. The general, catching the mood, tried a little rough banter.

'Need much improvement, then, your character?'

36

'I hope some improvement is possible. I look forward to the experience.'

'Any chance you might become a regular? I'm not speaking of the Education Corps. The Guards, a good cavalry regiment, that sort of thing?'

'The army could be my second choice of career, sir. But I hope the Foreign Office will have me, otherwise I wouldn't have applied.'

The general looked over the papers in front of him through half-moon glasses and sniffed. Benton had tried to sound sincere but now wondered if he had not been a little too pat.

'Poor show about the cadet corps, though,' the general said. 'It would have given you a head start even for National Service.'

It was clearly time for counter-measures, before the general became too inquisitive. Benton was cursing himself for his over-sight. The OTC. Of course. Only an afternoon a week, an occasional camp. He should have guessed it would one day be important, even critical.

'My father's old regiment have promised to take me in, sir. That should help.'

'Oh, your father was a soldier then, was he? A regular?'

'No, sir. He served throughout the War as a medic. Mentioned in despatches, I believe. The desert. Normandy. With the Ox and Bucks.'

Benton had difficulty stooping to 'medic' and 'Ox and Bucks,' but only the Chairman seemed to notice his pursed lips and he seemed on the whole to approve. The general's whisky-lined face relaxed.

'I wish you luck, young man. A fine regiment.'

Benton wondered whether the general too had been a light infantryman. It seemed too much to hope. He thought it unwise to add that he had been accepted for the Russian Interpreters' course and would spend the next two years usefully employed in a pleasant house near Cambridge. Far better to leave the impression that he would be slogging it out in the dripping rain on Luneberg Heath. With the regiment.

The Chairman glanced at the clock. 'Well, gentlemen,' he said. 'I see it's time to let Mr Benton go. Thank you for giving us so much of your time.'

Benton restrained an instinct to run. He rose as deliberately as he knew how and softly left the room. Behind him the Board shuffled their papers for the lunch break.

On the steps of Burlington House he took a deep breath. It was May, pleasant enough in its way but too soon for the full glory of London in early summer. He tapped his bowler hat into place and buttoned on his gloves. He chose to descend to Piccadilly by the Arcade, where the uniformed attendants gave him a knowing look. We know where you've been, they seemed to be saying. In Piccadilly he strode out, placing the tip of his umbrella between the corners of the paving stones. He glowed with the secret warmth of one who knew he belonged.

It had not been so difficult, after all. The Board was made up of men who, after all, were like himself. Men at home in Cambridge, in his great public school. Men who patronized Hatchard's bookshop opposite, and Simpson's of Piccadilly, and, though more rarely, Fortnum & Mason's. The men who ruled; the men who knew.

Halfway down to the grotty plastic-littered Circus, the first cold wave of doubt broke over him.

He could not have been a serious candidate. The questions were too obvious, questions to which answers could be worked up in advance. It was as if they had all been actors, all with prerehearsed lines. Façade had met façade. Hollow had responded to hollow.

Nothing had been tested, nothing that mattered. Not once had he felt the probe of curiosity. There was no serious interest in him, the essential him. It was obvious; he had been interviewed for form's sake, because his father was his father. He felt the cold clutch of failure in the pit of his stomach. Auditioned for a part he had been training for since the age of eight, he had been rejected for better candidates, those who had not neglected to join the OTC and whose translation of Rilke left nothing to be desired. The Chairman had been kind but it was obvious. Failure.

He turned into Lower Regent Street, heart beating, preparing for the next test, the real one. His father waiting for him in his club by the steps into the park. The famous surgeon, ready with his knife, knowing all the weak spots.

He would have to brazen it out. He would probably not succeed but he could try.

Yes, a reasonable impression, I think, Father.

The Board? Thorough but predictable. A bit amateur, really.

Of course I'd prepared answers. Most, at least.

Nearly all. Of course nearly all.

The majority, then.

No, no one we know. Total strangers. But then the Board was likely to be, wasn't it?

Father, please. It's the same for everyone. It's the system.

Yes, Father. Reasonably confident. Let's just wait and see, shall we?

The results would have to look after themselves. For the time being he would brazen it out. There was no other choice. His steps grew firmer. He threw his head back. His umbrella again came down smartly between the corners of the paving stones. In the distance he could see the Foreign Office across the park, intermittent among the trees.

He thought of his father, so contemptuous, so hard to please.

*

The time when.

To celebrate the occasion Sir Robin had driven the Rolls himself down from Hanover Terrace. He wanted, he said, a few minutes alone with the boy. He had been, for him, quite chatty.

'How old are you, my boy?'

'Fourteen, Father.'

'So let's see. It will be Jude's in 'fifty-three then. You'll be ready for us in 'fifty-six if I've got it right?'

'Yes, Father.'

'So it is high time you came down and had a look at us, got the feel of things. High time.' He nodded to himself fiercely as if registering the programme on his infallible memory.

At the Oxford Street lights he had another thought.

'Well, there's one thing at least. I'll be nowhere near retirement. I'll still be there when you join us at the hospital.'

'Yes, Father.'

Gareth gazed resignedly out of the window onto the crowds of shoppers. The idea seemed to grow on Sir Robin. He was positively beaming by the time he stepped long-legged from the car in his honoured space facing the main portico. He bounded up the hospital steps as if he owned the place.

In the high entrance hall, Gareth flinched before the smell of disinfectant. His father strode through the corridors like an Augustan emperor, deference oozing from the walls. The door of his office read simply 'Professor Sir Robin Benton,' an understatement as loud as trumpets.

The housemen were crowded into the outer office, the realm of Connie, an iron-grey spinster in white. They made way for him, murmuring 'Good morning, Professor' as he cut a path through to his room. 'Good morning, gentlemen,' he barked, ignoring the few young women. Only Gareth and Connie followed him through the door. He went straight to the cupboard to unhook his white coat and his stethoscope from behind the door.

'And how are things this morning, Connie?' he said, struggling into the coat. 'Anything interesting going on?'

Connie read crisply from her notes. Names of patients, incomprehensible descriptions of their condition and treatment. Sir Robin nodded fiercely at each new entry. He scrubbed his clean hands ferociously at the basin behind the screen, gave her a curt 'thank you' when she had finished, and strode out, vigorous, in charge, into the outer office.

'All right, gentlemen,' he said, 'let us take a look round, shall we? I have one or two surprises for you this morning. Shapiro?'

A slight young man with liquid Mediterranean eyes jumped slightly.

'Yes, Professor?' he stammered.

'Less guesswork today, if you please, less wild surmise. Logic, Shapiro, logic.'

'Yes, Professor,' Shapiro said humbly. There were smirks all round the room from the others, relieved that this time the barb was not aimed at them.

'And no hanging back the rest of you,' Sir Robin added with a

40

fierce stare. 'This is not a school for deaf mutes.' They looked abashed, but Gareth noticed a few elbow digs here and there. The old man was in form, they seemed to suggest; there should be some fireworks today.

They trooped behind him, even a couple of middle-aged registrars, like a group of schoolboys jostling behind the headmaster. Matron stood at the entrance to Bedale's Ward, eyes alight with apprehension, ingrained respect. Her little watch pinned to her starched apron trembled expectantly.

'Good heavens above, matron,' Sir Robin said, greeting her with seigneurial gruffness. 'Have you nothing better to do?' He sounded incredulous but it was evidently all part of the ritual for she took it in good part, with a relieved smile. There was a good deal of grinning behind his back.

'I just thought I'd give everything a final check before you arrived, Professor. Just making sure everything was all right.'

'And was it, matron? *Was it*?'

'Yes, sir. There were a few points to look into but nothing serious.'

'I'm profoundly relieved to hear it, matron,' he barked loudly so that everyone could hear. 'Who have you got first this morning?'

'Mrs Ellis, Professor. Third down on the right.'

Sir Robin swept into the ward, all eyes upon him. The floors glittered, unnaturally clean. Patients, scrubbed pink, lay in uncreased sheets, glowing coverlets. A ward sister stood by Mrs Ellis's bed, ready to swish the curtains round. The housemen tumbled through the swing doors, anxious not to miss the diagnosis.

Gareth watched his honoured father, always first, always the prize man, with wondering eyes. After a routine enquiry or two the patient ceased to exist as a human being at all, no longer gifted with a sense of sight or the faculty of hearing. They were just patients, mere clinical material. Sir Robin described the case from the bedhead, over the inert body. He posed the questions and listened to the answers, always ready to challenge the hesitant or the imprecise. Some were apparently almost right but there was always something to add, some similarity or dissimilarity with a previous case in his father's vast experience.

Some replies were treated with withering contempt.

41

'No, hardly that. Even Shapiro here could do better.'

'Logic, Shapiro, logic. Use your brains, man.'

'Think back. The problem's elementary. Third-year stuff.'

Later, when they were driving back to Hanover Terrace, Gareth asked a question.

'Which of those students will do well? Can you tell yet?'

'Oh, yes,' his father said coolly. 'Shapiro. He's in a class of his own.'

'Then why do you want to knock him off his perch all the time?'

His father thought about this for a while, manoeuvring the big car through the heavy traffic. 'Because he can take it. Because he's got to learn, I suppose.'

But Gareth saw through this. Shapiro was a rival and rivals, in his father's eyes, were to be treated ruthlessly, no mercy shown. Gareth had cause to know.

In the evening they dined alone at home. The place was unnaturally quiet, his father not admitting the existence of radio and detesting music in all its forms. They were left to the hum and swish of traffic outside beyond the railings and the tick of the grandfather clock within. They awaited the administrations of Florence, the latest of the succession of housekeepers since the death of Gareth's mother. Muffled scrapings could be heard beyond the kitchen door.

'You'll need a bit of help, of course,' his father was saying, 'a word or two in the right ear. But I expect with enough patience we could make a decent general practitioner of you.'

'I'll think about it.'

'I'm not promising, you understand. Early days.' His father paused, having only just heard him. 'Think about it?' he said incredulously. 'Think about it? What's there to think about? It's all planned: all we require of you is that you make the effort. It's all up to you. I can't do the work for you.'

The son said nothing, allowing the silence to speak for him. He was not risking further unhappiness.

'It's an honourable career,' his father added, having weighed the unspoken objections. 'None of your damned democracy about it. Medicine still has its standards. We stand no nonsense.'

'But suppose a patient dies?'

'He dies. We all die,' his father exploded impatiently. 'But while he's alive I decide how to keep him that way. The others can help but we'll have no majority voting, thank you very much, not as long as I can help it.'

'Anyway,' he said later, over coffee, 'there's no shirking it. Someone has to decide. In the case of St Matthew's Hospital,' he added with a snort, 'that someone is me.'

Later still Gareth lay in bed, watching his father on his round. The voice became curter, sharper, higher as patient succeeded patient. The curtains swished round bed after bed, the housemen increasingly restive, jostling uncomfortably around him. Father receded a long way off, a small gesticulating figure in paroxysms on a gleaming floor the size of a football field. He was quite alone, disarticulated, incoherent.

There was a pause. Blackness. Suddenly he was at Gareth's elbow, confiding. In his most natural voice he said, 'Who decides? I decide, of course. The others help. But I decide. That's the way it is, the way it always will be.'

'If you think about it, you'll see. That's the way it has to be.'

- GOSPEL -

All had sat for the Epistle of the Feast of St Thomas of Canterbury ('Brethren: Every high priest'). All now rose for the Gospel.

The cameras panned backwards from the trio at the High Altar who had between them sung the Gradual ('Behold a great priest') waveringly off-key. Slowly the scene widened to take in the roof arches springing so effortlessly from the clustered marble of the triforium. The cameras took in the high clerestory windows and the long narrowing perspective of the Trinity Chapel stretching behind the High Altar to the Corona. Above, then, the solid serenity of early Gothic: below, the glittering restlessness of a great crowd.

The Archbishop came down from the High Altar threading through the forest of mitres to the lectern. A domestic chaplain stood expectant, one of his soft white hands on the page indicating where to begin.

The Archbishop began in the clipped accents of the Anglican rite. At home in his own cathedral, his voice was perfectly adjusted to the acoustics of the place. His the English voice: one trained on Cranmer and Donne, on Keble and Pusey; heir to the generations attuned to the Authorized Version.

> *'At that time Jesus said to the Pharisees:*
> *I am the good shepherd . . .'*

The cameras panned forward again, trying to avoid the light glinting unpleasantly off his steel glasses. Even so they were unkind to his pinched clerical face, so unlike the serene spirituality of his Roman brother, the Cardinal of Westminster. But there seemed to be no alternative to the close-up enabling the millions to concentrate on the noble words. The cameras thus missed Welch, standing less than ten feet away.

Benton found it more difficult to keep track of him across all the standing figures. For an instant he wondered whether he had not been imagining things. For moments Welch seemed to have disappeared entirely, his clenched white face a figment.

But no. A bishop in the back row, Liverpool perhaps or Salford, moved his head slightly, unblocking the view. Welch was still there, indignant, even menacing. Benton looked around at the detectives scattered about among the civilian dignitaries. All were looking down the great church to the lectern, listening. A chill came over him. He realized he was alone. In the vast crowd he was alone, in silent struggle with someone he did not know, for reasons he could not know.

'. . . and there shall be one fold, and one shepherd.'

The Archbishop had ended.
'This is the word of the Lord,' he said after a pause.
'Thanks be to God,' rumbled from the congregation.

Welch made no attempt to evade him. He looked back, locking onto Benton across the sea of bobbing croziers, his black eyes glittering dangerously. At the words 'one shepherd' his lips curled in contempt. He turned abruptly aside to watch the Archbishop move slowly back to his appointed place on the right of the Pontiff at the High Altar.

The time for the incense had come.

-FATHER AND SON-

An evening in early autumn with the club room still warm from the sun. The great windows reflected a glowing pink sky over the park.

There was a scattering of other diners, bishops up for a conference, a tight-mouthed widower or two, a few scrawny bachelors peering myopically about through pebble glasses. Gareth and his father were at a corner table usually reserved for four, two tall lean Englishmen apparently at ease, gravely considering what to eat. Behind his reserve, Gareth was struggling to control his rising panic. He gazed without seeing at the multiple choices.

'Ah, Mary, good evening,' his father twinkled at the waitress. 'We've had our sherry, thank you. We'll be ready presently.'

Mary retreated, ruffled, to attend to a couple of ecclesiastics daintily picking over the menu a few tables down. Gareth watched her standing poised amidst the glowing teak, the portraits, the club silver. This was, he recognized, his father's world, the settled order of things, the framework.

His father challenged him, gold fountain pen in hand.

'Well? What's it to be?'

'Whitebait, I think.'

'Good, good. I may join you.'

Gareth watched the well-known hand, so sleek, so well-scrubbed, sketch out the first line of the order pad. The piercing grey eyes looked up at him, the bushy eyebrows commanding.

'And roast beef.'

'Never. Not the roast beef, never in the evening here,' his

46

father said with finality. 'It's been stewing since lunchtime. Kidneys might be better. Or at least fresher.'

'All right. Kidneys then.'

'And?' His father's pen paused irritably over the order pad. Gareth plunged on, heedless, anxious to get it over.

'New potatoes and cauliflower.'

His father completed the order with a masterly impatient flourish. He chose the wine, a good safe Burgundy, without asking for an opinion. As they waited for Mary he looked about to see if there was anyone he knew. 'Odd place, this,' he offered at last. 'It's supposed to be a club, but there's scarcely anyone one knows. And the food is getting steadily worse, particularly in the evenings.'

'Do you not think you might do better elsewhere?'

'Elsewhere?' his father barked. 'Elsewhere? Join another club, you mean? Good God.' He paused for a moment to think over the proposition. 'Oh, no,' he said at last. 'I don't think I'm likely to do that.' He looked around again before returning to the theme. 'I expect the members have complained about the place ever since it was founded. But I've never heard of anyone actually resigning. I suppose I'll go on, grumbling to the end.'

'Now then, Sir Robin,' Mary said when she saw the order, 'that is naughty. Not kidneys for goodness' sake.'

'For once, Mary, for once,' his father grumbled, already prepared to surrender. 'You know it's some years since I've had kidneys.'

'All that rich sauce, imagine,' she said. 'You of all people should know better than that. The whitebait will be bad enough. I've a very nice sole to follow, if you like. Very fresh.'

'Oh, all right then if one must.' He sighed. 'The sole. *Véronique.*'

'*Meunière,*' she said firmly, picking up the menus.

Gareth was astonished. His father had always seemed so unconquerable, above the rest, never less than first. It was impossible to imagine otherwise, to realize that somewhere down underneath all the titles and the honours was the schoolboy ready—happy even—to be bullied. Sir Robin caught his eye, then turned away shamefaced.

Fortunately the remedy was at hand.

47

'You must be pleased,' he said, watching the plump figure retreat towards the kitchens. He turned on Gareth with his most commanding stare. 'A not inconsiderable achievement, I've been given to understand.'

'I hope so. The Master wrote.'

'Did he indeed? Yes, I can imagine the College wanting to take part of the credit. The Foreign Office has always been regarded as difficult, I suppose with some reason.' Sir Robin's sniff was only just audible. Gareth cringed before the blow he knew was coming.

'And tell me. Where did you come in the final result?'

'Fifth, Father. I told you. Fifth place. Out of eighteen.'

'Ah, yes. So you said. Fifth place. Know any of the others?'

Gareth was in no doubt that his father meant only the candidates who had done better. 'Not really. Two were from Oxford, one from Edinburgh. I've run into Drummond from time to time.'

'Drummond?'

'The man who came out top. Trinity. He read Classics for Part One, Law for Part Two.'

'Clever man, would you say?'

'Evidently.'

'He should do well then, he and the others. You'll have your work cut out trying to keep up.'

'In his note the Master said it wasn't the Last Judgement. Anyone in the top ten should have a useful career.'

'Useful? Perhaps. But I imagine the Foreign Office will always retain a certain prejudice in favour of the best. For example, this, this—what did you call him?'

'Drummond, Father.'

'Yes. Drummond. In my experience there's no substitute for being top, being the first. Still, it can't be helped.'

Mary returned with the whitebait. Sir Robin watched stoically as she served the major portion to Gareth. He did not blink when, unbidden, she poured the wine. 'And a little water, Mary, if you don't mind,' was all he said.

'Still,' he added when she left, 'you must be pleased to have at least got in. There's a certain amount of competition, I believe, even these days.'

48

'Yes, Father. Reasonably pleased. There were twelve hundred candidates, I believe.'

'I suppose most were non-starters, though. That's generally the case with competitive examinations.' He finished the last of his whitebait with a certain complacency. He paused for a moment before laying down his knife and fork. 'Young Drummond,' he said. 'I wonder if I know him? I should write if I do. His father, isn't he the banker?'

Gareth, wincing, grasped wildly into the unknown. 'No, Father,' he said. 'He's a soldier. A major, I believe, in the Royal Artillery.'

His father remained unperturbable. He laid the cutlery down with care and thought for a minute. 'No,' he said at last. 'In which case I don't know him.'

'No, I don't know a Major Drummond of the Royal Artillery,' his father said, watching Mary spoon out kidneys for Gareth, *sole meunière* for himself. 'Funny, I could have sworn Drummond the banker had a son your age. The father was a contemporary of mine. At Trinity too, of course. Could be a coincidence.'

Gareth gritted his teeth under this search with surgical instruments. Experience had taught him it was better to lie still, to say nothing, to wait for the pain to pass.

'You're sure about it?' his father asked as Mary passed between them with the vegetables. 'The Royal Artillery? You're quite sure?'

'Yes, Father. Quite sure.'

A little later his father said, 'I might just give Mark Drummond a ring tomorrow. Just to be certain. It wouldn't do not to acknowledge his son's success if that, indeed, is what it is.' He relapsed into silence, delicately filleting the sole piece by piece. He grew absorbed in the task, at home with the scalpel.

'You'll need a wife,' he said in due course. 'Like a GP or a clergyman, you're bound to need a wife. Still, I suppose, plenty of time for that.'

'I've no one particular in mind, Father, if that is what you're hinting.'

'Of course not, my boy. I was thirty-four when I married your mother. Plenty of time yet. Better to lay the foundation of a solid career before thinking about that. Besides, you're less likely to make a mistake. There have been several unsuitable marriages among my friends' children recently. They all seem to marry foreigners or someone one has never heard of.'

'I'm unlikely to do that, Father.'

His father looked up with his dazzling man-to-man smile, the one reserved for his fellow professionals. 'Cheese or pudding after this?' he asked. 'I recommend the cheese.'

'Pudding,' Gareth said, imitating his father's smile as if nothing had occurred. 'I think for once I'll try the pudding.'

His father could not be outdone. 'Yes,' he said after a long enough pause, 'I'm sure you'll try to be careful over this wife thing. You've done your best so far. I'm sure you'll continue to exercise prudence. So important, in your chosen profession.' The smile was this time edgy, daring Gareth to try something new.

Mary arrived with the menus. 'My son would like the club pudding for once,' Sir Robin explained.

'I really wouldn't,' Mary said. 'Not in the evening. I've a nice fresh Stilton, just opened.' His father beamed in triumph, his eyes mocking.

So Stilton it was, among the portraits and the club silver, the settled order of things, the framework. Despite everything, Gareth hoped his father might offer some words acknowledging his achievement. But no. Instead, he said, 'Funny, isn't it? In my profession a wife is totally irrelevant. I have no idea if most of my colleagues are married or not and, if so, to whom. It just doesn't matter.'

'Do you miss Mother?'

Sir Robin thought about this for a while. 'I did. I distinctly remember missing her early on. It was so sudden, you see. Funny things those rockets, the watchamacallems, the V-twos at the end of the war. They came in so quickly you heard the sound of the approach after the explosion. She was dead before anyone heard it coming.'

'And now?'

'I wonder if I would recognize her if she were to pass me in the street. Which, of course, is impossible.'

The evening had darkened. A club servant went round switching on the lamps, which cast harsh shadows after the bloom of twilight.

-FIRST STEPS-

Anything should have been easy after Father but it all turned out to be somehow disconcerting, not quite as it should have been. All except the beginning.

Turning the corner from the tube station, Benton felt a stab of pure delight. Whitehall, empty by now of tourists, had turned sepia in the autumnal glow. There was a suspicion of mist down the longer perspectives producing effects not unlike those of a good Victorian water-colour. Soot stencilled in everything, riming every recess, crocket, pilaster. Only the Cenotaph seemed exempt, a dead chalk-white aglow with the fading wreaths of Old Comrades' Associations.

Benton had heard that in some fit of inscrutable snobbery the Foreign Office had never accepted the bowler hat. Post-Suez, the Anthony Eden was seen no more, and Benton thus went under the great arch into the thunderous courtyard in a soft brown felt number. This, he hoped, would be judged sufficiently incongruous for his new clerical grey three-piece. Only later would he learn that the very young went bare-headed, in scruffy nondescript suits. So, too, did the most senior, the Undersecretaries, bent under the weight of their children's university fees. Only the middle-ranking, the Heads of Department competing for their first ambassadorships, looked the part in tailored chalk-stripe. In the hot weather all worked in shirt-sleeves, preferably displaying expensive braces, the old-fashioned kind with leather tabs to attach to trouser buttons. In the park in winter there was competition for the oldest overcoat, the first in esteem being anything Edwardian, preferably country wear handed down from Grandfather.

He knew not to arrive early and thus had deliberately waited until the office had settled to its morning's work. In those days there was a laborious climb up the cavernous stairs from the opposite archway, the one facing No. 10 Downing Street. After the beetling façades of the courtyard dominated by mottled statues of forgotten heroes, the effect had been nicely calculated. From the bottom of the stairway Benton, for all his advantages, felt daunted and his heart quailed at each heavy step on the way up.

There was a large lobby at the top with a reception area over to the right. Two immense powdered ladies in twin-sets and pearls, so alike they could be sisters, sat at heavy polished desks behind the heavy polished counter. A tiny lady was seated mouse-like in the remotest corner compiling some sort of ledger.

One of the large ladies approached with an intimidating smile. 'Good morning,' she boomed regally. 'Can I be of help?' She was tall enough to look him straight in the eye.

'I was asked to report here this morning,' he replied in his driest voice, determined not to be put down.

'Ah, a new entrant,' she guessed. 'How very nice. Let me see.' She consulted a list, holding it at arm's length and squinting to make out the letters. 'You must be—Mr Benton. We have been expecting you. The others arrived a little while ago.' She was hooting scentily at him now, welcoming him to the family with only the faintest hint of reproach.

'I was asked to report to the Northern Department. To a Mr Hurrell, I believe.'

'Just so,' she agreed. 'Mr Hurrell, the Assistant. I'll have you shown up.'

Benton followed yet a fourth lady, this time in uniform, down the elaborately tiled corridor between the high doors. They passed the agency machines chattering out the stories and he had his first glimpse of the expanse of purple carpet rising up the Grand Staircase between the statuary. She turned the corner and in a moment or two dodged through a doorway into a plain stone lobby at the head of some stone stairs. There was an antiquated lift shaft of open steel webbing and a notice saying Automatic Service. She pressed the button.

They were joined by two fat porters in uniforms so faded as to be barely recognizable. From the shaft came the cymbal clash of steel doors echoing throughout the building. The fatter of the two porters gave the uniformed lady a squeeze.

'How far you going, Doll?' he asked.

'That depends,' she said, 'on how nicely you ask.'

The two porters haw-hawed suggestively, elbowing each other in the ribs.

'Two up,' she added, 'with this gentleman here.'

'Mind dropping us off halfway? We're a bit pushed, see.'

'That'll be all right, darling. You'd do the same for me, I expect.'

'Any time, Doll, any time.'

All three were guffawing heartily by the time the cage arrived. Dolly was left to struggle with the steel doors, as resistant as man-traps. The others looked on complacently, waiting for her to succeed.

'Get in, sir. You don't mind, I'm sure, about Fred and his mate here?'

Benton nodded stiffly, aware that he had no option. He was pushed to the back of the cage by the trolley, which pressed his hat flat to his chest. The two messengers squeezed in next to Dolly, who stood poised by the buttons.

'All right then, Doll?' Fred said. 'Two singles to West Ham.'

'Aren't you going to take me then?' Dolly asked with a giggle.

'It's 'im we're not taking,' Fred replied, nodding towards his mate. There was a further caw of laughter all round. The mate looked plethoric, as if he were having convulsions.

'Here you are then, my darlings,' Dolly said as the lift came to a stop. 'All right?' She tugged at the man-traps again until they parted. 'Mind how you go.'

'Ta ta, then, Doll. See you.'

'See you, Fred. You too, Stan. Take care.'

They manhandled the trolley out into the lobby, leaving Benton room to breathe freely again. Dolly tugged the doors together and they dropped unexpectedly down again. 'I couldn't of pushed the button hard enough,' she explained apologetically. 'This here is the temperamental lift. Not that the others are much better, I must admit.'

There were two distinguished silver-haired figures deep in conversation outside the steel gates. One reached out to open the outer gate.

54

'Do you mind, dear?' Dolly called out firmly through the bars. 'This gentleman here is late for his appointment already.' The two figures shuffled aside apologetically. They watched without rancour as the cage shot off again upwards to deposit Benton where he was going.

'Here we are then, sir,' Dolly said with a kind smile. 'Here at last. Better late than never.'

They emerged into a corridor cut into tiny cubbyholes through which they threaded their way back into the noble part of the building.

Allan Hurrell was sipping coffee from a chipped but expensive mug. He looked up over the rim as Dolly went in without knocking. He was small and pudgy with sandy hair, a huge forehead, and intelligent glasses.

'Ah. You must be Gareth Benton,' he said. 'We've been expecting you.' Again Benton thought he heard a faint hint of reproach. 'All right, Dolly, you can leave Mr Benton with me.'

Dolly gave him a conspiratorial grin and ducked out.

'I thought I ought to let you settle in for the day before coming to disturb you,' Benton explained evenly, taking his measure of the man.

Hurrell seemed unconcerned. 'No disturbance, old boy, I can assure you. We've had nobody on Romania and Bulgaria for a month. Thank God it was over the holidays. By now you're manna from heaven. Richard is very pleased.'

'Richard?'

'Richard Hallett-Brown, the Head of the Department. He's asked me to apologize for not being here to meet you but he's a bit tied up this morning. I'll take you in presently. Meanwhile I've been asked to start your briefing.'

One of the telephones on the desk rang. Hurrell automatically picked up the right one and began a long, incomprehensible conversation, something about Poland's pre-war debts. Benton looked around.

It was a small room with space enough only for a desk and a couple of chairs. A small coal fire burned in the grate and there was an old brass coal scuttle alongside on the hearth. Dominating everything was an enormous oil painting, much too big for the room, of a Victorian lady draped in decorative grief over an ivy-covered tomb. He could make out the inscription on its stonework:

> The remember'd voice of Father's love
> All hushed within the tomb.

The telephone conversation came to an end. Hurrell waved at the picture apologetically. 'Sorry about that,' he said. 'It's by someone called Bathurst. Ever heard of Bathurst? No? Neither have I. Frightful thing.'

'Why don't you have it moved?' Benton asked.

'I only notice it when I'm thinking about how many multi-megadeaths the Russians could inflict on us. And vice versa of course. Nice to remember a time when we took death rather more seriously.

'Besides,' Hurrell added, 'I expect the Office Keepers have forgotten where it is. They'd only make a fuss.'

Benton courteously waited for him to pick up the threads.

'You'll be working for me,' Hurrell said at last. 'I'm Assistant for the whole bloc except the Soviet Union. Jim Blakely next door is responsible for that. There are accordingly two third rooms, of course.'

'Third rooms?'

'Where you'll be working. Where the work's done. You'll see. You start everything off—well, nearly everything—and I look it over. Sort of sub-editor. Then it all goes to Richard as Head of the Department, who decides whether he likes it or not. It's all very simple, really. I'll explain it in more detail in due course. Care for some coffee? Milk? Sugar?'

Hurrell picked up another of his telephones and talked to someone called Maire who seemed to be in charge of the coffee. Benton was not aware of any orders being given, but there was a suggestion that somewhere surely there was a mug without a crack in it. This seemed to cause some merriment for Hurrell was grinning sheepishly when he put down the telephone.

'I take it Mr Hallett-Brown knows I'm a Russian speaker?' Benton ventured, not sure how far he could press the point.

'Richard,' Hurrell said firmly. 'His name is Richard. The first rule of this place is that only Ministers have titles. The rest of us have Christian names. And never call anyone sir.'

'Why ever not? Is there a reason?'

'I don't suppose so. Because we are not the army, perhaps.'

'Is there anything else I should know?'

'Never knock when entering a room. There's no reason for that either, as far as I know. But it's quite safe. There's too much to do to leave time for any hanky-panky with the girls.'

As if on cue, a tall lissome blonde came in without knocking, carrying a coffee mug on a tin tray. Her long slender arms were still a summertime brown. She had the dazzling smile of an equal which Benton found somewhat disconcerting.

'Ah, Maire,' Hurrell said. 'Coffee. Good. Meet Gareth Benton, our new recruit. Gareth, this is Maire Mollison, otherwise known as fairy-fingers. Fastest shorthand in the office.'

They shook hands. 'I've managed to find you a biscuit,' she said. Her voice bore traces of the flat accent of the northeast, Newcastle perhaps or Teesside. 'It's not a very nice biscuit but it's the best we can do. A leftover from the Soviet Ambassador's call last week, as a matter of fact.'

'Thank you,' Benton said, settling down again. 'That is really most kind.' He turned to Hurrell again, dismissing her from his thoughts. 'Are there any other rules while we're on the subject?' She and Hurrell exchanged sharp glances.

'I'll have that draft ready for you in half an hour,' she said, very clearly over Benton's head. 'Richard says he can't look at it until this afternoon anyway.'

'Fine, Maire, fine,' Hurrell said apologetically. 'I can't do much about it for the moment myself. And thanks for the coffee.' He watched her rustle out on her flat heels, hips swaying.

'You were saying?' Benton persisted. Hurrell seemed to have some difficulty refocussing. 'What?' he said. 'Where was I?'

'The rules. You were speaking of the rules.'

'Ah, yes, the rules. Well, there is a third, as a matter of fact, but I dare say you'll ignore it like the rest of us. Avoid the temptation to join the Traveller's Club. I can't imagine why we all go but we do. The place is like a works canteen at lunchtime.'

They passed on to talk more seriously about the East-West relations.

Later Hallett-Brown said, 'Well? What do you think? Does he look any good?'

57

'He's bright enough,' Hurrell conceded, 'but he looks as if he's been programmed since the age of eight. The rest of us don't seem to exist. . . . He was perfectly frightful with Maire. Treated her like a housemaid.'

'He may be a little shy. This place is fairly intimidating to begin with, we often forget that. Perhaps he'll improve as he gets used to us.'

'He hinted he would prefer something Soviet to the desk he's been given. He is a Russian speaker, after all. A good one, I believe.'

'Oh, no,' Hallett-Brown said. 'He must learn to crawl before he begins to walk. We can't let him loose on the serious stuff for a while yet. You'd better wheel him in.'

Later still Maire's train rattled southwards under the river. It was still warm enough for the windows to be open and the noise was deafening.

'Our new entrant joined us this morning,' she shouted at her friend, a girl from the next department. 'When's yours due?'

'Next week,' her friend shouted back. 'What's yours like?' Maire turned her thumbs down.

At Waterloo when it was quiet she said, 'He's a funny chap. I mean, he's super-looking and all. But there are not many men who treat me like I wasn't there. I'm not used to it.'

'Not like Allan then?'

'No,' she said softly, blushing with pleasure. 'Not a bit like Allan.'

Between stations, when it was too noisy to speak, she fantasized about Hurrell. From a bed of soft down she was watching His Excellency dressing in the morning, adjusting his cuff-links. The sun was shining in from a wide balcony sparkling with sea reflections. A breeze ruffled through his hair, thinning but elegant. She had a breakfast tray on her knees, a plate of tropical fruit, a silver coffeepot. Drowsy with sensual bliss, she watched him through half-closed eyes.

They got off at Clapham South where great lorries were throbbing at the lights.

'Pity he's married, your Allan,' her friend said, handing in her ticket.

'Yes, isn't it?' said Maire, undeterred. She shook open her umbrella and tramped off along the edge of the Common, the cold astringent London rain slanting through the streetlights. A couple in training splashed by leaden-footed, near the end of their run. She walked through the night without haste, dreaming of the future.

- MANDARINS -

It was a lovely May and the sun had gone down over Buckingham Palace, leaving the lake a glitter of pink mother-of-pearl. Benton waited gravely at the bottom of the steps while a troop of the Household Cavalry clattered by to their first rehearsal on Horse Guards Parade. Once under the trees of St James's Park he stopped on an impulse to watch the pelicans lumbering like aldermen beside the lake, gulping, it seemed, at nothing. And everywhere there were the ducks, ducks of every variety, bobbing silhouettes in contramotion to the speading iridescence of the water. He could identify one kind by its wicked jewelled eyes set in white in a quilt of vivid green and orange.

Mandarins. For a second he wondered whether the choice had been some royal gardener's idea of a joke, a subtle rudery against those who passed this way every day, sober-suited, on the way to the club: the Treasury knights, the soft-footed advisers in No. 10, the lean-jawed hierarchy of the Foreign Office. Mandarins all. Those who know; those who decide.

Benton was into his eighth month and was beginning to feel he could belong even though the system remained so unexpected, so unlike the image he had formed of it since his childhood. The pace for one thing was unbelievable. Everything, it seemed, had to be done now, this second, amidst the clatter of typewriters, the whir and click of photocopiers, the din of telephones. And there was no style, no attempt to keep up appearances. Visitors were received at the desk among the files: there would be three conversations going at once while yet a fourth figure would be booming confidences at a secretary. The only alternative was a stiff horsehair sofa in the corridor, where diplomatic exchanges took place with the girls clacking by on their stilettos.

He had been amazed to find that Hurrell preferred to work on a corner of one of his subordinates' desk in the uproar rather than alone in his room next door. 'Can't stand it, old boy,' he explained. 'All that silence. It's a matter of habit, of what you're used to. Like journalists, I suppose, who can only work within sound of the presses.'

'But this is meant to be serious. How can one make decisions in this atmosphere?'

Hurrell shook his head in puzzlement. 'Decisions? Oh, I don't know about that. Sometimes, I think, all we're doing is standing around the Tower of Babel telling each other stories. Nothing is ever decided—finally decided, that is. Nothing ever happens. I simply can't remember when a diplomatic problem was last solved.' Benton did not know whether to take this seriously or not but he noticed that the most acute and urgent problems of his first few weeks neither were solved nor went away. All that happened was that the urgency went out of them: they sank down in everybody's in-tray under the weight of more recent emergencies. He could not reconcile himself to this, or believe that this was how things should be.

Worse was the feeling that the system contained self-created obstacles, traps for the unwary. It was all somehow so ramshackle, so improvised. The telephones were not automatic and hours were spent going through the various exchanges. It was often quicker to walk about the huge building, trapping people in their offices for the necessary consultations. 'Keeps you fit' was all Hurrell would say when Benton complained.

Above all there was the daily struggle with the stencilling centre where briefs for the Foreign Secretary were reproduced. He tried to keep his temper but really it was not easy.

'No, dear,' the weary cockney voice would say. 'I'm afraid we're just too busy to take on any more work today.'

'But he's leaving tomorrow for Washington. He must have it today.'

'I know, dear, that's what you all say. It's always the same when he goes away.'

'What can I do then?'

'You can bring it up if you like. I'm not promising anything, mind . . .'

The Foreign Secretary's own copy was stencilled on a rich stiff paper that would not absorb the ink. The answer to this problem had been to erect washing lines around the stencilling room where the pages were hung out to dry. Officials coming with fresh work had to duck and weave their way, as if through a Monday morning wash, to the reception desk. Anthony Eden had hated staples, and ever afterwards the pages when dry had been stitched together with blue silk. Both silk and needles were available in every department, with one girl with a reputation for neatness deputed to carry out the delicate task.

'I know it's archaic,' Hurrell said, 'but you've got to admit the system's not without its batty charm. And the service we provide isn't bad, I think.'

Even Benton, watching the light fade from the lake, had to admit that the service was not bad. His prose had improved and his wits had been sharpened. He was faster and more accurate but not as fast and as accurate as Hurrell or any of the more experienced people. But he belonged; he felt he was beginning to belong.

The lights were coming on the length of Birdcage Walk. Behind in the distance the massed bands of the Brigade of Guards were running through their programme before a thin crowd of early tourists. The soul of the great city was stirring with the promise of early evening while Benton, self-absorbed, considered his prospects of advancement.

'What d'you think?' Hallett-Brown said the next day. 'You see more of him than I do.'

'One of the pricks,' Hurrell said, 'of which we have had too many in this department in recent years. Why can't we have one of the normal ones? Other departments seem to do all right.'

'I didn't select him,' Hallett-Brown said defensively. 'They're wished on me. And you can't say he isn't bright enough.'

'Oh, sure. His work's fine and getting better. But why can't he be human with it? Does he have to go round upsetting everybody? They hate him, you know: the girls, the messengers, everyone.'

'I know, I know,' Hallett-Brown agreed wearily. 'Too much naked ambition. It's as though he hadn't time to be civil.'

'The trouble could be ambition but I've an idea it goes deeper than that. You know—son of a famous father and all. He seems to be trying to prove something. Underneath it all I suspect he's frantic, too self-absorbed to relate to anybody. I sense a sort of panic there, don't you? A need to justify himself. Sad, really.'

'Perhaps,' Hallett-Brown ventured, 'perhaps after a couple of postings he'll have grown up.'

'And who was the last person you met who improved with age? I can tell you one thing, though.'

'What's that?'

'After a couple of postings he'll have to have lost his virginity or he'll be past saving.'

Hallett-Brown thought about this for a moment, tapping the ends of his fingers with a ruler.

'Have a word,' he said at last, 'but go easy on the virginity bit. He'll think that somewhat impertinent in the circumstances.' Hurrell looked startled. 'He's probably like the rest of us,' Hallet-Brown explained dryly. 'Wondering whether you're going to make an honest woman out of Maire. Poor girl, you'd better make up your mind soon. Otherwise she'll have been posted to Ulan Bator.'

'Ah, Gareth,' Hurrell said as Benton came in. 'Good. I wanted a word.'

'You rang when I was out, I believe? I received the message.' Benton sat down easily, bending forward straight-backed. Hurrell contemplated Benton's shoes, so thoroughly burnished they hardly looked of leather.

'Well, it's Richard really,' Hurrell explained. 'He thinks you've managed very well these initial months. They're always a little trying. New atmosphere and so on. But he thinks it's now time to relax a little, try to get on with people more, that sort of thing.'

'I wasn't aware I wasn't getting on with people. Are there complaints?'

'Not exactly complaints but the girls aren't very happy.'

'Ah,' Benton said, 'the girls.' He looked up meaningfully at Hurrell, who looked away.

'It's all the juniors,' Hurrell said, passing on quickly. 'You hardly seem to be aware of their existence is the general feeling and you do tend to blow up whenever you think things have gone wrong.'

'I like things to be done well. And I can't say from what I've seen that we get the service we deserve.'

'Yes, but there is a price to pay, don't you see? We're only part of the business. There's everyone else. Messengers, typists, cleaners, clerks, and so on. They're all part of it too. They can't be treated like furniture.'

'But we do the work,' Benton objected, stiff-backed. 'They're only here to help.'

Hurrell found it hard to suppress his irritation. 'But they're human,' he cried, 'and we're all only human, after all.'

'I'm sure I try to be courteous.'

'Well, try a little harder, that's a good fellow. Try a little humanity. It works wonders, you'll see.'

Benton considered this doubtful proposition, the modern disquieting heresy his father hated so much. The country had gone soft, even, it seemed, the Foreign Office. He saw his mentors with new eyes, part of the new cowering generation filled with flabby sentiment, uninsistent on standards.

'I'll try,' he said at last, 'if that's what you really want. I don't accept that there's anything wrong. But I will try, if you say so.'

'Richard will be pleased,' Hurrell said, unsure if he'd made any real impression. 'You see, this place is a bit like the whole country. It's so small we all have to invent our own version of it. We have one version, the messengers have another. There's only one rather pompous set of buildings, but really there are many Foreign Offices, all different. And we all have to get along, you do see that?'

'No. Frankly I don't. The work has to be done. We do it. The others help.'

Hurrell gave up. 'Let's just stick to the humanity point, then. Can I tell Richard you'll try?'

'Certainly. I've already said I'll try.'

'I told you, a real prick,' Hurrell said. 'The man's not human.'

'I can't see we can do much more about it,' Hallett-Brown replied. 'After all, he can do the work. You could even say he's got talent.'

64

'Let's pin our hopes on the women then. Perhaps they'll humanize him. If his thoughts should ever stray in that direction.'

'You're a frightful cynic, Allan,' Hallett-Brown said admiringly. 'God, what a cynic.' He shook his head, his mind already alight with an idea.

In July the Head of Personnel rang. It was the twenty-second consecutive day of rain and as he talked he looked out over the Mall lashed with water. There was a State Visit in progress and the flags of the two countries hung sodden from the flagpoles.

'Young Benton. What d'you think about Moscow? In September, of course. We've got a replacement lined up for him.'

'Too soon if you ask me,' Hallett-Brown said. 'He's still awfully immature. Bright but immature. He'd probably crack up. The strain is terrible there, you recall.'

'I wondered if it might be getting easier. And he does have the language. There's not a lot else available at present.'

'Well, he's not likely to forget his Russian and he could do with another hard language. What about Thai? What he needs is a small post where he has to muck in. He's still frightfully la-de-da with the juniors. They all hate him.'

'Can't you put him right?'

'God knows we've tried,' Hallett-Brown said. 'He's going to have to learn the hard way.'

'Actually Thai is a possibility, I see from the movements chart. We can probably make it fit if we hurry. .... All right, let's try that. Will you tell him, or shall I get one of my people to do it?'

'Let's keep to the appearances, shall we? It's for your people to do the postings, not me.'

Both sides were smiling conspiratorially as the telephones were replaced. The Head of Personnel looked up into the weeping greyness above the trees and sighed. He moved a couple of names around on the chart in front of him and picked up the telephone for his next move.

Benton heard the news with irritation in September. He protested, arguing for a more central posting, somewhere ambitious like Moscow. But in late November he was enrolled in the

Thai course in Bloomsbury, and the following year found him in sweaty Chiengmai lodging with a university professor for the stiffest part of the course. He became something of a figure in the town, moving awkwardly among the gently undulating masses. He kept to his books with ferocious determination, blotting out thoughts of the languorous Chiengmai women, the most beautiful of all that beautiful race. He was the object of much fantasizing, this prickly exotic creature from the cold lands of the north. At the gates of the British consulate many a garland was placed in vain on the statue of Victoria, stern but just, tutelary goddess of all affairs of the heart.

'Well, he may be a prick,' Hallett-Brown said a year later over lunch at the Traveller's, 'but he's a good officer. I hear he got the best mark ever in the Thai Higher. Practically interpreter standard, I believe.'

Allan Hurrell, on home leave from Paris, was paying. 'I can't say I'm surprised,' he said dryly. 'He would always get a hundred percent for determination. Is he any better otherwise?'

'Not much. Inhuman as ever, it seems.'

'Maire says she'd be surprised if anything were to change him now. I must say if Thailand can't do it, nothing can.'

'How is Maire anyway?' Hallett-Brown asked. 'Is married life suiting her?'

'She's not complaining. Or not to me she's not,' Hurrell said. 'Gosh, the food here's as bad as ever. This soup's a disgrace.'

A couple of others joined them to share in the gossip. The room gradually filled with the sober-suited, the incomprehensible hierarchies of mandarins from across the Park.

BERLIN

- CONSECRATION -

In the deepening silence the Pope bent over the communion wafer. The millions throughout Europe and the Americas saw the famous hands, the Fisherman's ring on the fourth finger of the right, holding the unleavened host. His lips approached so close that the microphones had difficulty picking up the whisper:

> *'For this . . .*
> > *is . . .*
> > > *my . . .*
> > > > *Body . . .'*

He stopped for what seemed an eternity, his gnarled hands whitening as he adjusted his grasp, before the genuflection.

This time there was no mistake. The bishops had bowed so low that Benton could only see the winged tips of their mitres, out there among the hundred croziers. Only Welch was standing, his eyes gazing on the wafer with horror, loathing, as at something obscene. As he rose, the Pope shot a startled look in the direction of the throne, a moment that was later analyzed in a thousand commentaries. He fiddled for a moment before lifting the host on high for all to see. Above the crossing, the bells in the Tower swung heavily, reverberating copper and bronze through the lovely stonework.

Again the cameramen bent over, focussing for the close-ups. Again Boniface's hooded eyes, his pursed lips.

> *'Take and drink ye all of this*
> *For this is the chalice of my blood*

Of the new and eternal testament.
The mystery of the faith:
Which shall be shed for you and for many
Unto the remission of sins.'

Boniface paused, lost in the mystery. The millions watched breathless, half afraid he would not recover. The world witnessed his slight start, almost a shudder.

'Do this . . .
in memory . . .
of me.'

All eyes came up to witness the genuflection and the second elevation. Despite his great age, he held the cup aloft, winking under the lights, until all had borne witness. The bells boomed muffled overhead. Gareth pictured the shock waves rolling out over the town, breaking over limp employment exchanges, sodden shopping precincts, glistening garage forecourts. Here was a blazing room with its matchless splendour of cope and crozier. There was a grey December where it was scarcely daylight before the night shadows began to assemble.

Boniface replaced the chalice before him and stood, hands apart, expectant. It was the turn of the Archbishop to his right, again to add the English intonation:

'Let us proclaim the mystery of the faith.'

A single male alto voice from the depths of the choir stalls took up a note. Two bars later the counterpoint began in the treble register, at first from the boy choristers, soon joined by the whole range of human voices. An indefinable slackening of tension settled on the crowd as they developed the theme:

'My soul doth magnify the Lord.'

The lighted hall. Gareth tried recalling how grim old Bede, the Venerable Bede, had put it in the beginning: Life is a bird, that was it. Life is a bird flying in and out of the darkness, flitting for a brief span in the lighted hall, going out again into the darkness. Here was the lighted hall, all right, the theatrics of the Word in the dead days of the year. How it glowed: how dark the rest.

The cameramen, growing restless with the motionless tableau at the altar, tried some artwork while the singing went interminably on. Cameras panned over the assembled dignitaries, first in long shot and then in composed groupings. There was a particularly fine-looking Royal Duke, representing the Sovereign, across the aisle from the Archbishop of York and his grandest brethren, Anglican and Roman. All grave men, faces etched with piety, looking splendid in the view-finder.

Later, it was discovered, some cameras had accidentally picked up Welch, chalk-faced, in the background over against the Archbishop's throne. It was possible, later, to imagine what was to come. At the time he was just a face in the crowd, a taller figure than most and unaccountably standing. But not visually of much interest: just a face, one more, in the crowd, part of the composition.

The voices tumbled through a succession of augmented chords coming to rest in perfect, inevitable resolution. United at last, they soared into the vault and rebounded, tingling.

In the afterglow the Archbishop waited for the silence to resettle. He then began his cadenced mellifluous flow:

> '.. Grant that we . . . may become one body,
> one spirit in Christ . . .'

As he came to the peroration Boniface was half-inclined towards him, drinking in the last of the words with a slight nod. They glanced at one another in mute understanding, joining the congregation in one emphatic Amen. Benton recalled their old association, twenty years before as Bishop of London and Papal Nuncio. There had been a joint letter to The Times, scandalous to both communities, on the Christian Expectation. Already, it seemed, forces had been at work leading to this moment.

Amen.

There was a long pause, charged, theatrical.

Boniface next turned to the Cardinal on his left. The voice was tremulous, spiritual, barely audible to Benton standing only twenty yards away. The old man under the lights, his hair blue-white, unimaginably fine, familiar to television audiences for half a lifetime.

'And so we, having no abiding city
But seeking one to come,
Pray that through this sacrifice . . .'

No abiding city. Becket's chosen text, days before his martyrdom in this place. Even Benton was moved.

He checked again over the restless forest of mitres. Welch's
bloodless face duly reappeared through the waving croziers still
framed by the sculptured throne. A giant's head, hair cropped
short, aggressive, military. A bully's cassock in plain dissenter's
black, unambiguous.

A body poised, not in repose: its time, whatever it was, not yet
come. Benton watched and waited. For fleeting moments he
could hope there was some mistake, that it was some trick of the
imagination. And surely the web of security was complete, not
evident but perfect. Everything, surely, had been looked into. It
was silly to fuss, silly and embarrassing.

But Welch's face, gazing across the forest of mitres, told him
what he already knew. There was to be no escape. Benton thought
he saw the lips pursed to form a word.

Amen.

Benton could not be sure but he thought that was the word.

Amen.

- PATIENCE -

He spotted Patience when lunching in the officer's mess with
Charles Napier his first October with the Military Government
in Berlin. By this time he was thirty-one, with his years in Thailand and a spell in South-East Asia Department in London
behind him. He was by now accepted, though scarcely liked. It
was time to settle down, to found a family. It was time for a hostess to preside at his dinner table beyond the candlesticks and the
bowl of cut flowers exactly in the centre. It was what was expected.
    Napier noticed his interest at once.
    'Pretty thing, what? Berlin is looking up. She's only just
arrived.'
    'How do you know?'
    'I was in the general's outer office this morning and there she
was, fresh off the plane. She's a Patience something-or-other.
Her father's a retired admiral—or is it an active admiral?
Anyway, no one you've ever heard of. Mummy has oodles,
apparently. Sussex somewhere, as you might expect.'
    'Gracious. And you've only just met.'
    'Beth was telling me, the girl sitting with her. I rely on her for
all the gossip.'
    'And how old, would you say?'
    'Twenty-one, maybe. Young enough to require Daddy to pull
a few strings to get her out here.'
    'Funny. I'd have thought he'd prefer her nearer home.'
    'You never know. Anne's pa likes nothing better than having
her over here with me rather than over there with him. But then,
he has other interests.'

Gareth had heard the stories. There had been a particular nasty divorce in which Anne's father had been cited as co-respondent. The papers ran it for days. There had been pictures: a Jumbo-sized husband, a Jumbo-sized lover, a tall aristocratic blonde outside the Law Courts in the Strand.

'Like an introduction? We could go over if you like.'

'Not here. Not in the mess.'

'Sorry. I just thought . . .'

Patience looked up from her cottage cheese salad to say something to the girl with her. She glanced over at the two young men, guessing she was being talked about. She smiled faintly at Charles. She used delicate fingers to pull back her hair, unremarkable in colour but obviously cut and handled in Knightsbridge. Gareth was struck by the startling blue of her eyes matching the blue of her jumper, soft as Harrods, or better. There was a clarity of jawline, a tilt of the head signifying position, school, class. She had the pale transparent skin of the English rose.

She returned to her cottage cheese, sipping occasionally at a glass of apple juice.

They followed her with their eyes as she left with the other girl. She had slender legs under a Black Watch kilt which rippled briskly over the calves with each movement. Napier recognized the stiff unyielding back of a virgin. Her friend sauntered behind trailing suggestion, promise.

'I'm not sure, Gareth, you wouldn't have more success with Beth. You should ask her for a dance at the next regimental effort. Talk about the vertical expression of horizontal desire.'

'When is the next dance anyway?'

'The twenty-fifth, I believe. It's the Green Jackets' turn. In-house. No dashing froggies or oversexed Yanks to worry about. All the captains are married, all the subalterns overgrown schoolboys. Absolutely no competition.'

'Will you and Anne be going?'

'Of course. Mrs General will be there inspecting all the marrieds for signs of infidelity. She thinks it shows. And Anne and I *are* married. To each other.'

'I might just ask that Patience girl. Could we make it a foursome?'

At his desk later that afternoon when the last telegram had

74

gone, Gareth stared out of the window overlooking the car park, twiddling a pencil. It had just started raining and the car roofs glistened but he did not notice. Instead he was thinking: Sussex. Of course Sussex. And clothes from Harrods, or better. Some good school, no doubt, but she would be brighter than short-hand and a few modest O levels would suggest, her parents having made sure that she did not give wrong signals to the market. A good home amongst the chintz and the Chippendale. A couple of retrievers about the place, a couple of horses in the paddock. Father would be neat and quiet in the modern naval way. Mother would be large and loud, her head full of country-club gossip.

And really she was awfully pretty. Someone who would look good at the end of a long dinner table; someone who could be trusted, even out of earshot, to say the right thing to important guests. Someone able to give that imperceptible sign which caused the ladies to rise and leave the men to their port and cigars. Her accent, doubtless, would be sweet and yielding with no false stridencies. With any luck she might have picked up enough French to get by, spoken in the no-nonsense English way which foreigners found so reassuring. Even the French.

Patience. Exactly the kind of girl he was looking for. Someone his father would approve of. Someone in keeping. Suitable. Someone fit to be his wife and the mother of his children.

The rain came down more heavily, hard enough to cause him to look up. It was sweeping over the old stadium, home of the 1936 Olympics, all granite purpose, battered survivor of earth-shaking events.

The following day Gareth found an excuse to call on the general's ADC on the mezzanine floor. When they had finished he passed through the outer office. There was a half-finished letter in the machine and an empty typing chair, a cashmere cardigan draped over the back. Her friend looked up, slyly malicious. He could not know he had already been the subject of much speculation, silent and shared. They knew his reputation for driving ambition and had already decided that he needed a good wife to soften the edges.

'Hello, Gareth,' Beth said. 'Is there anything I can do?'

'No. Not really. I—'

'You don't remember me, do you? I used to see you round the Office sometimes last year.'

'Yes, of course. You're Beth.' Gareth had remembered this much from his conversation with Napier the day before.

'That's right. Beth Porter, formerly in Protocol. You were on the second floor somewhere. Weren't you Burma and Thailand then?'

'That's right. How clever of you.'

She seemed to let this go unchallenged. She looked quick and funny, ready for anything. She had the perfect standard figure, long-waisted, light-boned. Gareth found her eyes a little too bright, her mouth a little too eager. She was clearly expecting something more, her small cupped breasts motionless in her tight jumper.

'How are you finding Berlin?' he asked lamely, unable to think of anything more promising. 'You've been here how long?'

'Seven months. Since Easter. It's all right, I suppose,' she said. 'The work's not very interesting, the same old thing day after day. I'll say one thing for it, though. It's miles better than Protocol.'

She laughed, throwing her head back and half closing her long lashes at him. Her gold-on-brown hair was tied back with a little feminine ribbon, adding dash to her appearance.

There was a pause. Gareth found himself staring at the tourist calendar she had hung on the wall.

'And,' she added softly, 'we all have our own flats here, instead of having to share like we do at home.'

Gareth caught the faint suggestive whine of London, the promise of experience, of wide good-hearted tolerance. He felt trapped, as if something more was expected of him.

'The social life isn't bad either,' she added, making eye contact again. 'You can have a lot of fun. Are you coming on the twenty-fifth?'

'Yes, I hope so. I was wondering . . .'

'Yes?'

She looked on the point of melting when the door opened and Patience came in like a breath of sharp county air. He felt relief, as if saved from himself.

'Hello,' she said, taking her seat and looking over the half-

76

finished letter in the machine. Her accent, as he expected, was perfect and her movements quick and purposeful but poised, in control. Perhaps it was her woollen dress, but she appeared a trifle broader in the shoulder than he remembered, someone who would thicken with age. Her skin however was radiant, clear-toned, as if she were wearing no make-up at all.

'I'm Gareth Benton,' he said, feeling awkward. 'We haven't met.'

'No,' she replied, 'but I believe you know my brother John. John Troughton? He says he was at school with you. He asked me to look you up when I got here. Patience Troughton.'

'Of course,' he cried, relieved to have a neutral topic of conversation. 'Of course I remember him. He joined the Navy, didn't he?'

'Yes, as a matter of fact. Of course he had practically no choice. What with Daddy and all.'

Beth looked on at this mating ritual, already excluded. Her smile lost none of its brightness but there was a shadow lurking in her eyes.

They first went down to Meddows the following April in the glittering Sussex rain. There was a copse of wet trees in early leaf between the main gate and the spangled lawns. The daffodils were at their best and the wallflowers on the terrace just beginning to appear. The house was unemphatic, at ease with itself under the downlands behind.

'It's not as old as it looks,' Patience said apologetically. 'The old place burned down in 1910 in Great-Grandfather's day and they had to start again from scratch. The land's pretty well gone too. I had a wicked grandfather. The usual thing—fast women and slow horses.'

She was dressed for the occasion, her tailored suit an exact blending of town and country, a bright Hermès scarf knotted at the throat, good sturdy leather shoes, flat soles. Her eyes sparkled with anticipation, homecoming. She seemed not in the least nervous, which spoke well of her parents and their affection for her. They had been warned she was bringing a friend and of course guessed that there was already more to it than friendship.

The admiral opened the door. He too was dressed for the part: an old flannel shirt, a club tie, an unkempt tweed suit of impeccable credentials. He was slight, almost insignificant. Only his hair, a distinguished silver grey, and his sharp eyes gave him away.

'Ah, there you are, old girl,' the admiral said. 'How's Berlin?' He kissed his daughter with evident affection. She was half a head taller and sturdier, more heavy-boned, but she had inherited his translucent skin. Both were laughing, arms entwined.

'Daddy? This is Gareth. Gareth, my father.' She beamed at them both.

'Admiral,' Gareth said, putting out his hand. Somehow the word came out a little too smoothly, as if he were claiming the same seniority. They shook hands a little warily, two dogs sniffing at the same bone. Gareth could tell at once that he had given the wrong impression, that he was not what was wanted as a son-in-law.

'Do call me Andrew,' the admiral said, more lamely than he intended.

'Andrew, then,' Gareth replied, smirking. They shook hands again, mutually resistant.

'Your general was over the other day, a great favourite of the family. I didn't tell him you were coming, of course.'

'Why ever not?' Gareth tried to keep the tone neutral but was aware he was betraying some anxiety he had rather kept hidden.

'Just keeping private and public life apart. Old navy habit. It comes of spending so much of one's life at sea. He knows you've been seeing one another. He had nothing but praise for your work.'

'Ah. The work.' Gareth wondered what else the general might have said. Patience started to bustle to cover over the awkwardness. 'Come and meet Mummy,' she said, clutching Gareth by the sleeve.

'Yes, do go on in, she's in the drawing room,' the admiral said. 'I'll get your things.'

'No, no. Let me.'

'Nonsense, Gareth. I may call you Gareth?'

'Of course. The general does.'

'So I believe,' the admiral said dryly. 'Do go on in and meet Helen, there's a good chap. I'll get your things.'

Gareth looked down from his great height on the diminutive

78

figure and tried looking filial. Patience dragged him away as the admiral went out to the car.

In the chintz drawing room a tall lady rose heavily from an armchair, grasping a stick. She looked out, sightless, slightly off-centre as the blind do. Gareth had been warned.

'Ah, Lady Troughton,' he said with affected warmth before Patience could speak. 'I've brought Patience home for the weekend.' He spoke too loudly as the sighted do with the blind.

'You must be Gareth,' Lady Troughton said, stiffening. 'Patience?'

'Yes, Mummy.'

'Introduce me to your friend, darling. Where are your manners?'

The two women were embracing when the admiral returned. One glance at his wife told him all he needed to know.

'Ah,' he said, summoning up his reserves of hospitality. 'There's just time for a drink before lunch. A little gin, Gareth?'

'Sherry if you don't mind, Admiral.'

'Ah,' said the admiral. 'Just so.'

'I suppose Patience knows what she's doing,' Lady Troughton said from the bed, listening to her husband undressing. 'But isn't Gareth a bit odd? I can't make him out. Such spiky manners.'

'A proper Foreign Office twit if you ask me, old girl. You'd think they'd pick them for their ability to get along with people. But no. They're all the same. Inhuman young swine.'

'Not all,' she objected. 'We met some nice ones in our time. Think of Washington.' In his prime the admiral had been Naval Attaché in Washington.

'Our luck, though,' he grumbled, 'to have Patience mixed up with this one. The general thinks he's able. All he needs, he says, is a good wife, someone with a sense of humour to slow him down. Too bloody ambitious, it seems, for his own good.'

'Well, you knew she might fall for someone like that, the moment you conspired with your friend to get her the Berlin thing. It was always a possibility. I mean, she's of an age.'

'I was hoping she'd meet a nice soldier. You know, one of our sort.'

'Well, you'd better get used to him, darling,' Lady Troughton concluded. 'I've a feeling she's been hooked.'

'Silly girl' was all the admiral could find to say.

And indeed the silly girl had been hooked. In her bedroom, all watery rose and powder pink, Patience lay awake, hugging her collection of soft toys in turn. She was still a virgin but only because he had never asked and in a way she liked that too, his sense of what was fitting. She could not imagine why he wanted to take her on but she knew she wanted that tall lean body next to her, the aquiline profile caught in the half-light. There had been difficult moments, times when his jaw tightened and his eyes blazed with impatience. But she had managed to humour him, and surely a little submissiveness was desirable in a wife. Part of the problem was that he was so clever. So clever and ambitious. He wasn't easy, she could see that, but he was her own, her very own Gareth. And for all his foibles, he had—she knew he had—a noble career to come which she would come to share.

She turned out the light and lay in the dark hoping to hear a soft shuffle in the corridor outside, an urgent scratching at the door signifying dependence, need, passion. Oh, come, she thought, come to me now. But the corridor remained silent, as in her heart she knew it would.

A full moon rose over the downs, flooding her window as it did when she was a child. She waited, one finger tucked in between her thighs, for the old sound of the screech owls from the wood, her own secret happiness in a happy life.

Tomorrow, she decided, she would go out riding.

-MARRIAGE-

The wedding took place the next year on a bright blustery day in March. By this time Patience had doubts. So too did Gareth. But they had their good days too, and they were now only doing what had come to be expected.

On their good days she thought she detected a little-boy-lost behind his official superior manner; and his crooked grin when he relaxed could stab her to the heart. On their good days he basked in a love that was almost maternal, a glow dimly remembered from the past, and the blue of her eyes could give him a shiver of aesthetic pleasure. There were enough good days for her to explain away his maddening obsession with order, the thing done, the way ahead. And his white anger when crossed. There were enough for him to forgive her for the minutes he had been kept waiting, for her unsettling opinions and for her obstinacy when she must, surely, have known she was wrong. They knew they looked good together, a handsome couple, and this too gave them confidence.

And so, on that blustery day in March, a hired Rolls pulled away from Meddows and purred down the drive where the few early daffodils nodded under the trees. Patience was of course veiled and gloved in white. She had lost a few pounds and the white silk ribbon round her waist was very becoming. White silk shoes peeped from the folds of her full skirt. In the High Street, the shoppers stopped to watch, wondering who they were, this stunning bride and the little man beside her in the splendid uniform.

As the car left the church, Gareth said in a tone of mild contempt, 'I didn't think we had so many admirals left. What do they all do, for heaven's sake?'

'I don't know,' Patience said, grasping his hand and gazing down at her own, complete with wedding ring. 'Oh, darling, what does it matter? I'm so happy.'

'I expect half of them are on the retired list like your father,' he went on doggedly, as if he had not been interrupted. 'They're glad probably to have the opportunity to put on a uniform again. Comical, really, the obsession with gold braid. Has your father—I mean, does he have an obsession with gold braid?'

'I expect so,' she said brightly. 'Give me a kiss.'

'What?' he said incredulously, as if the girl were capable of saying anything. 'Here? In the High Street?'

'Yes. Don't be stuffy. We're married, aren't we?'

He turned on her with suddenly blazing eyes.

'I resent the word stuffy,' he whispered between clenched teeth. 'I prefer to think it would be wrong to make a spectacle of oneself.'

She winced, as if she had been struck. They both stared white-faced out of their separate windows. She clung to his hand as to a piece of wreckage. Looking timidly upward, she could see the firm bunch of his jaw muscle with its tic of suppressed rage.

After a minute or two she tried a gentle squeeze of his arm. 'It's all right, darling,' she whispered at last. 'Honestly it is.' She looked with concern at the passive back of the hired chauffeur, anxious that he should not witness anything so shocking as a scene.

As if on cue the chauffeur glanced back through his rearview mirror. 'Go on, sir. Give her a kiss,' he said with an assumed NCO matiness. 'What's the harm? We wouldn't want to spoil the little lady's day, now, would we, sir?'

Their eyes met in the mirror, white-hot outrage on the one side, faint derision on the other. Gareth shrank inwardly, afraid of what the man might say next. Anyway, he could see her silent tears by now.

'There, there. Don't blubber,' he said, giving her a quick peck on the cheek.

'Oh, Gareth,' she said, melting. She took out a new lace handkerchief from her new white bag. The chauffeur looked on complacently.

'That's the ticket, sir,' he said. 'It's the little things that count. That's the secret of marriage.'

'Are you married?' Patience said, glad of something to talk about.

'Thirty years, ma'am,' the chauffeur replied. 'And it don't seem a day too much.' He grinned at them both reassuringly, just before swinging in through the gates.

A marquee had been set up on the upper lawn, the one with a view over the Downs, but the side panels had had to be fastened down against the wind. Empty, it smelled of canvas and warm grass and the first of the year's carnations. The hired staff stood about behind the champagne buckets waiting for the first arrivals. Gareth had prepared his speech thoroughly. He had rehearsed every inflection. It contained all the expected elements and he was easy in his mind about it.

When they came down the broad staircase the bride was in grey silk, the groom in grey chalk-stripe. They descended slowly, hand in hand, looking so right that even the admiral let his guard down for a moment, thinking that after all they might make a go of it. Photographs were taken on the steps. Lady Troughton left her stick in the hall and was escorted out by Sir Robin. 'Mustn't spoil the young ones' wedding photographs,' she explained, inclining approximately in his direction. 'I want them to have only happy memories of today.'

It was the best man who had the privilege of giving the bride a final hug before helping her into the car.

'Lots and lots of happiness,' he whispered. 'Let us know the instant you're back.'

'Thank you, Charles,' she said. 'Thank you for everything. And Anne too, of course.'

They drove away in a hail of confetti. Charles gave a final wave as the car disappeared into the trees by the main gate. He turned to Anne, standing a little ahead of the crowd on the steps. She was wearing a wide straw hat which cast a glowing amber light over her perfect features. Her eyes sought his.

'Well, what d'you think?' he said, knowing it was the question she was expecting.

She made a little *moue*. 'I wouldn't have,' she said, 'if I'd been her. Gareth looks fantastic but—well, you know. . . .'

'I know,' Charles said.

'A right one I had today,' the chauffeur said as he changed from his uniform. His wife was standing next to him, holding out his shirt. 'Treated his bride something shocking. She was really upset and such a nice little thing too. I can't see that lasting. . . .'

'Well, they don't, these days, do they?' his wife said complacently. 'Not like in our day.'

'True, true,' the chauffeur said, buttoning on his shirt. 'Still, you'd think he'd make the effort. To begin with, anyway.'

A leaden weight fell between them as the car nosed its way through the Sussex lanes towards the main road. She felt desolate, fearful, as if there were already nothing left to talk about. Here she was in her beautiful new clothes, with her beautiful new luggage sitting next to her beautiful new husband, and it was raining in her heart. She could not understand it.

'Not a bad speech from your father, I thought,' he offered, to break the silence. There was no reply. For a moment he thought she was asleep. 'I said it wasn't a bad speech, your father's,' he repeated, this time more loudly.

'What?' she said, coming to. 'Yes, not bad. They were all good, really. Charles was very witty.' The silence was renewed as he negotiated the roundabout that put them on the main road.

'Yours was very nice,' she added loyally, not looking up at him, 'very polished. I just wish Uncle Edward wouldn't go on so.'

'Schoolmasters usually do. They're used to a captive audience. Perhaps we should have asked Father instead. He's famous for it.'

'I imagine so,' she conceded wearily.

There was again a heavy silence until she could bear it no longer. The subject had to be raised and as he never had, she would have to raise it. She did not think it was fair. She thought that sometime during their engagement he would have taken the initiative. But he hadn't, so she would have to.

'Darling,' she said, fingering her wedding ring.

'Yes, darling? What is it?'

84

'It's going to be all right? You know, tonight?'

'Most people seem to manage. Maybe not right away but after a while.'

'You're not expecting too much, I hope, not right away, not at the beginning. I mean I never have, you know. . . . You'll have to teach me.'

'I understand.'

She waited a minute or two, but he seemed to think there was nothing further to say. She looked at him, hardly daring. He was looking intently out on the tail-lights ahead. But she had to know.

'Have you? I mean, have you ever . . .? Oh, Gareth, don't make it so difficult for me. But you've never said. We've never, you know, discussed—'

'I don't think you want a reply to that,' he said stiffly.

'But I do, I do,' she cried with exasperation. 'I think I've a right to know.'

'Please let the subject drop,' he insisted. 'It's not . . .'

'Not what?'

'Proper,' he said shutting her out again. 'Decent. What one expects of a wife.'

'Oh,' she said, thinking that perhaps after all he was right. They drove the rest of the way in frigid silence.

They had chosen the country hotel from the Guide. Three stars RAC and three centuries old, comfortably settled, part of England. The tankards above the bar winked like country gaffers and the food, plain cooking over which not too much trouble had been taken, reminded them of their own, the real world. Wine had softened them both, the wine and the subdued lighting which took the edge off things. They took coffee in the lounge, where the firelight, too, helped.

She looked into the fire, holding her coffee cup to her lips. Flickers of light and shade played with the contours of her face. He caught himself thinking that she might actually be perfect, totally flawless, the way he remembered his mother. Ridiculous, he knew, but the possibility had to be faced.

'I wear contact lenses,' she said dreamily into the fire. 'I hope you don't mind. I meant to tell you but—well, there it is. You've married an old four-eyes, I'm afraid. Do you?'

'Do I what?'

'Mind?'

'Not in the slightest.' He hesitated a moment before beginning. 'Look, Patience . . .'

'Yes?'

'You asked me a question today.'

'I remember.'

'I should have replied. I'm sorry.'

'No matter.'

'No, I should have. It's not fair otherwise.'

'Oh,' she said, 'fair. It never has been fair. There have always been different rules for men. Even my mum told me that.'

'No, you misunderstand,' he interrupted quickly. 'The plain fact is that I . . . I . . .'

'You? Yes, darling, what about you?'

'I never have either.' It was out at last. 'Don't laugh. It's stupid, I know. But somehow I never thought it would be right. One would be sort of—trapped. Put in the wrong position.'

'You don't have to apologize to me. I just wondered, and it is important, isn't it, to be clear? I knew. Somehow I knew.'

'Does it show?' he asked, unable to conceal his anxiety.

'Sort of,' she replied with a short laugh. 'Never mind. We'll just have to learn together, won't we?'

'Do you mind?'

'Not especially. It might have been nicer if you'd had some experience. It would make it easier for me . . . I think . . . I don't know really. At least I don't have to share you with anybody.' She looked doubtful. 'Here, let's have another cup of coffee,' she said, rousing herself. 'There's heaps left.'

There were twelve steps of Axminster carpet up the stairs to the long corridor of bare, creaking oak. They tiptoed to their room like burglars. She had never seen Gareth look so foolish, so human. She suppressed a desire to giggle and to cover him with kisses at the same time.

'Sorry,' he said. 'I'm terribly sorry.' He was, she knew, sincere enough but he sounded as if he were apologizing for a muffed shot at tennis. She was hurt, outraged even. After all, she could hardly teach him how. She had done what she believed was expected of her. All she knew, anyway. She thought he might have taken the trouble to find out what to do.

She lay, with a corner of a sheet between her teeth, half afraid
that the truth of the matter was that she just was not attractive
enough. She hoped she was. She had gone to a lot of trouble.
But it was almost as if he was repelled by the contact of skin on
skin. Her skin. Even now he lay on the other edge of the bed, as
far from her as possible. It was a nightmare, a living nightmare.

'Perhaps we're both tense,' she said, when she had thought it
over and decided how she could help. 'Perhaps the excitement
of the day, you know, the wedding and everything . . .'

'Do you think so?' he said, moving back to her side. 'Do you
really think that might be it?'

'I expect so,' she said, cradling his too-lean head in her arms.
He was bonier, more resistant than she had expected, the articu-
lation not quite right. 'We need practice,' she said finally.
'Happily, we have a lifetime ahead of us to practise in.'

He looked up into her face, anxiety lurking in his eye. 'Yes,
that must be it. Sorry.' He looked so boyish, his crooked grin so
apologetic, she felt her heart giving way.

They fell asleep at last, holding hands. It was a restless night,
all the same, since both of them were used to sleeping alone.

He came in after breakfast the following morning as she was
kneeling to unpack his suitcase. She glanced up, guiltily clasping
a book she had come across under his shirts. In her honeymoon
clothes she looked barely attainable.

'Oh, I say,' he protested. 'I do think you should leave a chap's
things alone.'

'No,' she replied with a firm nod of the head. 'I'm your wife,
darling, remember? I've got to get used to looking after you.'

'Yes, but I mean. I ought to have a choice. I mean I don't go
through your things, now, do I?'

'You can if you like.' She laughed. 'At least you won't find
anything like this in my belongings.' She opened her arms to
him.

It went a little better this time, at least for him. Cradling his
head in her arms, she ran her fingers through his hair, comforting herself with the thought that it might, after all, come right in
the end. It wasn't, so far, anything like she expected, the way it
was in books when Mr Right came along. None of those girls had
any difficulty. And what about Beth? She never had any

problem. She could not believe she was doing anything wrong. Surely it was for him . . .?

'Is it a good book?' she asked, looking down on the top of his head, realizing he was already beginning to go thin.

'Mmmm? Is what a good book?' he said. 'Really, you do ask some strange questions. What's this about a book?'

'You know. That book. I mean, does it help?'

'He's said to. He's a well-known authority. It's what's recommended.'

'By whom, for goodness' sake?'

'Charles, of course.'

'Oh, Charles. Of course.'

Her fingers twisted his hair into short ringlets. He relaxed under the scratch of her long nails.

'Could we read it together?' she said. 'I mean, it might help.'

'Good God, no. What a suggestion.'

Her fingers froze. It was as if she had stopped breathing. He looked up but her face was twisted away towards the window. 'Patience?' he said. 'What is it now?' He sounded genuinely concerned, almost contrite, she thought.

'Nothing. Go to sleep. It's all right.'

He nestled again in the crook of her arm and yawned. 'I see no reason why you shouldn't read it by yourself, though,' he said, composing himself for sleep. 'I'll leave it around. It's worth reading thoroughly, I believe. I have been studying it myself.'

Patience tried to blot out visions of his high forehead furrowed over the illustrations.

'Thank you,' she said simply. 'I will do my best.'

Gradually his breathing grew more regular. This is a mistake, she thought, this whole thing is one ghastly mistake. The hired Rolls, the new clothes, the hired staff behind the champagne buckets in a tent smelling of warm grass and early carnations. She'd played her part but it was hollow at the core; there was nothing there. Something society invented to prevent worse.

She bit her knuckle to avoid crying out. Through the window she could see grey clouds trundling out of the west across the glass.

Two days later they were on the Roman Wall, deciphering the excavations with the help of an official handbook. It had always been his ambition, he had explained, to walk the wall from one end to the other. So she tagged on behind through the swirling mists bringing rain out of the west. They slept in village pubs where the walls were too thin to make the act of love possible. They were both surprised to find it was a relief in a way.

-HIS AND HERS: THEIRS-

The world, judging as ever by appearances, considered them a success as a couple. Particularly as a couple: more than the sum of the constituent parts.

Sit her between that wet young subaltern, what's his name, and that frightful Kraut. If anyone can make that situation jell, she can...

You know Gareth's quite witty when he remembers to relax. He was charming the pants off Mrs Minister after dinner. Such a relief, I can never think what to say to her. . . .

Young Benton had a bright suggestion at prayers this morning. Can't say I like the fellow but I can't deny he has brains.
    Too big for his boots, though, wouldn't you say?
    Oh, yes. Much. But she goes a long way to make up for it. Awfully sweet with the other wives.

A useful couple, too, the world judged, because so evidently correct, under control. Perhaps a little too studied, being too impeccably dressed too often—even for tennis or, what was worse, for sailing. They never wore an old favourite pair of shoes or flung a threadbare cardigan over their shoulders. A couple, in short, with faultless taste, if a trifle conventional. Discreet, too: people who could be relied upon.

Nice to have you back, Major, if only temporarily. And how are things in the Whitehall shop?

Underpaid, General, underpaid. It's nice to be back, if only temporarily, to somewhere I can afford the gin. Particularly with a chance to take a peek over the other side again.

Take the Bentons with you, I would. So much safer that way.

Right, sir.

No uniforms, I take it? Out of the question.

Strictly mufti, sir.

Well then. Good luck. Try not to get caught. So embarrassing when you chaps get caught.

I'll do my best, sir.

It was as a foursome plus military driver that they went through the double barrier in the June sunshine. At the checkpoint they flashed their identity cards through the windows as they had been taught to do in their first days in Berlin. During one of the earlier confrontations, probably the Khrushchev–Kennedy round although no one was now sure, the Russians defied Western protests and had their own khaki-clad guards replaced with East German *Volkspolizei*, now invariably known as Vopos, in their olive green. The Western powers would not give up their rights of access to East Berlin but refused to recognize the Potsdam government either. When the dust settled there was no alternative but to find a compromise: access by vehicles of the military governments only on condition that identity cards were flashed in the direction of the Vopos deemed not to be there. Thus grew up one more arcane practice to add to so many others invented since the winners fell out after the victory.

'Gosh, this is new since I was last in Berlin,' the major exclaimed, pointing to the double concrete barrier through which they were threading their way. 'Is there any explanation?'

'Does there need to be an explanation?' Patience replied. 'Just one more structure in the madhouse you've all been so busy making here since the war.' Benton looked at his wife with some surprise, even alarm, as if she were being disloyal or at the very least insubordinate.

'But you know why, darling,' he explained patiently. 'It was put up last year after those young people stole an MG and crashed through to our side under the barrier. The East had to do something.'

'A madhouse,' Patience said, unrepentant. 'I told you.'

'True,' agreed the major, 'but it keeps us all in groceries.' He laughed, a short dry laugh which died when he found it was not reciprocated.

'Don't be such a cynic,' his wife said to cover the awkward silence. 'You know it doesn't suit you.'

'Oh, but it's true,' he protested. 'What would I be doing if it weren't for all this?' He waved vaguely over the vast paraphernalia of the Wall. 'Selling chocolate bars or soap, I shouldn't wonder.'

'Still,' he added reflectively after a moment's thought, 'that'd be fairly innocent, I suppose. There's nothing sinister about soap so far as I'm aware.'

'Not much there isn't,' said his wife, 'in this country anyway. You're not at home now, remember.'

'Sorry,' he replied. 'I forgot for a moment. Krautland. God.'

They were picking up speed again on the straight run-in between the stained stucco apartment blocks rebuilt as a thin cover for the desolation behind: acres of spent grass punctuated by ruined buildings, black as decayed teeth. The wind was blowing in the wrong direction, from the east, bringing with it the sour exhausted smell of lignite, the brown coal used in the power stations.

'As dreadful as ever, I see,' said the major. 'This bit always reminded me of a film set. A Russian film set at that, the gloomy buggers.'

A couple of minutes later the brown stucco started to thicken into a town where life struggled again into existence. There were blond children playing hopscotch in side streets, flaxen-plaited girls jumping ropes.

'I wonder if they ever did manage to do anything with our old embassy site on this side?' the major said. 'It was sinister-looking in my day, I remember. Would you mind our taking a look?'

'Isn't that rather frivolous?' said Benton. 'I thought you had something serious to do tonight.'

'True, old boy,' came the reply, 'but there's no way you can avoid being noticed. Take a look behind and you'll see what I mean.' There was a large old-fashioned black saloon keeping pace exactly a hundred yards behind them. 'A driver and three passengers,' the major said without turning round to look. 'The driver is bare-headed; the passengers are all wearing what I think used to be called fedoras.'

'I thought they'd have given all that up by now,' his wife said wearily. 'So time consuming.'

'Why should they?' the major answered. 'It keeps them in groceries too. And there's precious little else to do over here. They're a bit short on chocolate and soap. What there is sells itself. They don't need the salesmen.' This time Patience joined him in his laughter.

'I think I'm beginning to like a touch of cynicism now and again,' she said. 'It's some evidence of sanity.'

'The only thing to do,' the major went on after a short pause, 'is to appear as if you don't care. Driver? Stop at the old place, will you? Perhaps they'll think this is why we've come. Fat chance.'

'Right, sir.'

The site lay on the left-hand side of the boulevard, a single massive mound of overblown grass browning in the late sunlight. Beyond there were vacant lots and bits of burned-out property all the way to the Wall. From the top of the mound they had a panoramic view of the desolation as the men in the fedoras looked at them through field-glasses. 'Cheeky buggers,' was all the major would say, turning his back on them.

'You're standing, ladies and gentlemen, on what used to be one of the most expensive pieces of real estate in the world,' he went on, after a pause to let them take in the empty acres. 'Under your feet are the remains of balconies, balustrades, splinters of chandeliers, and doubtless an odd filing cabinet or two. The old British Embassy, chewed up in the war and left to rot. Horrible, isn't it?' Benton was reflecting that despite his insouciant manner he could scarcely be anything else but a British army officer in mufti. His moustache alone would have given him away, even the military dubbin on his brown shoes. There was something insolent in his combination of expensive brown overcoat and black bowler hat—as if he regarded the opposition as complete idiots. Benton began to feel uncomfortable, exposed out on a mound being spied on by men with field-glasses.

'I really think we've seen enough,' he said grimly. 'I must ask you to come away. Now. Immediately.'

The major took no notice. Instead he pointed to the mound next door, this one neater, almost parklike.

'Formerly the Reichskanzellerei,' he explained to the two women. 'Hitler's bunker is still over there, I believe, but unfortunately just out of sight. The Russians might have blown it up, of course, and of course they never will say just what they've done with it. Beyond it was the Hotel Adlon. My old man used to stay there before the war. Has the fondest memories of it, has the old chap. Funny when you think of it. This used to be one of the centres of the fashionable world like the Rue Royale, Bond Street, Fifth Avenue. Can you imagine it? The carriages, the jewellers, the expensive crowds.'

Patience shivered. 'This is becoming macabre,' she said. 'Can we go?'

'Certainly, my dear,' said the major gallantly. 'I didn't come here for entertainment. I need to remind myself occasionally of what can happen if we're not very, very careful.'

Life, even if it were make-do down-at-heel life, began again in earnest in front of the *Komischer Oper*, where they joined the hurrying crowds. True, Benton reflected, the men could only manage cheap blue or grey drab and the women homemade lurex sheaths, but at least there were lights as in the West and the billboards were gay with posters. The successful production that year was Felsenstein's *Love for Three Oranges*, and on this evening the billboards nearest the box office showed a silhouette of Prokofiev, looking puckish, even sardonic.

Once inside, the major closed his eyes and took a deep breath. 'Can you smell it, darling?' he asked. 'How it all comes back. Here I've been missing it for ages and I haven't even known I've been missing it.'

'What?' his wife asked, amused.

'Carbolic,' he said. 'Carbolic soap. Just like at school after rugger. I told you, they only make one kind of soap here, saves on salesmen. If you led me blindfolded to this spot, I could tell you instantly where we were.'

'The school changing rooms perhaps?' his wife said with a laugh as they passed under the arch into the stalls.

In the dark Benton could forget himself. The brilliance of the scenic invention made up for the irreducible fact of the music, which meant nothing to him. At the end he glanced round, irritated the moment the East European rhythmic clapping began. The seat next to Patience was empty. The major's wife, seeing the alarm in his eyes, whispered, 'He'll join us at the Lucullus. In about half an hour. Don't worry, he's in good hands.' Benton felt exposed, at risk, involved in something beyond his own ordering: the real world of conflict, entrapment, terror. The slow decanting of the crowd was nearly intolerable to him; he had to restrain an instinct to bolt. Recognizing the signs, Patience took his arm to keep him in check.

'This was a mistake,' he murmured to her, not taking his eyes off the exit door. 'I should never have let myself be talked into it.'

'Sh,' she murmured back. 'You really have no alternative but to go through with it. You do see that.'

'Oh, yes,' he said, 'I do see that. A bunch of cowboys.'

'I like him. He's amusing.'

'That's not the point.'

'What is, then?'

'It's not proper. The fool.'

'Oh. That.' Patience kept her eyes firmly on the back of the lady in front as they slowly edged towards the door. Knowing she had to keep control, she concentrated on the clumsy stitching round the lurex collar. I must not let go, she said to herself, I must not let go.

'If this goes on another minute I'm leaving,' Benton said, white-faced, his eyes ablaze. All around them East Germans were placidly forking through their plates, napkins tucked in their collars.

'Sh, sh,' Patience said. 'The service here is always this bad. It's no better at the other place.'

'It's not the service. Where is he? I thought,' he said, turning to the major's wife, 'I thought he was to be here in half an hour. No?'

The major's wife was serenely sipping her aquavit, as though nothing in the world was wrong. 'It's all right, Gareth,' she said, 'really it is. He'll be here presently. Why look, here he is now. I told you there was nothing to worry about.' She scarcely seemed surprised, still less relieved. Things were turning out much as expected.

The major made it from over the other side of the room. He advanced with a great grin, his mission evidently successfully accomplished. 'Have you ordered?' he asked before sitting down. Then, seeing them nod, he added, 'Good. Darling, did you order the schnitzel for me? Good. Good. They do an excellent schnitzel here, as I remember it. The dear old Lucullus. Ah, the good old days, what?'

'Well. And how are things?' Benton asked in his most cutting voice. 'We seem to have been here rather a long time. I hope it was worth it.'

'Sorry about that,' said the major, not the least bit apologetic. 'Things are fine, you'll be pleased to hear. Couldn't be better.' He beamed at them all before his eyes lit on the small decanter in front of him. 'Oh, I say,' he said. 'Is this vodka for me? How very thoughtful.' He knocked back one small measure and poured himself another. 'Here's health to all ze fridom-loffing pipples of ze vorld, ja?' His German accent was appalling but it made the women laugh.

Their three watchmen, hatless, sat uneasily at a table in the corner nursing a beer each. The major twinkled in their direction before turning to the serious business of the wine list. 'Darling,' he said, 'do they still have it, whatchamacallit, the Georgian white?'

'Yes, darling,' his wife answered, 'and Gareth here ordered a couple of bottles. One for you and one for the rest of us.'

'That's nice,' he said. 'Have you been waiting the statutory forty-five minutes? We used to time it in the old days. It was always forty-five minutes, not a second more or less. Prussian efficiency to the last.'

'The waiters disappeared into the woodwork some time ago,' his wife replied sourly, 'but I'm afraid we haven't been keeping track of the time. Gareth here was a little on edge. He was getting anxious for you.'

'Anxious? Gareth? Good heavens,' said the major, 'I was in good hands.'

'So we've been assured,' said Benton drily. But even he was taken with the major's irrepressible high spirits.

They all breathed a sigh of relief when the barrier went up and they were through the checkpoint into the American sector. It was one o'clock in the morning, but none of them felt particularly tired. There was a sort of exultation in the air, a sense of having done something rather clever. Even the driver seemed pleased.

'Well, now then,' said the major, 'how about a *boîte de nuit* to round off the evening? Fancy a little champagne from Champagne, France, as opposed to Georgia, USSR?'

'No thank you, Major,' Gareth said quickly. 'We have a busy schedule tomorrow. Thank you all the same.'

'Sure you won't change your mind?' The major looked at him, waggish.

'Sorry, but no.'

'A pity.'

When they drew up to the Bentons' door the major said, 'I see the Foreign Office still have the best houses. I suppose we poor soldiers still have those awful little boxes down the way.'

'I'm afraid so,' said Patience. 'It does seem so wrong in a way. But we simply go into whatever we're provided with. There's no such thing as a choice or anything.'

'When I was here the Berlin authorities told us that if we ever move out the first thing they'll do is pull up our married quarters. Can't say I blame them. A blot on the landscape.'

'I don't suppose,' said Benton, 'there's much chance of our moving out in the foreseeable future. The question's rather academic, I should have thought.'

'Too true, old boy. Nothing I heard tonight would lead me to think otherwise.'

They watched the car pull away before turning in at their gate.

'What was all that about?' Patience asked.

'All what about?'

'This evening. Everything.'

Gareth stood for a moment looking up at the house. 'I haven't the faintest idea,' he said at last.

'Oh, Gareth,' she said, bursting into laughter and taking his hand. 'I told you. It's a madhouse. Berlin is one great lunatic asylum. Only it's the patients who are in charge.'

Although she could not see it, she knew his brow was furrowed at this novel thought. As so often, she reflected, he missed the obvious. What was the point of all his cleverness?

'I wish,' he said, 'I could persuade you that this is a serious mission involved in serious work.'

'Oh,' she said. 'Sorr-ee,' she said.

-HIS AND HERS: HIS-

Willett, then the Press Secretary in Berlin, had his feet up on his office desk reading *Die Zeit*. As usual he seemed to have all the time in the world. He had lunched well with a couple of newspaper cronies and was looking rubicund, beaming as cheerfully as the weather, the mid-July of Middle Europe before the heavy heat of the holiday season.

'I wonder if you could spare me a minute?' Benton said coldly. 'The general's asked me to review our press policy again. In his opinion it can be improved. Or, to put it more frankly, it leaves something to be desired.'

'Wants his name in the papers again, does he?' Willett suggested. 'You might propose another of what he's pleased to call his "hearts and minds" campaigns. You know, give a few books to the Polytechnic? Big ceremony. I'll lay on plenty of photographers, never fear.'

Benton paused, allowing his incredulity to show. He looked down in icy contempt on the irrepressible Willett, by now beginning to quail. 'Fear?' he said evenly, the thunder only just over the horizon. 'Perhaps you'd like to explain those ideas personally to the general tomorrow at ten? Alternatively, you could let me have some more useful reflections on the problem by this evening, say six o'clock? Should the Information Department have any, that is.'

'Sorry, Gareth,' Willett mumbled. 'Just a joke. I'm sure we've got something on this already. Our last report on the state of the press is here somewhere—' By now Willett was fishing around among the untidy piles of paper on his desk. 'Where is the blessed thing?' He pulled out a slim document gingerly from a particularly chaotic collection at the far end. 'Ah, here it is. Our very latest thoughts.'

'I see.' Benton sniffed, glancing up and down the pages as if there were something wrong with them. The report was, in fact, extraordinarily well done, he could see that, but he was not going to be joshed by Willett or anyone else his junior. 'Perhaps,' he concluded, 'you could by six o'clock come up with more considered views?'

Later Willett discovered that Benton had already approached Klaus Dutton, his Anglo-German assistant, with the thought that Dutton, with his more intimate knowledge of the local scene, might like to put up his own paper direct to Benton to ensure it was properly considered. Willett was pale with rage. As usual when dealing with Benton, it was as if the sunlight had gone steel-hard, leaving no pleasure in the day. He went to Wilfred Cross, the Head of Chancery, responsible for co-ordination.

'Dutton's in my department. If anyone consults him, I do. What's Dutton to think? That the general doesn't trust me?'

'There, there, David,' Cross said evasively. 'You know it's only Gareth. It's just his way. He doesn't mean any harm.'

'No, that's too easy. You must tell him. I don't go around behind his back with suggestions he isn't up to the job.'

But they both knew it was no good. Cross was afraid of Benton's tongue as everyone else was. He knew, they all did, that Benton had the general's ear, that Patience was already un-official lady-in-waiting to Mrs General. Had not the general and Mrs been at the wedding as friends of the family?

'God, he's newly married,' Cross confided to his wife that evening, 'and still he's causing trouble. As if we don't have more serious things to think about.'

'Hurry up or you'll be late,' his wife said, her mind on other things. 'It's the Komischer tonight, remember? My treat? The driver's waiting.' They had not yet got used to the idea of being driven anywhere but, under the byzantine rules governing the four-power occupation, a military chauffeur was essential to navigate civilian passengers through Checkpoint Charlie into East Berlin.

'I fear,' said Cross quietly as the sullen Vopo waved them through the barrier, 'we're soon going to have more to worry about than bickering in the office.' He nodded to the left and right. There were four Russian tanks drawn up just off the ruined Friedrichstrasse. T54's, the latest thing, their crews milling about waiting for instructions.

His wife drew her breath in sharply. 'What are they doing here?' she said. 'What on earth does it mean?'

'Trouble,' Cross said. 'This Czech business is beginning to look serious. We all think the Russians will decide they prefer Dubcek to the alternative, but you never know. I mean we're all agreed, all except Gareth.'

'Gareth?'

'Yes. He believes we're all barking up the wrong tree. He says the Russians take the primitive view that what they have, they hold. On their own terms. He may be right.' Cross waved back at the tanks now behind them. 'They're starting to send up signals. The papers know something's been going on but so far they haven't guessed how serious it is. They'll be in no doubt tomorrow.'

'Do I turn back, sir?' the driver said without turning his head. Cross noticed his knuckles whitening on the steering wheel. 'No, I think not,' Cross said. 'My wife booked weeks ago.' They all smiled but it was impossible to disguise the general anxiety.

At midnight the Russian tanks looked more purposeful, battened down, ready to start up. There were also four tanks drawn up south of the barricade in the American sector, their white stars clearly visible under the sodium lighting. The silence was almost tangible, as if the earth had ceased turning.

'Driver?' Cross said calmly. 'I think you'd better drop me off at the office before taking my wife home.'

'Yessir,' the driver said, in a way which revealed that the rumours had reached the lower ranks days before, picked up by that osmosis common to all large organizations. He knew he would contribute to them in the morning. He turned in from the main road.

The old stadium, lightless, loomed sullenly against the luminescent sky to their left. After the checkpoint, there was a black hole to the left where the outdoor pool lapped, empty of NCOs at this time of night. But the office, ahead of them across the car park, was ablaze with light.

A world crisis, viewed from a diplomatic mission, always begins in the same way. The teleprinters, churning out the routine correspondence, stutter for a moment into silence. There is a pause of several seconds, perhaps as much as a minute, as if the machines are gathering strength. And then it comes rolling in, the tidal wave of telegrams from a dozen capitals at once, all signalling the onrush of frightening events. No one is ever completely taken by surprise, the possibility of trouble being in everyone's mind for weeks or even months before. What is always surprising is the irresistible flow of words, as if a dam had suddenly given way, driving all before it. 'A war of conflicting fantasies,' Charles described it later. 'Hostilities without weapons.'

To begin with, all that happened was that the working day grew longer. Charlottenburg, the British diplomatic ghetto, emptied earlier of its men and single women: up and out often before the daily exodus of children to their various schools. Dinner parties carried on for a week or so, often with only the wives present, but were soon abandoned by tacit consent. All those not directly involved were in any case glued to television sets as the events unrolled. At night the leafy streets were deserted, totally silent except for the occasional mew of an unhappy cat or the distant bay of one of the larger dogs. A blackout could have been imposed without inconvenience. A blackout was not imposed; street lamps continued to throw a steady phosphorescent gaze on unresistant avenues, devoid of all movement. And then, at midnight or so, there would be the sound of approaching cars, headlights dipping and rising with the contours of the underlying land. Car doors would slam, irregular as undisciplined musketry. Hall lights would show and garage doors shine in the headlights. A certain revving of engines and clunking into first gear. More slamming, this time of garage doors with space enough—just—behind rear bumpers. The crunch of good leather soles on gravel; bass and soprano voices in sequence; and then the closing of doors on personal lives, each entirely individual, without parallel, like none that had ever existed before.

By early August it got worse, as they all knew it would. The teleprinters battered away all night. No sooner did the Washington and the Havana traffic close down in the early hours than the Peking traffic began again, followed shortly by the latest developments in Moscow. Nobody seemed to be sleeping at all in London and Paris, and odd bits of information were coming in from the most unlikely places: Wellington, say, or Tokyo. The communicators worked longer and longer shifts until London took pity on them and sent reinforcements, grey figures seen blinking on the tarmac at Templehof at the foot of the aircraft stairs. Some people were, however, irreplaceable: the general, for instance, and all his senior people, who had cots made up for themselves in their offices and moved in with supplies of shirts and razor blades. The secretaries took over the canteen as a dormitory, although meals continued to be served throughout the day at Formica tables amid the sleeping bodies of the night shift.

For exercise there was the old Olympic diving pool tacked on to the office block at the end of a long corridor. Gareth found the water an astringent remedy to the increasing physical and mental fatigue. He took to going there every day about noon when for a full half-hour he would plough up and down in his pedantic way, scarcely aware that there were other swimmers. A great part of the pleasure, he reflected, was the momentary release from all human contact.

'Hello,' Beth said, drawing up beside him and taking her pace from his. She laughed. 'Do you come here often, as we say at the Palais?'

'Hello,' he said, panting. 'I try to put in half an hour a day.'

'Gracious. I didn't think anyone had the time.' They swam a few lengths in a silence becoming increasingly companionable. He felt her physical presence imposing itself on him in a way he could not quite define. Something to do with the silence between them, the regular rhythm of the strokes, the pause at the turn at each end. He became conscious for the first time of her long slender arms, cream-pale from the enforced confinement of recent weeks. She had plaited her hair into a thick rope of gold-on-brown, revealing a clear brow glistening with moisture.

After a few more lengths, by tacit consent they turned to the steps. She waited for him at the top, half turned towards him, thin-boned as a gazelle. Their eyes met in some mute, surprised recognition and she shrugged her delicate shoulders as if to say she had known all along. In her bikini she looked columnar, almost weightless, physically irresistible. They walked side by side towards the dressing rooms. He found it touching that she hardly came up to his shoulder, as if she was in need of his protection.

'That was very nice. Thank you, Gareth,' she said on a half-sigh, turning to go. He could scarcely hear the words in all the echoing clamour of indoor swimming. Their hands met.

'Must you?' he said. 'Must you go?'

'Yes,' she said, lip-reading. 'Yes. I must.'

'Tomorrow?'

'Maybe. It depends.'

'On what?'

'Lots of things. What's going on. The general. Lots of things.' If this was meant to be resistance, he thought, her eyes told a different story.

At this moment the general emerged from the men's dressing room. Despite the pressures of the last month he was still bronzed and fit, the jagged scar of his old war wound across his shoulder only emphasizing his boundless physical health. He looked up, surprised, his shaggy brows indicating at once that he realized something was going on between them. They instinctively moved apart.

'Hello, you two,' he said. 'Had your swim? Good. You'd better cut along quick now. We've just heard. The invasion's on. Don't smirk, Gareth, I know you've been telling us all along it would be. Anyway, I'm having a dip for five minutes. God knows when, if ever, there'll be time for another one.'

That night Russian tanks clanked and roared across the Czech border to put an end, in August, to the illusions of spring. The Soviet Ambassador went down to Prague airport and from the control tower there personally directed the stream of huge Ilyushins bringing troops and their equipment to bear on a defenceless population. Within the next three days a million and a half Soviet troops were on the ground in Czechoslovakia, several times the maximum estimated possible by the Western military planners. The world held its breath, not knowing the ultimate aim of the deployment and what Western reactions to it might be. In the general uncertainty, the risks of mutual misunderstanding grew ominous, a looming overhang of mind-numbing anxiety.

'Mutual madness,' Napier would say to anyone who would listen. 'They install tanks at the checkpoint. We install tanks at the checkpoint. They forbid the Yanks access to the East. We forbid Russian access to their War Memorial in our sector. They're called signals but we're just a lot of children out of our depth. Next thing is we'll be exchanging tactical nuclears. After all, they're only little ones. Madness.'

'Yes, Charles,' Benton replied, finally irritated by this, to him, emotionalism. 'But try to restrain yourself at the general's meetings. He's beginning to get worried about your soundness.'

'Stuff the general. He's as bad as any of them. He thinks it's going to be like the Second World War all over again. Difficult but manageable. He hasn't the faintest.'

'Perhaps. But he's in charge here. He would like you to keep cool.'

'Can't stand the old duffer.' Charles nonetheless looked abashed. 'All right,' he said finally, 'I'll try.'

'Good. I'm sure it will be for the best.'

The British communications centre in Berlin was subject to a constant deafening battering, as though the machines had suddenly assumed a brief manic life of their own.

The short telegrams were the worst, carrying without qualification the gravest possible news. At such moments everyone had the sensation of a noose tightening, a trapdoor opening at their feet. The longer telegrams showed the adversaries more reasonable, more willing to explain. These were read with a deep reassuring breath, a moment's relief before turning to the next instalment of threat and counter-threat. There were times when it seemed the desks would be submerged beneath the paper, when everyone had the feeling, as in a nightmare, of swimming upstream, all strength ebbing.

The marrieds phoned their wives once a day for mutual reassurance. Like wartime letters subject to censorship, the conversations were very general, very ordinary, neither side wanting to say anything too personal on the open line.

'All right then, darling? Kids tucked in?'

'Yes. Jamie's got toothache.'

'Oh, dear.'

'What's that?'

'I said "oh, dear." Give them a kiss for me, won't you?'

'They want to know where you are. I tell them you're at the North Pole putting in a good word with Father Christmas.'

'Yes. Well. Take care of yourself, now.'

'You too. You'll call again tomorrow.'

'Of course. Of course. Love you.'

'Love you too.'

Click. Someone else's turn.

Benton occasionally had the impression that the whole episode followed the course of a terminal illness. There were moments of elation when the strain would suddenly ease, a quiet shared excitement when everyone would exchange brief nods and eyes flashed in common relief. There were other moments when the strain grew intolerable, when there appeared no remedy, when the unimaginable was just about to happen to them and their fresh-faced wives and perfectly formed children: a millionth of a second of unfathomable pain and all their ashes becoming one with nuclear ash churning up millennia of history.

'It's times like these,' Napier shouted against the clatter of the machines, 'that one longs for a desert island.' He tore off the latest telegram. 'Preferably one,' he added, 'we haven't made radioactive.'

The chief communicator grinned. 'You watch,' he shouted back. 'The Russkis have got what they want, i.e., the poor sodding Czechs, and they sure as hell don't want a tangle with the Yanks. And vice versa for the Americans. There's a lot of old hoo-ha, but when it comes right down to it they're all chicken. Thank God.'

'I hope you're right, Jimmy.' Napier sighed. He flicked the telegram with his thumbnail. 'When you read this kind of thing you begin to wonder.'

Jimmy shrugged. 'Come off it,' he protested. 'I was here in

'forty-seven, 'forty-eight, time of the airlift. We had problems in those days, all right. But this Brezhnev character, old Eyebrows, he isn't a patch on Uncle Joe.'

'I'll tell the general,' Napier shouted. 'He'll be relieved to hear it.' There was a crow of laughter around the room as this was passed round above the uproar. All eyes turned back to the machines, on watch for the next gnawing item of news.

'The real problem,' Napier suggested to Benton, 'is the feeling of helplessness. We none of us can do anything for the Czechs, we know that, still less for poor old Dubcek. But we also know that if there's not going to be a world war, it's going to be settled at the top between a couple of peasants. It's some sort of symbiotic thing they have developed. They need each other to stay on top even if they have to risk everything once in a while to make it work. At times like this, all the rest of us only look busy, protesting to the other side about this, liaising with our own side about that, mobilizing the other. But basically we're just a crowd watching a couple of heavyweights slugging it out.'

Gareth had been thinking of the swimming pool and the harmony of slow concerted rhythm and the pause on turning at each end. He frowned, annoyed at his own lack of concentration, wondering if it showed.

'Cheer up, Gareth,' Charles said, 'the lower decks have decided. It's Peace tomorrow.'

And peace it was. It came suddenly a few days afterwards, late at night, with a short telegram from Washington, the kind they had come to dread. They all gathered in the general's room. Even he was haggard by now but still, in the circumstances, surprisingly spruce and clean-shaven.

'It's beginning to look all right,' the general said, 'but we still need confirmation from over the way.' He nodded in the direction of the Wall down the road a few miles. 'I don't know. It all looks too good to be true. What's happened about the tanks at the checkpoint? Not a word in here about the tanks.' He read the telegram again to check this was so.

'The Americans have just telephoned,' Cross said. 'Both sides are withdrawing about now. The Russians are to be allowed over tomorrow to man their war memorial in our sector. The travel restrictions on the Americans in the East have been lifted. It's back to the status quo, it seems.'

There was a perceptible sigh of relief round the room. Charles winked at Gareth, who glanced quickly back to the general lest this should be thought frivolous and he a party to it. But the general was staring out of the window at the night, tapping his reading glasses on his blotter. 'A damn near thing,' he said, 'a damn near thing. Let's have a drink.'

And it was true. The first news was followed by a flood of telegrams from all over the world piecing the story together. Then it was the turn of the commentators, the BBC, Voice of America, Radio Moscow, all giving their version of the events. A couple of days later the cuttings service circulated the editorials from the main London dailies, *Le Monde*, *Die Zeit*, and the *International Herald Tribune*. The *Economist* trundled up last with its magisterial, if not entirely helpful, reflections on where to go from here.

Like a particularly violent summer storm, the thunder rolled round them ever and ever more distant until by the end of the year it was as though it had never been. There was a reminder on December 31 when, as part of the Review of the Year, the newspapers published by-now familiar pictures of bewildered-looking Russian boys in the turrets of tanks surrounded by protesting Czechs, of sinister-looking columns of those same tanks crumping down the boulevards of Prague. There was another reminder the following day when *The Times* published the New Year's Honours List. The general was made a Knight Grand Commander of his Order and the Minister, his deputy, was the pleased recipient of a Knighthood in his. There was even a smallish medal for the chief communicator for exceptional service. The young men, Cross, Napier, Benton and Willett, got nothing but good marks with Personnel Department.

Just before the group broke up and the office cots returned to the storeroom the general had a word with Gareth.

'Don't think I want to interfere,' he said, 'but I thought you'd be interested in a little story. During the war everyone took a turn at fire-watching on the old War House roof. It was cold and dark up there, the blackout you see, and—well, a lot of friendships were formed up there. It was the stress of the times, the long hours, everyone far from home. Led to a lot of divorces, a lot of unhappiness. Very unprofessional, of course, what went on. But then we didn't think we'd survive, most of us. You do see?'

'I see.' Gareth's lips went white, but he knew enough to keep his voice low and even. 'And so?' They had, he thought, been extremely discreet. Their meetings had been few and furtive, mere whisperings in corridors or the accidental sharing of a table over lunch which was not quite accidental, or a few snatched minutes alongside each other in the swimming pool. He had assumed no one had noticed in the press of public events, but evidently he had been wrong. The general had noticed. Or someone had noticed and told the general? Gareth could feel a gulf yawning under his feet, as if the ground were giving way.

'It's very understandable,' the general continued. 'She's a fine-looking girl. Odd circumstances. But it's back to real life now. Go home. Take a couple of days off. You need to get all this'—the general waved a hand to embrace the whole building—'all this out of your system for a while. Get back to that bonny wife of yours.'

'You're not suggesting—?' Gareth began. He was wondering who had noticed. Charles? The general himself? Surely Beth had not confided in anyone?

'I'm suggesting nothing, old boy,' the general interrupted. 'But I thought I owed it to you both to say. You with a career to make. And Patience too, of course. Almost a member of the family, you see.'

'Thank you.'

'*Pas de quoi*,' the general said. 'Give her my love, won't you? Perhaps you'd like to come to dinner next week. Thursday, I believe, but you'd better check with my ADC. The Defence Secretary's coming out. He calls it a morale-building exercise, hah-hah.'

'Thank you. I'm sure we'll love that.'

From his window above the car park Gareth watched her leave. The autumn sun rising deliquescent through the first mists shone weakly on the departing saloons, all the bustle of general evacuation. She was carrying a small suitcase and his heart almost stopped at the sight of her slender clenched wrist, her hair, gold-on-brown, shaken loose in the early morning air. She was dawdling, advancing with that almost imperceptible undulation of one willing to be caught. She reached her Mini and bent to place the suitcase on the back seat. Straightening, she looked up at the façade as if searching for something.

Their eyes met. He instinctively drew back into the shadows. She froze, one hand clutching the car roof, the other to her mouth. When she had at last understood she got quickly in and roared off down towards the incline and the main road.

Gareth was surprised at the sense of celebration he felt on the drive home. It was still a little before seven o'clock and the roads were empty. He drove fast, as if this would blot out memories of nightmare weeks. He thought it pretty decent of the general to invite them to meet the Defence Secretary, giving them the chance to shine before someone who, rumour had it, would be Foreign Secretary next time round. He could feel his life taking on a fresh, a renewed order, the priorities reestablished, even his own sense of himself restored. He blocked out memories of a touch of hand, of a plaited rope of gold-on-brown, their brief, desperate clingings in the eye of the storm. Instead he thought of Patience, wondering whether she would be in her housecoat, the pretty one that came with her trousseau, the one with ruffles setting off the pink bloom of her neck. He smelt the new morning, warmed to the sunlight sparkling irregularly through the leaves. He imagined fresh coffee and fresh bread, and Normandy butter from the Economat in the French sector. It was, he decided, the happiest moment he could remember, this return to normality, to a life under control, just the two of them with his the guiding hand.

Patience, Patience. She would meet him at the door, her arms opening to him. She would be tugging him gently up the ponderous staircase and across the mock minstrel's gallery to their bedroom. Her hand would already be on the silk ribbon at the throat, the ribbon she would pull the moment the door closed behind them. She would be bed-warm to the touch.... Somehow, at this point, the image of Beth would superimpose with that shrug of delicate shoulders as if to say she had known all along.

He parked the car in the drive. As he got out he looked up at the heavy German house they had been allocated, as into a comfortless face indifferent to his desires. The windows were closed. The curtains were drawn, only their blank linings hanging lifelessly being visible from the garden. For a moment cold clutched his heart, a spasm of inner panic. It was a house of total strangers. Worse, it was as if it were uninhabited, where nothing ever happened because it was a house where nobody real lived.

He opened the front door with his latchkey and stepped over the threshold. Here, at last, was reassurance. All was in place, all as it should be. The telephone directories were all neatly arranged under the small hall table. Her horse pictures in their discreet frames hung evenly against the dark panelling. The blond official-issue furniture, incongruous in the sombre pomp of prewar Germany, gleamed with new polish. In the drawing room the newspapers had been folded. The kitchen, the only modern part of the house, shone with uncluttered surfaces. It was home as he would have wished it, satisfying in its order and propriety, in its absence of the unkempt, the awry. She was, as he always knew she would be, the model wife, knowing how things should be.

He climbed the stairs and crossed the gallery to their bedroom. The bed was made, looking as if nobody had slept there. Ever. Patience came in quietly, wrapped in a bath towel. Her eyes were puffy with fatigue and her face was rough-grained, green. 'I feel rotten,' she said thickly. 'I've been sick all night. Poor Gareth, just as you finally get home.'

'You sounded all right, last night on the telephone,' he objected.

'I couldn't lie down. I slept in a chair. Could you make me some tea?'

'All right.' He tried to sound grudging but she was too ill to care. She sat down on a chair again, avoiding his eye. 'Please,' she said quietly and he had little choice but to go.

Ten minutes later she came across him in the kitchen, head down on the table, fast asleep. She turned the steaming kettle off and got him somehow to bed. When he awoke late in the afternoon there was a note on the hall table:

Bazaar meeting, I'm afraid, with Mrs General. Then there's the Chevrille party—I mentioned it on the phone last week, remember?
Love, P

No. He could not remember. He found their *putzfrau* in the kitchen, a still handsome war widow with a good skin and S.S. past. She was, of course, incurably sentimental.

'You poor, poor soul,' she wailed. 'How ill you look.'

'Not ill, Frau Henze. Just tired. Bone-weary, as a matter of fact.'

'You must eat. I prepare you something special, something very German, *ja?*'

'Oh, all right.'

'Poor Prague.' She sighed, opening the refrigerator for the eggs. 'Poor Mr Dubcek. No one to help. No one. Munich 1938 all over again. Your Chamberlain. Same thing now with the Americans, *ja?*'

'Yes, well,' Gareth said, once again at a loss for something to say when confronted with Frau Henze's selective memory.

She served him a small potato omelet and salad as he sat, punctilious as ever, at the dining room table, its immense blond surface set only for one. He could not see anything particularly German about the omelet, but the strudel that followed was the real thing, as light and sugary as Frau Henze's character. He noticed she had red eyes. She had been weeping silently in the kitchen amidst all the glittering Formica.

'It is Heinrich I have been thinking about,' she explained, dabbing her eyes with a small lace handkerchief. 'He died, you know, in the East, fighting the Russians. 1943.'

'I'm sorry.'

'Such a waste.' She sighed. 'Poor Prague. We could not stop the Russians. And now this.'

Patience got back only in time to shower and change. She looked better but there was a greenish touch to her temples. He tried looking meaningful but she only said, 'There, there. The Chevrilles, remember? Hurry up or we'll be late.'

'I thought you were sick. Couldn't the bazaar meeting have waited?'

'Darling, you know it's next week. There's a million things to do.'

'I don't think the bazaar comes before your duty.'

'Darling, the bazaar *is* my duty. Besides, you're making the other seem so soulless.' Seeing his brow threaten, she tried coaxing. 'Besides, there'll be time tonight. You'll see.'

'We won't be able to get away until midnight,' he explained, as patiently as he could, but it was clear to her that his voice was being kept deliberately under control. She had got used to that clear clipped enunciation which meant menace, danger.

'You can always say you're tired. They'll surely understand. After all, they've been as busy themselves. You can ask to leave early, surely?'

'Certainly not,' he said. 'There'll be several senior people present. You know we can't leave before they do. It's never done.'

'Surely for once?' she pleaded. 'It's very informal. It's her birthday. Last week she was wondering whether she'd have another birthday at all.'

'I couldn't possibly,' he said, his jaw shutting firmly. She said nothing. She was putting on her dress. She turned her back on him with just a hint, he thought, of titillation.

'There,' she said. 'All ready. Can you do the zip?'

'No,' he said petulantly, 'I can't do the zip. Do it yourself.'

'All right,' she replied evenly, trying to put on a brave face despite her welling eyes. 'You'll see. It will be all right when we get back. I promise.'

He said nothing but his eyes danced with rage. She flinched inwardly, half-expecting violence.

'Oh, come on, Gareth,' she said incredulously. 'It's only a few hours.'

He strode out, clutching the car keys. 'Come on,' he said grimly. 'If you're not at the front door in thirty seconds, I'll go by myself.'

She followed him down the corridor, a little shaken, prepared to be humble. They put on their overcoats by the front door, neither saying anything, each in a private world. She felt small beside his tall shoulder, grudgingly accommodating itself to his overcoat and scarf.

In the car on the way to the party she told him about the baby.

'That's why I'm being sick all the time,' she explained. 'I'm sorry, but there you are. Late March or early April, the doctor says.'

'Rather soon, isn't it?' was his reply. 'I thought we had agreed to wait at least two years. That's usual, I believe. What's normally done.' It was her turn to control herself. 'What went wrong?' he asked.

'Nothing went wrong,' she said very distinctly. 'We were just a little careless, that night after the Russian party. That night, you remember, when we were forced to drink all that vodka. All those toasts, remember? Friendship between our two peoples? Peace in our time? Funny, when you come to think of it.'

'It couldn't be helped,' she said, after a pained silence. 'Or I couldn't help it, at least.'

'I had hoped we might have kept to our decision to wait,' he said doggedly, knowing it was a mistake but wanting something, anything, to hurt. 'I did think you could be relied on to that extent—why, whatever is the matter?'

She had let out a howl, uncontrollable, defensive, uterine. He could scarcely believe it from one so evidently well-bred, trained to restraint, politeness, manners. Through her torrents of tears she managed to stammer, 'Gareth, it's a baby. *Something Real. Ours. A Baby!*'

'I see,' he said, seeing only that he was in too deep to retreat. 'I think you had better stop now. You'll have to make your face up. Tegel is the next turning, look.'

This to him self-evident observation was greeted by a fresh outburst of sobbing, as if she would never stop. It was only years later that, remembering this scene, he suddenly realized that if only he had had the sense she would have forgiven him anything at such a moment. All she was waiting for was the right words. The irony, he reflected, was that at the moment she was telling him about the baby he had felt a gush of human warmth like none he had ever previously experienced.

- HIS AND HERS: HERS -

A year later, with the baby born and a time of relative peace in Europe, the marriage should have been going better. The Crosses, mindful of staff morale, thought it was their duty to hold a dance twice a year for all the under-forties, civilian and military, the singles and the marrieds. Their house was ideally suited and the garden, being larger than average, was an additional asset, at once a refuge for the shy and an opportunity for the amorous. 'Sugar,' the voice on the tape recorder crooned for the third time that evening. 'Sugar, sugar.' Someone had turned the lights off to allow the dancing couples to snuggle closer together. It was a still hot night, not unusual for Berlin in August. The long windows had been set wide, allowing the scented bushes some small scope against the Chanel of the women, the men's aftershave.

They sat together in their separate unacknowledged misery on a swing seat in the garden, letting the music eddy around them. It was Saturday night, their first pause since they had left for church the previous Sunday morning. During the week he had breakfasted alone. She had plenty to occupy her with the baby, even though a nanny was expected shortly and Frau Schmidt babysat meanwhile, while they went about as a young couple from the British Mission.

You know, the handsome pair, very British. The tall one with the delicious English wife, all peaches and cream. Had a baby a few months ago. A boy, I believe.
    Ah, the whatchamacallems. Batesons? Batemans?

Bentons, mon cher, *the Bentons. Gareth and Patience.*
Funny name, Patience. Très jolie, d'ailleurs.

As the Bentons, they had eaten seven lunches in the week, one
at home, but never alone. There had been six dinners with a
little bridge and tennis, two National Days, and incessant cocktails. Between times he had slogged away at the telegrams and
the twice-weekly bag to London. When the baby slept midmorning she leafed through *Country Life* or *The Field,* dreaming of Meddows. In the afternoons she had gone about with
the general's wife: Patience Benton, everyone's favourite, if
thought a trifle cool by the shrewder judges among the non-
diplomatic wives. But all were agreed, if not for the same
reasons, that it must be a great help to have a wife like that.

He should go far, young Benton. A clever young man with a
charming wife, a real sweetie. Our sort.
    But he's hateful! Such a bully. Thinks a sight too much of
himself, does our friend Benton.
    They say she's gone a long way to humanize him. Pretty little
thing.
    I hope so. There was a long way to go, you have to admit.

They entertained well, with proper place settings and handwrit-
ten menus propped up in silver holders and a bowl of well-cut
flowers halfway down the table. Theirs was not a place for the
informal buffet followed by charades or the rougher English
house-party games—'Sardines,' say, or 'Are You There,
Moriarty?'—which so mystify foreigners. They gave their
dances like everyone else, but even then there was a noticeable
straightening of uniforms before pressing the front doorbell.
The obligatory Russian First Secretary and his wife who were
seen everywhere conspicuously failed to get drunk as they
usually did, and the girls soon found out that the music chosen
never quite got things moving. Gareth with his wretched sense
of rhythm and Patience with her slightly glacial air and her
pre- and post-maternity wear were not at their best on these
occasions. But at the formal dinner party, with candles lit
and helped by staff moonlighting from the Army Catering

Corps in white gloves, they were considered the best of their generation.

Frightfully nice Frenchwoman I was sitting next to last night at the Bentons.

I know. But you didn't have to make it so obvious. Everyone noticed.

No, really? D'you realize her brother is Secretary General at the Quai? The food was very good too. And first-class wine. We'd better have the Bentons back soon . . .

Darling? Did you hear me?

Of course we shall. Darling.

Eighteen months had passed quickly enough, what with the wedding and the baby and everything. The first few weeks had been best, when she had been buoyed up by her new status. Her wedding ring would catch on the soap in the morning bath. Through the steam she would look at it, soap and all, for minutes on end, reflecting on how handsome he was, how clever everyone said he was, how lucky she was to have made such a match. He was difficult, she recognized that, but clever people were said to be difficult, weren't they? She had read that somewhere. She was sure she had read that somewhere.

Not many weeks into the marriage she learnt the danger signals: the knotting of the jaw muscles, the slight firming of the voice into the treble register, the assumed air of weary patience belied by unsteadiness in the eyes.

'I do wish you'd watch what you wear, Patience. That was really most unsuitable.'

'Sorry, Gareth. I do try.'

'But if only you would ask me, there would be no difficulty. Did you see other wives in a short skirt? It was a long-dress occasion. Clearly.'

'I'm sorry.'

'It's all very well being sorry. Next time I'll choose for you.'

'No. Not the Egyptians this time. We're having the Israelis, remember? You haven't invited the Egyptians?'

'Yes, as a matter of fact I have invited the Egyptians.'

'Then you'll just have to de-invite them, that's all. Tell them you've got the date wrong. Tell them anything.'

'You *do* know the Portuguese have broken off diplomatic relations with India? You've got them sitting together, look.'

'But the wives play bridge together. They're the best of friends, Gareth, honestly.'

'We've got to get it right. Cross is coming and that wife of his. They're bound to notice. They'll think we don't know the rules.'

'Not at all. Janet Cross plays bridge at the same table too.'

'Darling, how many times do I have to tell you? A dinner party is a formal act. There are rules. Wilfred Cross knows them. I know them. I won't have him reporting that I do not.'

She tried submissiveness but this only made things worse. He would icily press home his advantage until she would burst into tears and flee from the room. After ten minutes savouring his triumph he would come after her, passion spent.

'Sorry, darling.'

'That's all right.'

'Don't cry. It makes you very plain.'

'Oh, Gareth. I'm sorry. I'll learn.'

'Of course. I'm always here to help, remember. You can always ask if you're the least bit unsure.'

When she wrote to her father recounting the latest incident he would reply that the first couple of years were always difficult. Why he and her mother . . . they had walked out on each other scores of times. But her father's letters did not seem to help.

Essentially, she concluded just before the crisis took Gareth away for a few weeks, it was the sex thing that made all the rest so difficult. She had studied his wretched book, but it scarcely made any difference. Most of the things recommended were too ridiculous, really weird. Gareth would gravely try some of them in an experimental sort of way, but she could see his heart wasn't really in it. If only he could let go, she thought, if only he would come alight, she would have tried anything.

As it was she approached the marriage bed every night with dread. Had he not been schooled in persistence? Every night in the bathroom she would remove her contact lenses and put them in their little case. Every night she would take out the bigger case and prepare everything for the insertion. She would wash off the surplus jelly, telling herself it was all right, one of these days it would work out, just give it time, as her father invariably wrote. She would open the bathroom door and fumble unfocussed towards the bed, unable to see whether he was lying on his arm watching her approach or absorbed in one of his impenetrable books.

On the good evenings she was allowed to snuggle next to him, to gaze at whatever page he was on with puzzlement in her eyes.

'What is it? Is it fun?'

'Mmmm? Hardly fun. Interesting for those who might be interested. Hardly your cup of tea, I'd have thought.'

'Go on, tell me. How d'you know I'm not interested?'

'Really, Patience. I'm trying to concentrate.'

'Go on, go on. Tell me.'

He looked up to the corner of the room and sighed audibly, as if calling on heavy reserves of patience. 'Well,' he said, 'if you must know it's an account of the conversation between Bethmann-Hollweg and von Bülow on the fifth of August 1914.'

'Oh,' she said, deflated. Then, brightening, 'What did they talk about?'

'The German is a trifle elliptical when it comes to the fine detail. The main point is that Bethmann had now realized, too late of course, that the invasion of Belgium was a mistake.'

'Yes,' she said, thinking this over. 'I expect it was. Good night then, dear.'

'Good night.'

He allowed his cheek to be bent to her kiss but he did not take his eyes off the page.

She could sense the bad evenings from the door, long before she could see anything from the bed. It was as if there were something about the heavy German panelling that vibrated on a different wavelength. Oh, dear, she would think wryly, here we go again. Going round the bed to her side she would pass his chair where his pyjamas would be folded neatly, almost pedantically, as if laid out for the school matron's inspection. As she popped brightly into bed he would put a thin arm round her, using the other to lift her nightie.

'Hello,' he said, striving for an intimate tone, as deep and throaty as he could make it. 'And how is little Patience tonight?'
  'All right,' she answered, 'I think.'
  'Really? I mean you're not . . . you're not?'
  'No. Next week; end of this, perhaps.'
  'So it really is? All right?'
  'Yes,' she whispered. 'Yes, it's all right. Honestly.'

There seemed to be an awful lot of fumbling, a lot of digging about with unconvincing fingers which did not produce the effect described in the book. And as the book said, when he was out there riding on his own, she tried to keep the rhythm going but never quite got the hang of it. She tried to blame herself for this, but in her heart she knew that physical coordination was not really his thing.

  It hardly took any time, she was prepared to admit that. The whole thing was really quite endurable if only she had not been so shaken up, so left with her thirst. The compensation was the thought that she had given him something he appreciated, doubtless had need of, although he seemed to get on quite well without it before they got married.

'Thank you, darling.'
  'That's all right, dear. Go to sleep, now.'
  'Was it as good for you?'
  'Oh, yes. I enjoyed it.'
  'Did you? You know, did you?'
  'Not exactly, darling. But it was nice. I feel fine.'
  'These things take time. It says so in the book. You've just got to learn to relax a little, apparently.'
  'You're right, dear, I expect. Go to sleep now.'

The world crisis, when it came, thus brought her only relief. She awaited his telephone call every evening with the same concern and worry as the other wives. Like them she could feel through his carefully neutral words the throb of world events, the yawning anxieties in the telegrams. But for the rest of the time, she had to admit, there was happiness in having the house to herself, his oppressive presence removed. She found the need to gossip with Frau Henze, who grew temptingly confidential in the absence of the master of the household. She would find herself drawn to the kitchen about eleven o'clock each morning, by which time the house was swept and burnished with a teutonic hand. Frau Henze seemed to be able to sense her coming, for there was always a cup of coffee waiting for them both. She had a fine skin and soft blue eyes. Her ample bosom promised maternal comfort, understanding, warmth. Even her faint wrinkles were disarming, suggesting experience of this world, unblinking tolerance.

'Your husband, Frau Benton, he telephoned last night, *ja*?'

'Yes, Frau Henze.' Patience suppressed a sigh. 'He is quite well, thank you.'

'It is times like this I think of poor Heinrich. Lying there somewhere in the Ukraine, forgotten by everybody. And for what? Nothing. Always the same thing, the Russians.'

'Not forgotten, surely? Not forgotten by you, Frau Henze?'

'No. I have not forgotten. Poor Heinrich.'

'What was he like?'

'Like?' Frau Henze was holding a mug between her knees. She had a clear brow, Patience noted, and her piercing blue eyes, normally restless, birdlike, smoked over with reminiscence. She laughed softly. 'A proper man,' she said at last. 'Never satisfied. Never.'

'Gracious.'

'Yes. A proper man. I liked it best when he would steal in behind me when I wasn't looking. Washing maybe the dishes. Then—oops! You know?'

'I know,' Patience lied, but Frau Henze, alight with fond memories, did not stop to notice. 'How he liked it when I washed the dishes,' she said as they both burst with laughter. Frau Henze rocked backwards and forwards on her stool, making no effort to control herself. Tears, half of joy, coursed down her cheeks until she checked them with the back of her sleeve.

'Was he your first, Frau Henze?'

'Not so, my dear. Just the best. I had plenty to compare him to, otherwise I should never have known.' They giggled, like a couple of schoolgirls at the back of the class. 'I liked them best when they had a little car, an Opel maybe or a Volkswagen. You waited until the windows steamed up so nobody could watch. The what d'you call them?'

'The Peeping Toms perhaps?'

'*Ja*. The Peeping Toms in the parks. Awful. Sometimes they rocked the car, knocked on the windows maybe. We didn't care. We were young.' Frau Henze shrugged her still pretty shoulders. 'But married to Heinrich, that was the best. So handsome in his uniform. The S.S. but shh . . .'

'Was it awful when he died?' Patience asked. She found herself admiring the clarity of Frau Henze's skin.

'After he died,' Frau Henze replied, 'after the news came, I didn't care anymore. I slept with everybody, with anybody. We knew the war was lost anyway. It was not unpleasant, sleeping with a man, waiting for the end to come. One more night, we used to say, only one more night.' Struck by other memories, she paused a moment. 'And then it was the Russians, no longer nice German boys. Animals. And then the Americans for a bar of chocolate or a packet of cigarettes. Americans always chewing their gum, even when drinking beer, even when making love, imagine. Ugh.'

Patience hardly dared to ask. 'And after that?' she managed at last, drawn inexorably into the spell.

'After that, my dear,' Frau Henze said, 'no more men.'

'I see.'

'Too much hurt. No pleasure. Only girls now.'

'Did I shock you yesterday?' Frau Henze said. 'I am sorry if I shocked you. It's the truth.'

'I know. Poor Frau Henze.'

'No. Not poor. There is still life. I have life. It is poor Heinrich who is dead.'

'So you don't really remember him? I mean, now.'

'Nothing lasts, nothing survives the absence. I remember how it was but no, I do not remember him. Not any more, in bed with another—person.'

'Do you hate us?' Patience reached out a hand and stroked Frau Henze's cheek. She did not know why she did this but Frau Henze took her hand and looked at its strong sensible nails.

'You must call me Margrethe,' she said. 'You understand?'

Patience, bewildered, tried to withdraw her hand. 'No,' she said thickly. 'I don't understand. Please, Frau Henze, I—'

'Ah,' said Margrethe, 'I see you do understand. Shall I call you Patience?'

'No,' Patience said after a long pause, looking into Margrethe's eyes as if searching for her soul. The final barrier gave way. 'Of course you must,' she said at last.

'I hoped you might say that,' Margrethe said, leading Patience out of the kitchen and across the heavy hall to the ponderous stairs.

'Tell me about the war, your war.'

'Another time, dear. Shh, now.'

'Now I show you my uniform. Would you like I put on my uniform?'

'Not especially.' Patience lay on her back looking at the ceiling, trying to recall it rocking as the pleasure between them mounted and they went thrashing over the top.

'I brought it especially. Usually it is hidden away. Please.'

Patience was not sure about the uniform, but she was too content to care much either way. 'All right. If you want to,' was all she said. But Margrethe was already padding barefooted to the bathroom door.

'There,' Margrethe said. 'You like?'

Patience burst out laughing. 'Oh, Margrethe. Oh, my dear. It's too absurd.' Margrethe looked bewildered. But it was true. She was still a handsome woman but she had filled out since her teenage years. The black skirt stretched awkwardly over her too-full thighs and the tunic looked as comfortable as a straight-jacket. The once-fetching stand-up collar with its sinister emblems on each side of the throat no longer met in the middle, giving the whole outfit a slightly raffish air. Even the high-prowed military cap, once the terror of Europe, looked dated, theatrical.

123

'Come,' Patience said kindly. 'Come here if you want to.'

Margrethe looked down on the young girl, who looked back through half-closed eyelashes. 'You're delicious,' Patience said, wondering. 'Do you still need it? Really? That uniform?'

'More than ever, my dear,' was all that Margrethe could say. 'More is the shame. I keep it to remind me what it was like. The excitement of it all, the dressing up, oh, the lovely dreams. But then—afterwards—the things we did. In the East.' The tears flowed down her cheeks. 'I am so ashamed, so bitterly ashamed. There are no words.'

'Put it away,' Patience said, lifting a wondering hand to brush away the tears. 'You don't have to say. I understand. You wanted to belong. You would do anything to belong.'

'How old are you?' asked Margrethe, wonder in her voice.

'Twenty-two, nearly twenty-three. Why?'

'So much you know already.'

'I have been studying.'

A week later Patience missed her period again and two weeks later, on the eve of Gareth's return, she started to be sick. It was incredible, as if the waves of passion she was floating on had somehow opened her up. Then she remembered the Russian evening, the night Gareth and she had been forced to toast everything under the sun: Universal Peace, Brotherhood, Friendship between the Russian and the British peoples. Everything.

'It was awful,' she whispered to Margrethe in the dark. 'There was nothing we could do. Gareth thought it was his duty.'

'Poor darling,' Margrethe whispered back, giggling. 'Come to Mutti and tell her all about it. A bad evening for my dearest, then? There, there.'

'The worst of it was that when we came back here we went straight to bed. Even Gareth. Imagine.'

'Was he good to you then? Did he give my darling pleasure? Tell Mutti.'

'No. Not then, not ever. Only I forgot the thing. I realized the next morning, of course. But by then it was too late apparently. God, I'm going to be sick again.'

They were using the guest bedroom, and when Gareth returned the following morning he found his own bed unslept in. Margrethe had kept out of the way until he was safely asleep.

'How do I tell him?' Patience asked. They were in the kitchen sipping the coffee that had brought them together, by now almost a sacramental rite. They were holding hands. 'It's not in his plans, a baby.'

'Do you want Mutti to take care of it? I can, you know. I have addresses.'

'Good God.' Patience, even in her state of lost innocence, was shocked. She withdrew her hand. 'Of course not. It's a baby.'

'Yes,' Margrethe replied quickly. 'It is my darling's baby. Of course you must have it.'

'Darling Mutti,' Patience said, patting the hand to Frau Henze's cheek. 'How well you understand. No one else has. Ever.'

'I would have liked a baby myself,' Margrethe replied, 'but it was not to be. The war, you see.'

The pregnancy was interminable. After the weeks of green-sickness during which she felt repellent to everybody, there were the months of swelling out and ever more awkward lumbering about the house. She could not say she was surprised when Gareth told her that Margrethe had given notice. It hurt terribly, but she could not say she was surprised.

For some reason there was no cocktail party that evening. There was an hour or so to kill before the inevitable dinner party.

'I'm slightly surprised,' Gareth said, pausing to look up from his newspaper. 'I thought she was reasonably content here. There are only two of us. We pay the going rate.'

'Did she give a reason?' Patience said, apparently intent on her petit-point. 'Was there anything special?'

'No. She just said she had personal reasons. I did not enquire, of course.'

'Of course.'

'Didn't she mention she was going to you?'

'No.'

'Funny. I thought you two were getting on reasonably well. No? You haven't done anything to upset her? That would be too provoking. She's a good woman. Dependable.'

'No, I haven't said anything to upset her. We were getting on reasonably well.'

'Strange. I don't understand it.' Gareth returned to the Home News and the article on the impending by-election everyone thought so critical to the Government's survival.

'Oh, Mutti, Mutti,' Patience wailed. 'Must you? Must you go? I know I'm hideous. I'll not always be this shape.'

'No. It is not right,' Margrethe said calmly. 'You have a husband. He is back already.'

'A fine time to think about that. It's the baby, isn't it? Tell me. I can stand it. It's because of the baby.' Patience could scarcely focus through her streaming eyes. It was as if Margrethe was dissolving in front of her, as if she would soon be no more.

'It is the baby. I did not expect the baby.'

'Neither did I,' Patience sobbed, 'neither did I. I can't help it. Please, please—'

'Goodbye, my dear. You should not feel sorry for yourself. You are so—protected. No Russian animals. No Americans chewing their gum. And now'—Margrethe could not remove the bitterness from her voice—'this fine baby to look forward to.'

'Oh, Mutti, Mutti,' Patience cried, knowing it was no use. 'Don't go. Don't leave me. I'm so alone. So abandoned.'

'What?' Margrethe was incredulous. 'But you have a husband. You now know how to make him into a good husband. One like Heinrich, who had me here.' She pointed to the palm of her right hand.

'I wish I thought I could,' Patience said, finally realizing her predicament for what it was.

Nonetheless, she tried. Of course he must be disappointed a baby should come along so soon, she told herself, and she tried to show him she was sorry. She ruefully acknowledged to herself that her small lapse into carelessness was not like inviting the Portuguese to the same party as the Indians, something that could be got out of somehow. And then there was Margrethe on her conscience, something she had to live with, something she could not deny had happened. Something indeed she would have to leave behind, no matter what the pain, if the marriage was to work.

And so she submitted. Whatever he asked of her she did. He

seemed to be getting the hang of the lovemaking thing at last but there were shadows. He was, as always, too correct and methodical, with none of the raw gaiety and laughter which Margrethe brought to the business despite her past sorrows. At first her earliest memories of the marriage caused her instinctively to flinch and, of course, he could feel it, which did not help. Later, as she was getting used to it, she became too heavy, too clumsy, to take such an active part. Worse still was the restless play of her fantasy, substituting women, not necessarily Margrethe, as partners. She felt she was letting him down but he was careful to make no complaint, as if he too were working at the relationship. She would look down on his thin head wondering whether he, too, had fantasies he dared not confess.

It was all such an uphill task. He seemed to have a devil in him that could not leave well alone. While he could look pleased with her, his little-boy smile lighting when she waddled into the room in one of her small collection of smocks, the clouds would gather, suddenly, without warning, over the most trivial detail of their domestic life. Underneath it all she could not help feeling that he, too, was deeply, inarticulately dissatisfied with her because she was who she was and not someone other. But who? That was the question to which she could find no very satisfactory answer.

She shared her anxieties as usual with her father—for who else could she turn to without arousing harmful gossip damaging to their standing in the small British circle, where they were permanently on parade?

Her father replied in the New Year, much as she expected, full of evasive advice and assumptions she knew to be false. Surely, she thought, things ought not to be so difficult. All right, everyone talked about the difficulties of early married life in the diplomatic goldfish bowl. But this difficult? Her common sense told her this was absurd. Surely it was his singleminded, almost frantic pursuit of his career which was responsible for much of the nervous strain; why else the endless social round he felt obligatory to their not very exalted position?

'Darling? I've been looking through the diary,' she said, sitting fatly in the passenger seat. It was darkest January, and raining. He was peering through the swish of the windscreen wipers and could not escape even if he wanted to. It was one of the longer journeys into the farther reaches of the American sector.

'Have you, darling?' said Gareth, scenting danger. 'And what have you been thinking about?'

'Do you realize that we haven't had a night at home since Christmas? I mean, really.'

'It's the life. It's what we have chosen.'

'We used to find time. Sometimes. When we were going out together.' She did not have to look. She knew his jaw was tightening. She did not care. She trusted to her reputation in the family as a bit of a daredevil, someone who would take any fence in Sussex.

He said nothing.

'I said,' she repeated clearly, 'we used to find time. Before we were married.'

'I heard what you said.'

'And?'

'And what? What am I supposed to say? You know the rules. We're invited. We accept. We go. Unless we've a previous engagement. Or either of us is sick. They are the rules. They always have been the rules. They always will be the rules. Look at the general. He does twice as much.'

'But they've had their silver wedding. We're just married. And I'm pregnant.'

There was silence except for the swish of the wiper blades.

'I said we're just married. And I'm pregnant.'

'So I believe. That is scarcely my fault.'

'And so you don't think we should have any time to ourselves?'

'There are always the holidays. Otherwise there is this, the life we have chosen.'

'You have chosen, you mean.'

'I have chosen, if you like. But then you have chosen me.'

By the time they reached the house of their American hosts they were screaming at one another like things demented. Somewhere in the torrents of reproach, he had taken a wrong turning, giving her temporary advantage. She took it greedily, all of it, glad of an opportunity to cut, as she herself had been cut so many times since her marriage.

The car stopped. He looked at her coldly.

'Here we are then. Are you ready?'

'I need a moment to make up again,' she replied in kind. 'I can't be seen like this.'

'No. But don't be too long. The general has arrived, look.' Gareth pointed to the staff car, the sergeant driver sitting to attention in front, apparently devoid of thought. 'We're supposed to arrive before him, remember. That's another of the rules.'

'They'll have to wait,' she said. 'You can always say you took a wrong turning. It's the truth, after all.'

'I will this time,' he said, 'but just remember in future. I didn't make the rules. I follow them, like everyone else. And like everybody else I will be judged by how well I did so. *We* did so.'

She used his driving mirror to put on fresh lipstick and to touch up her cheekbones with a light brush. His gloves gripped the steering wheel until the knuckles showed. He seemed to be counting the seconds, straining at the starting blocks.

'All done,' she said, giving him an uncertain smile and putting her hand over his. 'All right then, darling?' He readjusted the driving mirror with exaggerated care and got out heavily, satisfied that, however silently, he had made his point. By the time they reached the house they had their party faces on. His was the thin-boned, ironic Englishman of legend, older than his years but promising agelessness later on. Hers was the soft accompaniment of the English rose, warmer and more yielding than when a virgin but essentially retiring, repelled by too open an admiration. The men warmed to the bloom of her cheek; the women melted at her change of shape, snugly emphasized by her party smock.

'Hello, Al,' Gareth said with his best, most crookedly endearing smile. 'Sorry we're a bit late.'

'Never too late, Gareth. Just as long as you bring the mother-to-be with you,' Al replied with apparently homespun honesty. 'Here, let me get you both a drink. You'll find my bride over in the corner talking to your general.' Gareth caught the general's eye and shrugged an apology. The general's raised quizzical eyebrows relaxed into a wink. Thank God, he seemed to have concluded, young Gareth's taken my advice. Not many of them do. And young couples had more to do with their early evenings after the office than attend cocktail parties. Even his hard-eyed wife, surrounded by young officers in the other corner, was deceived by their excellently mannered appearance. A little late in the pregnancy, she thought, but what's the harm? She recalled it being physically rather awkward, like shaking hands in boxing gloves, her husband had said with a grin that melted her heart. Awkward but also physically rather magnificent, as she remembered it, and such a comfort to know one was still wanted at a time like that.

Only half-consciously Patience developed her own armoury over the next few months. He was not, after all, invulnerable.

Dressing for one of their own dinners, Gareth paused, sock in hand.

'Little Whittam came up with some hare-brained notion today at the general's meeting. Some rubbish the Americans had fed him about the Russians being behind the unrest at the Polytechnic. Ridiculous, as if the Russians weren't aware that the students' brand of Marxism poses the greatest possible ideological threat to their own in the East there. I could see the general was tempted but I think I've managed to scotch it. The Americans see a Russian hand behind everything.'

'Oh, really? Mrs General seems to think George Whittam's doing well. She says he has the most charming manners. I see what she means.'

'Patience? What is that supposed to mean?'

'He's easy with people. They don't feel threatened. He scores more points that way. According to Mrs General, anyway.'

She waited for this to slip between the chinks. Then, when he was bent over tying his shoelaces:

'You should try it,' she said, thoughtfully, as if trying to help. 'Daddy always says it's one thing to be right. It's another to persuade others that you're right.' She watched him pause over his shoelaces, seeking to master himself. 'That's his opinion anyway.'

'It is, is it?' Gareth said at last, retiring into one of his sulks.

He telephoned from the office, biting the words off very distinctly to make each one tell.

'What's this? You've invited the frightful McLevens?'

'I thought I should. He's been so helpful.'

'I thought we'd agreed on the Napiers. I don't invite the American Number Two and Burgermeister Schultz to meet one of the clerks. You haven't actually invited the McLevens yet, I hope?'

'I have, I'm afraid. We see the Napiers all the time.' She quailed a little inwardly, imagining the thunderous pulsing at his temples. 'There's no harm,' she wheedled, 'honestly there's not.' Still silence at the end of the line. 'Besides, Rhoda's in the Dramatic Society. She played opposite Al in *Guys and Dolls*. They're good friends . . . Darling, are you there?'

'This is supposed to be teamwork,' he said coldly. She could hear him keeping his voice down in case it should travel through the office walls and let everyone know they were quarrelling again. 'Next time I'll give the list to my secretary. She at least I can trust.'

After that dinner party they sat at their fireplace sipping iced water. She could not resist.

'You see? The McLevens were fine. He and the Burgermeister got on famously. They seemed to spend most of the evening cracking Anglo-German jokes.'

'Very unsuitable, most of them.'

'No one seemed to mind. And Rhoda was a big success. You know she used to be a ballet dancer? She's still very pretty.'

A spasm crossed his face. 'A vulgar little piece,' he said. 'A vulgar little piece with a loud laugh.'

'At least someone was enjoying themselves, someone was making the effort to be entertaining.'

'But I had something to ask the Burgermeister. There were a dozen things I wanted to discuss with Al.'

'You can always go and see them tomorrow. Besides, if you'd invited the Napiers he'd only have pinched your contacts. You know what he's like.' She hoped this would finish the argument. Instead his face went very grave. He stared into the fire, not wishing to confront her directly. 'Look, Patience,' he said, 'if this isn't working out, you just have to say so. I'll understand.'

'Oh, darling,' she said with a pang. 'Was it really so bad? Was I really so bad?'

For he, too, was not without weapons.

'Yesterday.' The famous voice strained slightly beyond its natural register. 'All my troubles seemed so far away.'

The couples grew even closer. In the darkness there was some furtive kissing, discreet enough, it was hoped, to deceive the marriage partner. Fantasies were everywhere afloat.

'Oh, I believe in . . . yesterday.'

They sat miserably in a swing seat in the garden, saying nothing. Perhaps, she thought, perhaps life always is so difficult. Perhaps nothing better could be expected. She had freely chosen, after all.

She took his hand in hers and patted it absentmindedly in the darkness. She encountered no resistance, but then, neither did she feel any comforting warmth. It was, she reflected, just a hand, anybody's hand. She counted off the fingers separately and recounted them shut.

'I heard from Margrethe today,' she said.

'Who?'

'Frau Henze.'

'Oh, yes. And?'

'I think I'll invite her to tea next week. Unless you have an objection.'

'She wasn't—well, was she, she wasn't very loyal? She walked out, just when you needed her most. With the baby on the way, I mean.'

'No. Not very loyal. But I think I'll invite her to tea anyway.'

'Perhaps she wants the job back. But she's no better than this new woman, Frau Schmidt.'

'Perhaps. Let's just see, shall we? It can't do any harm.'

'All right. Anyway, it can't be for very long. We're not here for much longer.'

'What?' She gasped, feeling the cold clutching at her heart and thinking only: Margrethe.

'I have been meaning to tell you all night. We're posted back to London just before Christmas. Sorry. Is it a bore for you?'

'Not particularly,' she said calmly, wondering how much he knew. 'When shall I start packing?'

-ENVOI-

Young Benton's been posted home, have you heard? The general's very put out.

Stupid fellow. He can't keep him forever.

I imagine Mrs General will be equally upset.

Probably. What's he going to do then, in the Office?

I don't know. Something East-West I expect. No one's forgotten he was right about Czechoslovakia.

It'll be a relief round here, I can tell you. Supercilious young bugger, no one can stand him.

Able, though.

Oh, yes, able. But I'd have thought Patience could have done more to calm him down. What with the baby and everything.

They seem pretty well suited to me. She's very nice.

I don't know. I sometimes think there are hidden fires there. Patience, I mean.

Funny, I was thinking that. Odd isn't it, really? Somehow you can tell.

Such was the judgement of the world as Berlin settled down for the Christmas season. The general gave them a splendid dinner the night before they left. He made a witty little speech full of playful allusion to the magnificent contribution both had made to the British Military Government, Berlin. Benton replied with a few carefully prepared sentences expressing admiration for his Chief, blended with deference and respect for his lady wife. They left with the morning convoy to Helmstedt: mother, baby, and accomplished diplomat certain by now that he was being groomed for the top.

The guards at both checkpoints of the Autobahn were khaki-clad Russian soldiers, with the olive-green Vopos in the background, another of the obscure practices invented by the victorious powers. By this time, however, they were so familiar with the rules that they handed their identity cards over automatically, their minds on other things.

The baby was warmly dressed and his little pompon hat was new. As Gareth took back the identity cards he said, 'That's nice. Where did you buy it? Very becoming.'

'It was a present,' she replied leadenly. 'A present from a friend.'

'Oh. Who?'

'Margrethe.'

'Ah,' he said as if he expected this answer. 'Frau Henze?'

'Frau Henze. My friend. She came to say goodbye, yesterday. I couldn't refuse.'

'I see,' he said, conscious of dangerous waters. 'Of course not. A good woman.'

But by then they were being whistled through to take their place in the convoy that would take them at one invariable speed all two hundred kilometres to the border with the West.

All the way there Patience could feel her heart being torn up by the roots.

MOSCOW

- DELIVER US, LORD -

The time had come for Pope and people.

Boniface turned to face the pilgrim steps, bowing low in homage to the Chair of St Augustine at the summit of the rise. He opened his arms to those looking down, bidding them all to stand. He turned again, arms wide, to the vast crowd stretching down through the presbytery and the choir beyond. They too rose for the Lord's Prayer, recited together, the voices of the concelebrants clearly audible in the microphones above the thunder of the congregation. Two Englishmen and the Italian, their voices not quite synchronized.

All fell silent as the choir took up the Amen, first in the soprano register, later enriched by the alto and the tenor, the bass finally coming in to complete the affirmation.

The Pope waited for all sound to die away before intoning:

> *'Deliver us, Lord, from every evil*
> *And grant us peace in our day . . .'*

Ah, yes, Benton thought, peace in our day, the cry of every generation. Easy enough to pray for; impossible, it seemed, to attain. His eye searched out again over the bobbing mitres.

His heart juddered. Welch had gone. The space by the throne was empty. A gap had yawned open.

A move had been made.

This is nonsense, Benton thought, this cannot be. He sought out Daly, head of the security detachment, hoping for reassurance. Daly stood, head bowed, over against the Sudbury tomb on the other side of the altar, utterly useless. A Catholic, especially

137

chosen to guard the Catholic Pope but now lost in his devotions. Benton looked impatiently for the other detectives carefully interspersed in the crowd. It was unbelievable. All stood stone-faced, watching with sightless eyes over the bowed heads, noticing nothing.

The cameras were trying a few close-ups, alternating Pope, Archbishop, Cardinal. All three, hands on altar, bowed in silent prayer. The choir in honour of another tradition took up the old Lutheran hymn, sung softly in unison, the sound floating through the great space to greater spaces beyond:

Ein feste Burg ist unser Gott.

Growing bored with the inactivity, the cameras now began playing with the monuments of generations. They flicked over the heads in the Trinity Chapel to the tomb of Edward, the Black Prince: the replicas of his helmet and sword, his battle corselet, his gauntlets and shield. They soared into Bell Harry to pick out details of the fan tracery invisible a hundred feet below on the crossing floor. They selected roof bosses: the arms of the see of Canterbury, the red rose of Lancaster, the martlets of Edward the Confessor, or on azure. So busy, so inattentive they missed the first moves.

There was a quick furtive shuffle out behind the croziers, something discordant, inexplicable. It was Welch down beside the lectern at the end of the aisle. Their eyes met and Benton at once understood.

His warning was brief, a barely perceptible shake of the head. Welch nodded in acknowledgement but did not seem convinced. No one else seemed to notice.

The hymn came to a close, so quiet it could have been a sigh. Boniface stretched out his arms again to invoke the Kiss of Peace. He embraced first the Archbishop and then the Cardinal, a movement repeated in all parts of the church.

A great tropical bird, Benton thought, shaking out its plumage. The choir sang, in Latin this time, to the Lamb of God.

Unnoticed in all this quiet commotion, Welch began his slow shamble down the aisle.

A quick-witted cameraman, realizing something odd was going on, was the first with the news for the watching millions. He did not notice Benton, his eyes on Welch, willing him to stop.

- FRUNZE -

For Gareth, who had slogged it out a full six years in the Western European Department in Downing Street the news of his posting to Moscow was at once a relief and the realization of a long-standing ambition. The Head of Personnel was fairly beaming with the thought that, for once, he had got it right.

'Thank you, Roland. What splendid news. I've always wanted Moscow.'

'We'll give you a month or two to polish up your Russian again. Patience can take the beginner's course.'

'What about the wives? I've heard Moscow is sometimes difficult for wives.'

'Most of them manage. Besides, in this case, you take over the Faradays' house. Marvellous place. Lots of character. We were lucky to get the lease when we did.'

Her response, for the daughter of an admiral, was to him entirely unexpected: indeed, shocking.

'I'm not going. It's no good, Gareth. I'm not going.'

'Oh, but you are. It's your duty to go. You know it's your duty to go. I've been offered the job. I speak Russian. And it means promotion.'

'No. It may be my duty but I'm not going to Moscow. The idea's crazy. To spend years of your life in another madhouse, worse than Berlin—'

'You enjoyed Berlin. You often say how much you enjoyed Berlin.'

140

'I enjoyed it for entirely fortuitous reasons. It was still a mad-
house. I only enjoyed it because of my friends.'
'Maybe you'll make friends in Moscow.'
'German friends. I can hardly hope it will be the same.'
'Hardly.'

'Patience. I need you. There might be raised eyebrows if you
don't come. The posting might be cancelled, anything. Don't let
me down.'
'It's mad. You're mad. They're all mad. It's impossible, that's
all.'

'Don't snivel.'
'I'm not snivelling. I'm crying. It's different. Crying and sniv-
elling are different.'
'You're just feeling sorry for yourself.'
'Yes. If you must know, I'm feeling very sorry for myself.'
'But you are coming?'
'To Moscow?'
'Yes, to Moscow.'
'I'm thinking about it. I haven't said I will.'

Things were not made any easier by the briefing officer, who
had, of course, to warn them about one feature of Moscow life
which they would come to know well.
'You must assume, the pair of you, that everything is recorded,
everything analyzed. It's big business over there. Absolutely no
shortage of resources. None whatsoever.'
'But it's appalling. Such a waste. Surely they can see it's pure
madness.'
'If it's madness, Mrs Benton, there's method in it. Do please
believe me. Please.'

'I know it's not reasonable. Nothing about Moscow is reasonable if you don't accept the premise. Look on it as a challenge.
That's what most people do. They develop a sixth sense about
what to say and what not to say. Otherwise they carry on as
usual, treating the whole thing as a joke.'

'After all, when you think about it, there's not much to hide.

141

We're all human after all. No one expects perfection. There's inevitably a sort of rough-and-tumble about married life—I'm not speaking about yours, of course, particularly. Anyone's. The only thing is to relax and pretend it isn't happening.'

Patience had looked serene throughout this episode, sitting on the edge of the chair so as not to crease her smart linen suit. She had smiled as she put her questions and Gareth had found it difficult to judge whether the briefing officer had noticed how brittle she had become. He had had to admit she was every inch the admiral's daughter then, with her clean jawline and her crisp enunciation. She still bore traces of her old Head Girl manner, a credit to himself and the service. It was only afterwards that she revealed her true feelings.

'What? All the time? Day and night? Gareth, I mean . . .'

'Apparently. Of course you never really know. I suppose even their resources don't stretch to a full twenty-four-hour treatment for every foreigner in Moscow. It's just that one cannot take any chances.'

'But how is one supposed to live?'

'People do.'

'It's obscene. Gareth, you can't tell me we're going to live the next four years of our life, twenty-four hours a day, under a microscope? It's absurd.'

'I didn't invent it. It's the price one pays. Someone's got to go. And it is promotion.'

'I do see that. But life's surely quite difficult enough without that.'

'We'll manage. We always have.'

Patience had to admit that they had always managed. The six years in London had gone by for her without incident. The atmosphere was always tense between them but she had learned to live with this. To remain always on the alert for the danger signals, the hard light dancing in his eye or the slight bunching of his jaw muscles. To know when to submit, when to distract, when to stand firm. It was often very tiring, this constant living on the edge of some emotional catastrophe, but somehow she had got by. She sensed impending disaster this time but in her more optimistic moments she could imagine that even Moscow, with a bit of effort, might be manageable. In the face of duty she

squared her shoulders, as she had been taught to do since she
left the cradle.

'Patience. And just what did that sniff mean?'
  'What sniff?'
  'Darling. Don't play games with me. Your sniff just now.'
  'Oh, that sniff. I was thinking of that frightful briefing fellow
we went to see. In Personnel.'
  'What's wrong with him? He looked perfectly all right to me.'
  'Do you remember what he said? He said we'd come out of
the Moscow experience strengthened. It's the adversity, he said,
it brings out the best in one.'
  'So?'
  'That's why I sniffed. I was thinking about that. About what
he said. Has he ever been to Moscow?'
  'Yes, as a matter of fact. He had a very good tour there. He
and his wife. Of course they both speak Russian.'
  'Oh.'
  'So will you?'
  'Will I what?'
  'Enrol on the Russian beginner's course?'
  'I suppose so.'
  'That doesn't sound very enthusiastic.'
  'Yes, then. Yes. Yes. Yes.'
  'Thank you.'
  'It's nothing.'
  'Yes it is. Thank you.'

'You're sure you want me? In Moscow, I mean?'
  'Of course. We're married, aren't we?'
  'I'm promising nothing. I've told you I'm not strong.'
  'What does that mean, not strong?'
  'Weak, if you must know.'
  'Meaning?'
  'Oh, never mind. Human if you like. When do the packers
come?'
  'End of next month. Perhaps you'd like to go down to
Meddows before then.'
  'No. I'll go at the week-end with Charlie. I've too much to do
to leave London.'

143

'What, for instance?'
'The Russian course.'
'Ah.'

So they had been warned, but from the very beginning the feeling of being under a microscope was worse, much worse, than they had feared. And the feeling began at once, from the moment of arrival. It was palpable, part of the atmosphere, like the mixture of sweat and the acrid burnt cardboard smell of the *papirosy*, Russian cigarettes in their tubes of coarse paper, smoked by the older people.

They were met by the Embassy duty officer and his wife, one Mr and Mrs Honeysett, gentle people with gentle regional accents, Worcestershire perhaps or Herefordshire, who man-oeuvred them adroitly through the formalities. There was a long wait for the luggage and thus plenty of time to fill with arrival talk, the same the world over. Moscow wasn't too bad, they said, once you got used to it. The social life was fine, very active among the embassies; gave you a chance to make good friends. They would be sorry to leave, they said, honestly they would. Both, however, looked pale, at strain. It had been a hot summer, they said, a lot of dust about, rather hard on those with asthmatic kiddies. They hoped the little boy—Charles, was it?—didn't suffer from asthma. No? That was all right then.

The conversation in the Embassy car nosing through the dreary suburbs was relentlessly cheerful too. Cheerful but as im-personal as the straight avenues of featureless apartment blocks stroking by, the colour of prison walls. Yes, Moscow architec-ture was dull, they had to admit, but after a while you got used to it. You sort of forgot it was there. After all, Moscow wasn't for a lifetime and there was the bonus of home leave every year which was nice for those with ageing parents or young families. They grinned at Charles, who was squirming crossly in his new clothes.

They wondered if the Counsellor and Mrs Benton—oh, all right then, Mrs Benton, Gareth and Patience; we're Jack and Lucy—would care for lunch with them? Stewart Sherstone, the Housing Officer, would pick them up after lunch to take them to the house. The house was lovely, they said, very central, walking distance from the office. They were sure—er, Gareth and Patience would love it as much as their predecessors had. Really the Embassy had been lucky to get the lease when they did, just after the War when we were all such friends.

Mr and Mrs Honeysett—Jack and Lucy—were childless and thus had been allocated a particularly nasty little shoebox stacked up against other little grey shoeboxes in the outer suburbs. The birch trees outside had been spaced by some municipal hand and would take years to grow to a size which would soften the severity behind. The street stretched endlessly in each direction, a wide corridor of grey slabbing without contrast or relief. Only the air, the untameable air, had character: the wind, blowing from the west into the concrete facing, had created sharp local turbulences, shaking the yellowing birch leaves into spasmodic life.

The elevator, built for six, contained the little party and a thin young Russian in his early twenties who pressed the button for the top floor before turning to give them a friendly, impersonal nod. He stood courteously aside to let them out at their floor, stepped back in and was gone. The elevator doors closed on his smooth, pleasant face, his neat head, his cheap suit and his clumsy shoes.

'One of them,' Mr Honeysett explained. 'It's one o'clock, the time they change the watch.' Seeing a look of puzzlement on Gareth's face he explained. 'The boys with the headsets. Listening in. Everyone in the block is a foreigner, mainly diplomats. Our friends can't be too careful, or so they think.'

'Goodness,' Patience said, wide-eyed.

'But we were warned,' Gareth replied. 'Don't you remember, darling?'

'Of course we were warned,' she said with some slight irritation. 'Only I didn't think it was all so obvious. Blatant.'

'They've no shame at all,' Mr Honeysett said. 'They don't care that we know. I sometimes think they rather like it. That it's only to keep us all on edge, stop us settling down.'

By this time he had fished out a key and was opening the front door into the little shoebox they called home.

Stewart Sherstone turned up when they were having coffee. The Honeysetts had run out of cheerful things to say and were beginning to look morose as the gaps in the conversation yawned wider. Sherstone had thin shoulders and a moustache painted thinly on the narrow band above his thin top lip. Even his hair was thinning. He looked cheap, something acquired by the Service from another ministry which had not known what to do with him. Benton conceived an immediate distaste for the man, something he had no intention of disguising. Even Patience, normally so tolerant behind her slightly glacial manner, thought him over-eager to please, just like the local estate agent at home, the one Daddy sought to avoid at the golf club. They knew that they were in his hands and that he could make all the difference to the comfort of their Moscow years so they bore with him, smiling through gritted teeth.

Sherstone, fresh to the task, had no difficulty keeping the chatter general, noncommittal, all the way in to central Moscow.

'Mind if I smoke?' he said pulling out a flat silver cigarette case sporting his monogram. No one spoke. 'Ta,' he said, lighting up. The car was passing a gigantic hotel on the edge of the river. From the speeding bridge Gareth caught a brief glimpse of the twin bends of the river flexing between low banks. The car now arrowed into the gap between the massive ministries.

'Ever lived in a long-lease job before?' Sherstone asked, turning confidentially round to look at them from the front seat. 'No? You'll like it, you see. You're better looked after in your long-lease. The slightest thing goes wrong and *toute suite* they send an army round to put it right. They insist on keeping everything tickety-boo with your long leases. Isn't that right, Volodya?'

Volodya, the uniformed driver, grinned as if he understood. 'Doesn't speak English. Not a word,' Sherstone explained. 'I hope.'

'Just off the Prospekt here, see,' Sherstone said. The avenue had narrowed after crossing the second ring road, and now the driver was twirling into a short high-fronted street of frowning houses. They decanted onto the sidewalk and Sherstone led the way up a flight of steps to a high front door.

'You see,' he said waving a proprietorial hand in both directions, 'practically the only street left in Moscow with some character. This is only a duplex, of course, but we have the best two floors plus the basement and the garden. Dead lucky we were to acquire the lease when we did.'

'So we've been told,' Gareth said dryly. Sherstone gave him an odd look as if he didn't quite know how to take it.

'But it's lovely!' Patience cried when Sherstone flung open the double inner doors leading into the panelled hall. 'I didn't expect anything like this. Such—personality.'

Sherstone, pleased with the effect, grinned.

'You haven't seen the half of it yet,' he said. 'Where'd you like to start?'

'Anywhere,' she said happily. 'Oh, Mr Sherstone, anywhere you like.'

'The name is Stewart,' he said, opening the high doors to the right leading into the drawing room. 'Stewart spelled Eee Double-you. This is said to be one of the nicest interiors in Moscow. They're so keen on what they like to call Reconstruction that it's a wonder anything is left. I think they'd reconstruct the Kremlin and the Bolshoi given half a chance. Wait a tick and I'll open the shutters.'

'How has it survived?' Gareth asked after him, trying to keep the edge out of his voice. 'Some unexpected efficiency on the Embassy's part?'

Sherstone stopped halfway in the gloom. 'Inertia, I assume,' he said with a dry conciliatory laugh. 'Besides ...' he pointed silently with a circulatory gesture everyone gets used to in Moscow. 'They know where they are with us. Good payers, the British, quiet like, and we're all so ... well settled.... Get me?' Again the same gesture meaning: microphones.

'Oh,' Gareth said.

'Everyone likes to know where they stand, wouldn't you agree, sir?' Sherstone went on drawing the blinds back. 'And here, we all know what's what.' A stream of gentle September light poured through onto the polished parquet, a million motes spiralling in the still air. 'Funny, that,' Sherstone said, batting uselessly at them and only causing them to swirl more quickly. 'The place has had a good spring clean. Or rather autumn clean. It's been a long hot summer, loads of dust. Your kiddie doesn't suffer from asthma, does he? No? Good. I thought he looked as if he might be the type.'

147

'It's simply enchanting,' Patience said hastily before Gareth rose to the bait. 'Look at the lovely moulding on the ceiling. And there's even a piano, a full concert grand, I do believe.'

'Used to be in the Residence years ago,' Sherstone explained, 'until they shipped out a new one. Your predecessor used to say this one had a better tone. I can't tell myself but he was very good on the piano, was Mr Faraday. Very much in demand he was for Embassy smokers and whatnot. I believe he went in more for the classical, but he was very popular when he let his hair down. Very comical.'

'A pity neither of us plays,' Gareth replied stiffly, running his finger along the lid and making a trail through the dust. For a second he was back in Cambridge and Jeannie was blowing the ends of her fingers at him.

'As I say, it had an autumn clean,' Sherstone said apologetically. 'An awful lot of dust in Moscow in the summer. No rain, you see. It makes up for it in the winter, mind.'

'Perhaps we could learn,' Patience said, anxious to see the rest of the house. 'Can we see upstairs, Stewart?'

'Certainly, madam.'

'Patience.'

'Patience, then.' Sherstone grinned at her, sure they would get along fine. He was not so sure about Mr Benton. An odd sort of fish, he thought, sort of tense—know what I mean?

Gareth was staring at the ceiling moulding, wondering where the microphones were concealed. Devilish clever of them, he was thinking; there was simply no trace anywhere.

'This is your bedroom,' Sherstone said, throwing back more shutters. 'There's even a balcony, look. It's a mite narrow but you can just see the Prospekt at the corner if you crane a little. Mr Faraday used to walk up the Prospekt every morning to the office. He said his morning and evening walk were worth a fiver a day to him. Of course you're lucky here, living so close. Most of us have to live in concrete boxes miles away and drive in every day. A hard slog in the winter, as you can imagine.'

Sherstone bustled about, opening and shutting cupboards as if he owned them. Patience noticed the vast imperial chandelier.

'It was here when we took the place, I believe. They say this was the ballroom. Part of, anyway. The rest is your bathroom on one side, the guest suite on the other. Pretty grand, wouldn't you say?'

He passed through to the interconnecting bathroom, turning on all the taps to demonstrate they worked. All the fittings were gigantic, huge brass taps fitted to brass piping worthy of a steam yacht, a bath big enough for the tallest, leanest Englishman, the kind of Englishman that appeared in school photographs before the First War. Patience was taking in every detail, recording the position of everything in her infallible domestic memory.

'And to think this is on a long lease. Not expensive for what it is. We're charged the earth for the concrete boxes out in the suburbs. The earth,' Sherstone reminded them.

Sherstone was showing Patience the third bedroom before they noticed Gareth was no longer with them. They looked at each other and shrugged their shoulders in mute surprise. They found him gazing moodily at the walls of the master bedroom. Had they been able to walk silently, they would have caught him searching the surface with his hands, as if he had lost something.

Sherstone made the circular movement. 'We've often tried to do something about that,' he said, 'but we've never been able to get at the root of the difficulty. As we say where I come from: What can't be cured must be endured.' He had put on a broad Yorkshire accent which was startling after the flat suburban London he had spoken so far.

'I didn't think you came from the north,' Patience said. 'How funny, I'd have sworn you were a Londoner.'

'Yorkshire was a long time ago,' Sherstone said apologetically. 'We left when I was a nipper. It's London now, out by the airport. Hayes, actually. Woodruff Road facing the bowling greens.'

Gareth seemed not to hear. He was pacing the room looking up in all the corners of the ceiling.

'Lovely plaster work, isn't it, sir?' Sherstone said, only half concealing the malice.

'Come along, darling,' Patience said quietly, aware how much he was already on edge. 'There's still the kitchen to inspect. And the wine cellar.'

'And the garden,' Sherstone reminded them. 'It's small, mind you, but it's a real treat here in the centre of the city. We provide a lawn-mower and a few tools. But you'll need to buy bedding plants next May when the ground starts to unfreeze.'

'Come along, Gareth. We mustn't keep Stewart all day,' Patience said.

'I don't see why not,' Gareth replied, ushering them out of the room. 'Isn't this your job, Sherstone?'

'True, sir. Only too true.'

Gareth smiled inwardly at this, his first little victory for order, hierarchy. Sherstone would just have to wait until he was dismissed for the day. But Sherstone, too, was smiling inwardly, having got the measure of the new arrivals.

They moved in the next day when Anna the cook and Natasha the maid returned from their holidays, traditionally taken between occupants. Anna was ash-grey, evidently blond in her youth but still with a lovely taut skin all pink and ivory white. She walked with a quick bobbing motion. For her age she had a neat trim figure and must, Patience thought, have been stunning thirty years before. Natasha was built like a bolster, with the arms of a market porter and the giggle of a schoolgirl. Both cooed and clucked over Charles, who clung to his mother's skirts.

For the next week the house was a riot of wooden crates, old newspaper and miscellaneous kitchen junk. By now they were old hands at the business of unpacking and the eruption slowly subsided, leaving behind something which, for all its faults, looked familiar, even reassuring. Patience's horse pictures took their traditional place in the entrance hall to remind her several times a day of the rides around the hills above Meddows.

Thus did their Moscow life begin, as it always does in a diplomatic post, insecurely based in former realities; gradually, almost imperceptibly eroded by the days into something quite new, unsuspected: something of an entirely different shape and character.

The layout of the rooms soon ceased to be strange and the furniture unfamiliar: it was as if they had always lived thus in the grand, rather gloomy duplex in a street of high-fronted houses, practically all that was left of the old domestic Moscow before the Revolution. They were soon no longer conscious of the peculiar old-fashioned smell of the floor polish, imported from Finland and cloyingly sweet as if made from raw beeswax. Only a little later did they lose the mixed smell of sweat and

papirosy—Belomor, mainly, with their cardboard mouth-
pieces—which had hit them like a wave that first morning
outside the depressingly sanitized airport. The hours themselves, the normal hours for sleeping, working, eating, began to
seem inevitable, what was always done, even though they were
like nothing they had experienced before.

Charlie, entered already at the Anglo-American school, was
soon clattering down the staircase every morning, his oversized
satchel across his thin back, while his parents had breakfast.
They were listening out for him, welcoming anything that would
break the thickening wall of ice between them. He seemed quite
oblivious that there might be a problem. He was also quick-
witted enough to keep even Gareth amused for a few minutes.
Patience, in her housecoat, would invariably walk him to the
front door, where she would bend down and kiss him.

"Bye, Mum.'

"Bye, darling. Be good. You know we won't be here when
you get back tonight? Anna says she'll look after you, give you
something special for supper.'

'Yes, Mum. You'll tuck me in when you get home?'

'Of course, darling.'

She would watch him run up the street to the Embassy bus,
proud in her heart of his aquiline profile, the etching of his
nostrils, the mop of golden curls she deliberately left long. The
bus, throbbing at the corner, would take him in and roar off to
collect the next child on the roster.

They could then settle down to discuss the day's programme,
already seasoned veterans in the art of managed lives.

'My diary has you lunching with the Italians.'

'That's right. Here's the card, look. They've their Inspectors
in town, who've asked for some outside opinions on conditions
here.'

'I seem to be free at lunchtime. Good, I can catch up on some
correspondence. It's ages since I've written to Mummy and
Daddy. And then it's tea with Lady A for the senior wives.'

'Followed by cocktails with the Algerians for their national
day.'

'I've got the card and a map. It should take us about twenty minutes. Leave here at quarter past? We don't want to be the first.'

'All right. But I do want to catch Klaus there. He has something he doesn't want to discuss on the telephone.'

'And then dinner with the Johnstones for someone called Antoinette Darwin. Who's she? A ballet dancer?'

'Somebody in medical research. I've got the details in my office. Presumably we're invited because of Father.'

They were at their best then, calm and professional, with Natasha waddling between them with the coffee. As they bent over their respective diaries, something of the old courtesy of the pre-married days would return and nothing was said that would leave Natasha with the impression of hidden strains. As the days grew colder, Patience picked up a little more fresh colour on the doorstep while watching Charles gambolling to the street corner and tumbling onto the bus. There was thus increasing animation to her cheeks and a brighter sparkle to her eye. They could not know it but at such moments they were as a couple an object of pride to the sloe-eyed Natasha and round-eyed Anna in the kitchen awaiting orders. They were like a throwback to a distant half-remembered past when there was hierarchy, style, and a church with its incense and candles in every street.

Ten minutes before the hour, exactly to time, this tall, excellently clothed Englishman would emerge on the top of the street steps in his expensive English overcoat and carrying his lightweight attaché case. It was his habit to gaze up and down the street as if looking for something before pulling the front door to with a rich, satisfying clunk. He would button his gloves of a supple black leather and adjust his hat brim before setting off to the corner of the Kalinin Prospekt, all blue and ochre in the dying days of the Moscow autumn. There was still a lot of dust about, the remains of summer, but already the wind was changing and there was a hint of the great cold preparing itself out there on the endless steppes of Central Asia.

To any observer, assuming there were any, he was virtually indistinguishable from his predecessor. A little taller perhaps, a little more tight-jawed, but as long-shanked and narrow-headed, with his hair as softly brushed and his attaché case of a similar Bond Street elegance. His route, too, was identical. Turning right he walked up Kalinina to the great heavy Lenin library and right again along Marx Prospekt past the Metro station with its thin scatter of students and museum visitors, past the commanding old Pashkov mansion towering on its grassy knoll facing the west wall of the Kremlin. There could be a long wait on the corner of Frunze when there were official limousines streaming across the square into the Borovitsky Gate of the Kremlin. He manifested no impatience on such occasions, standing quietly gazing out above the squat group of Muscovites until the lights changed and he was free to move on, up onto the Bolshoi Kamenny bridge which crosses the river and from which he could see the British Embassy facing the Kremlin towers on the other side of the water.

He gave every impression of enjoying the walk among the disciplined, anonymous strollers making the most of those last days before winter: part but self-evidently not part, not one of them, a foreigner with a foreigner's thin-soled shoes and silk tie. At any rate he did not give up the habit, morning and evening, as the days shortened. By late October he had added a scarf, and, three weeks later, when the weather had drifted into the first snows of winter and the river started to freeze, he changed his London overcoat for a bulkier Russian one. He finally surrendered to overshoes and an Astrakhan hat in early December, when he just might have been taken for an aristocrat of the former regime or the scion of some old merchant house.

And the walk, in truth, was for Gareth the best of the day. Shutting the door on the insoluble problem of Patience, he could rejoice in the cleanliness of the streets, in the litterless Metro stations of polished marble like the glistening entries of underground palaces, in the discipline of crowds waiting their turn to cross at the street corners. For a few minutes each day his thoughts were his own and outward conformity evidently all that was required. He assumed he was being watched but outdoors, here in the Moscow streets, he enjoyed the liberty of the exercise yard.

It somehow did not seem to matter whether he was being watched or not. There was no intrusion, and in any case he wondered whether the watchers would be able to differentiate between Englishmen of his age and class. Beneath an indistinguishable exterior, Faraday, his predecessor, had been voluble and effusive, so full of phrases like 'Thank you *so* much' or 'How agreeable' that he could have been some figure hovering on the edge of Bloomsbury in the twenties. He was a fanatical balletomane, which explained his interest in Old Russia and the Russian language. Faraday had married an Irish girl, a passionate redhead of radical views who made a point of quarrelling with him in public as if they were facing each other on different sides in the House of Commons during Question Time. Everybody knew they were still madly in love and the marriage was as sound as any in the Service. They had three wild children just waiting to break the bonds. Yet, walking tranquilly from home to the Embassy in his London clothes, Gareth could have been Faraday's twin brother. When he changed, in the second week in November, into a heavier Russian overcoat he was following an identical pattern; when he surrendered to an Astrakhan hat and overshoes in early December the exterior likeness was uncanny. Gareth wondered what the watchers made of it all. Perhaps, looking down on convicts in uniform in the prison yard, warders come to see them as all alike, differing only in the numbers on their breast pockets. Halfway across the bridge one morning this thought came to him from nowhere, and his face broke into a brief ironic grin at the absurdity of it all.

No. It was not the watching, if any, that undid them but the listening, if any.

-LISTENING, IF ANY-

'How do you make this thing work?' Patience was on her knees in front of their shortwave radio. Gareth was reading *Pravda*, which was still trying, in vain, to cover over the widening fissures in the Politburo. 'Press the button marked ON,' he said from behind the paper. 'To turn it off you press the button marked OFF.'

'Now, Gareth,' she said quietly. 'Please. I need help. I simply can't get the thing to work. Be reasonable.'

'I am always reasonable.'

There was a short tense silence until he turned the page. 'Well?' she said at last, knowing he was waiting for her. 'Are you going to show me?'

'What? What is it this time?'

'Are you going to show me how to turn this thing on?'

'Not if you take on that tone.'

'What tone?'

'You know what tone.'

Within minutes the storm reached its full height. For the first time in years she raged at him, her words tripping her up, her eyes welling. He in contrast grew quieter, icier with the minutes, but his eyes danced with a black despair.

'Shut up, you bitch,' he said at last, slapping her savagely across the face. She fell to the floor while he stood over her, daring her to start again. She was weeping silently when he suddenly recollected where they were. Moscow. Under the microphones. Without looking at him, she could tell what he was thinking and she too realized that the quarrel simply could not go on.

'Sorry,' he said. 'That was unforgivable. Let me show you. It's quite simple, look. It works from the mains and you haven't switched on at the socket.'

'I see.' She sniffed, dabbing her too-bright eyes with a handkerchief. 'That was really rather silly of me.'

'Anyone could do it,' he said. The radio sprang to life with a series of pops and wheezes. 'I'll just tune it for you. Then all you'll have to do is press the button for ON.' He smiled at her. 'Or OFF, as the case may be,' he added.

'Thank you,' she said, smiling wanly, if only for appearances.

*

Appearances. They were good at appearances. There were some, there always are some, who suspected that all was not well between them, but their performance had become expert with the years. Sometimes, remembering Margrethe, Patience asked herself whether appearances were all and the thought somehow comforted her. In London she used to catch herself watching a couple of women shoppers on the top of an Oxford Street bus and wonder whether they were what they seemed, a couple of neighbours shopping around for curtain materials, or whether in fact they were lovers sharing a stolen afternoon. The pain of separation from Margrethe, however, had left her so shaken that she preferred the world of appearances with Gareth. She had begun to look back on Margrethe with wonderment, almost as if the experience had happened to someone else. She had been left raw, bleeding internally, but being young her heart was healthy and she healed with time. The pain, the pain—she could summon it up again at will like some awful ghost—but as the London years proceeded she did so rarely.

Margrethe had, however, taught her something about herself, had aroused the essential her, which could not be denied. Patience had joined the library which, being in Hampstead, was the haunt of others like her; and eventually an evening class meeting every Wednesday evening—or so she said—to study creative writing. She would leave him to the *au pair*, an unattractive Dutch girl who would prepare supper in her negligent way, singing along with the groups on Radio Luxembourg between bouts of painting her toenails. Over supper, alone, he would leaf through the latest novels Patience had left lying about: lent, she said, by other members of the class, novels invariably written by women.

And then there were the week-end seminars whenever the urgencies of the flesh became too great.

'What? Another one?'

'But it's three months since the last. And the speakers are first class.'

'It's funny, though. I never seem to see any creative writing. An awful lot of talk, it seems, without much result.'

'I'm studying. You can't write without a lot of thought.'

'Trash. I've seen them. Nothing but trash.'

'Well, I know it's not your Bethmann-Bülow, or anything.'

'Bethmann-Hollweg.'

'Same thing.'

There was, however, no apparatus left lying about the house, and while he might suspect, there was no proof. Besides, he was too frightened of what he might find to make a scene. And all the while she played her part as dutifully as she had been taught for the sake of appearances.

It had helped to be in London, where they saw each other only in the evenings and there was so much to distract. The work kept Gareth so busy in the day, so exhausted in the evening, that his edge was blunted. She cooked for him with the fitful help of the *au pair* and looked after Charlie. A cleaning lady came in every day for most other things. They played week-end tennis with their neighbours on light summer evenings on the Heath, strolling home through the Hampstead streets where the lamps would just be coming on. There were grandparents to visit two or three times a year. Sir Robin had retired to a college-owned house on the edge of Cambridge, an honoured guest in Hall, with a world-wide network of former pupils now leaders of the profession. Meddows remained Meddows, a peaceful retreat of church-going and naval gin before Sunday lunch, and if father-in-law and son-in-law still detested each other, they could at least be civil for the sake of appearances.

'What? Now?'

'Yes. Now.'

'But you know how nervous it makes me with Mummy and Daddy down the corridor. I know it's silly but that's how it is.'

'Don't be silly then. They must know. There is the boy, after all.'

'Yes. There is the boy. Oh, all right then. Just let me fix the thing.'

'Thank you.'

'I shan't be a tick.'

Not happy then but then not precisely unhappy. Protected by that special sort of privacy, the English privacy, that made appearances possible.

On his office desk in Downing Street he had a photograph of her in a wind-cheater and walking shoes, sporting a bright Hermès scarf. It had been taken one threatening afternoon on the Yorkshire moors in the course of one of their short holidays together. She was smiling affectionately at the camera and anyone looking at it would get the picture: a good English marriage between two civilized people with much in common, including a passion for long punishing walks, alone together in the rain.

There were some, nonetheless, who had brushed against him in the office in Downing Street, and had seen his jaw clench. Those who had witnessed the hard light dancing in his eye caught themselves wondering how she managed to stand it.

Honestly, darling, would you?

He's awfully good-looking, you've got to admit that.

Yes, but you don't see it like a woman does. We can sort of sense things like that. He's an awful bully. I wouldn't be surprised if he chooses all her clothes even.

Maire? You are the most frightful gossip. Darling.

You've forgotten, darling. I used to be in the Office. I know all about you men when you get together. You go on about us women but you're worse gossips, all of you. Much worse.

*

Somehow it all seemed manageable in far-away London. Here in Moscow it was very different. There were no barriers high enough to shut out the listening, if any. Their lives had to be played out nakedly, without pretence, behind bars like animals

158

in a zoo. They were left without corners in which to hide. Fish in an aquarium under the gaze of a prying public.

'Not tonight, Gareth. Please.'

'Don't tell me. Another headache.'

'No. Not another headache. You know. . . .' She made the gesture meaning: microphones. 'I just can't,' she said, 'not with all . . . that. Not tonight.' She was wearing his last present, the one that made her heart turn over when she had opened it to the sounds of Christmas morning: a ruffled nightie in old-fashioned lawn, a gesture, she felt, almost of yearning. He could feel the familiar stirring, provoked as ever by her bed warmth.

'When then?'

'Tomorrow. Tomorrow I might be, you know . . . stronger. More used to the idea.'

'But it can't go on like this. It simply can't.'

Her eyes widened with alarm and he pointed more frankly this time into the corners of the room. He turned the light off and they slipped with common accord under the blankets.

'I said,' he whispered under the bedclothes, 'we simply can't go on like this. We are, after all, husband and wife. You can get used to it if you try. We were told to ignore them.'

'Oh, yes,' she whispered wearily back. 'We're husband and wife. On holiday in sunny Moscow.'

'It's your duty,' he hissed. 'It's what you promised.'

She said nothing. After a minute's silence they needed to come up for air and the blankets were rolled back.

'Good night,' she said distinctly, for all to hear.

This time it was his turn to say nothing. The space between them grew wider as both stared at the ceiling, wondering how much the machines, if any, had registered. There was a long pause, there in the darkness, only their respective breathing audible.

'God. This is too humiliating,' she said at last to no one in particular. She sat up and stripped off, feeling for his nearer hand, which she placed against her soft rib cage.

Ten minutes later the bed creak became rhythmical, the gasps for air more urgent. A short while later there was silence.

'You're right,' he whispered in her ear. 'It's no good. It's simply no good . . . with all . . . with all that.'

'Too bad,' she said, 'but I did warn you.' They clung together under the implacable gaze until sleep overwhelmed them.

Later on they grew more reckless. It was as if, by common accord, they had decided that if microphones were unavoidable, they would play to the microphones, if any. If no walls could be built high enough, what was the point of any walls at all? They could feel, day by day, the old, the English restraints cracking under them. It became a challenge between them, a new sort of relationship with a new bated excitement born of the impossibility, any longer, to lie.

'Oh, that. Not again.'
  'It's natural, surely.'
  'Oh, yes. Natural.'

'What does that mean?'
  'What?'
  'That sigh.'
  'Nothing.'
  'Well, will you or won't you?'
  'I'm thinking.'

'Sometimes I get the impression that you aren't—well, natural.'
  'No, since you ask. I am not what you call natural. I'm sorry but there it is. I prefer making love with women.'

'Well, you did ask.'
  'I didn't ask.'
  They lay in the dark, panting, both of them shocked. Suddenly she laughed bitterly and said very loudly, 'There. That's given you something to think about.'
  'Shut up,' he said.
  'Not you. Them,' she replied. 'Out there. You've known all along. But you've never wanted to admit it, even to think about it. Well, think about it.'
  And by the time this had simmered down, through sheer exhaustion, it was three o'clock in the morning. They woke, hollow-eyed, with the hysterical wish to expunge the night hours, to wipe them clean as they could a cassette tape.

She began timidly one morning in December, in a quiet moment when he was in the office and the pressure was off. She tried humming to lighten the heavy silence of the drawing room and found herself wondering what it might sound like when played back on a tape recorder. She tried remembering the words of favourite hymns, those of the school chapel on hot bright Sundays in the summer term when she had felt fragrant, almost newborn in her light summer dresses. She recalled the innocent compulsions of the flesh on those days, the warmth of her womb, the daydreams of the good man, the man of principle, someone to give her straight-backed sons, graceful, lissome daughters. The man who used to come to her those mornings in the school chapel, smiling crookedly at her through tender eyes.

'It's all a lie,' she said aloud, standing in the centre of the drawing room. 'Marriage is a lie.' She turned to the corner of the room and addressed the ceiling. 'I hope you heard that,' she said as clearly as she could. 'I said that marriage is a lie. It is a lie we make up to deceive ourselves. Funny, that. What's more, there's no one to warn us we're telling lies.' She stood in the silence, imagining tape recorders coming to a stop. Then she remembered the cut-glass decanters ranged on the sideboard in the dining room, each with its silver necklace, the general's wedding present.

She soon found that a couple of nips of neat gin took the edge off things. She would swill the liquor through her teeth, savouring the sharp bite of juniper, knowing that within minutes the demons with which they were surrounded would be transformed into friends, confidantes, father confessors. Since nothing could be hidden from them, she reflected, they might as well have the whole story, the explanation, her side of things. One of their merits was their total, passive silence. After the third or fourth nip she read into this an intuitive understanding of her position, even approval of the views she found no difficulty, then, in expressing.

And thus it was not long before she was wandering the house making faces into all corners of the ceiling. She liked standing in the middle of a room best, loudly declaiming for all to hear, enjoying the sensation of apparently talking to no one.

161

Natasha came across her once in the drawing room. She was standing, one hand on the piano, the lieder singer's pose, addressing the empty drawing room in her most forthright, cutting, English voice. Seeing Natasha, she stopped in mid-sentence with a shy, conspiratorial half-smile. 'It's a rehearsal,' she confided in her halting Russian, 'a rehearsal of my speech tomorrow to the Embassy wives.'

But Natasha saw that her eyes told a different story. 'Ah,' she said, 'just so.'

'You may go,' Patience said firmly. 'There are I believe many things to attend to before my husband returns. I shall continue with my rehearsal. Alone.'

'My point,' Patience said from the piano to nobody in particular, 'is a perfectly simple one. My life is intolerable. You know it is intolerable. You have heard him. He is intolerable. I am a prisoner of his intolerable notions of order. He has been programmed—yes, programmed. Smile. Shake hands. Time for dinner. Time for bed. Yes, time for *that* tonight. Please to get ready. One, two, mark time. Over you go. One, two.'

'Ladies,' she said, clearing her throat. 'You ladies out there can surely sympathize. You have heard us preparing for *that* in bed. I could take all the rest if only *that* were better. Not so serious, methodical, you know? God, what a plodder. It is, I hope, better wherever you are. I myself have known better but shh . . . not a word. We will upset his notions of the suitable. The proprieties. What is done. Appearances.'

'We shall quarrel again tonight. You shall hear us quarrel again tonight.'

'I am tired now. I shall go to bed. You may switch off now.'

'Thank you. You have been very understanding of my position. Which, as I say, is intolerable.'

'Gareth? Are you sure Patience is all right? She's looking awfully peaky just recently. She could hardly keep awake at H.E.'s dinner last night.'

162

'She's fine, Anthony, just fine. I don't think February in Moscow does much for her. Not enough exercise. She's a girl who likes plenty of exercise.'

'Ask her if she'd like to join the ladies' broomball team. A good game, broomball. Invented here, you know. She played hockey at school, I take it? Lacrosse, that sort of thing?'

'Of course.'

'I'll speak to her at the Norwegian do tonight. Must not get run-down here of all places. Got to keep active.'

'I might join the broomball team myself. I'm not much good at games, though.'

'There are plenty of teams. We can find you a slot at an appropriate level. Bit late in the season, of course, but we can arrange something.'

'Thank you.'

'You'll have to watch it. Broken bones and so on. The doctor's always going on about it. You'd think we'd all contracted VD. But it's something to do in the winter. There's even an Embassy broomball team in Ulan Bator. Not to speak of Budapest and Helsinki.'

'No,' Patience said firmly, 'I do not want to play that whatever-you-call-it.'

'Broomball.'

'That broomball thing. I've decided what I want to do. I want to go home at Easter. I want to go home and find Charlie a good school.'

'But he'll be going to my old school. It's already arranged.'

Patience had difficulty, but she found she could with an effort just manage it. 'The trouble, Gareth,' she said quietly, 'is that everything always is arranged. I am afraid that this time I want a hand in the arrangements. I shall go home and find a school for Charlie.'

'I see. And may I ask why?'

'Because I want him to turn out in an entirely different way than we have.'

'I see.'

Gareth strode out. She could hear him clumping up the stairs evidently in some state of shock. She was surprised how easy it was, how little fuss he had made. Despite her firm tone she had been trembling inwardly, expecting violence. He had stepped a pace nearer but had obviously thought better of it. She had made that little circling gesture with her hand. He had glanced into the corners of the room, turned his blazing eyes on her and simply walked out.

She sat and waited for his next move, certain there would be one. She sat very still listening for sounds overhead. It was eerily quiet.

He came down half an hour later, dressed for the evening cocktail party. 'It is the Norwegian party,' he said coldly, 'but I shall go alone. I shall tell them that you are not well.'

'I see,' she said. 'Yes. Do that.'

'It is the simple truth after all,' he added, with a despairing wave of the hand.

'You don't have to explain,' she said calmly, almost as if she were in a dream.

'Good night. You don't have to wait up. I shall dine out.'

'Good night then.'

When the door slammed behind him with enormous terrifying force, she waited a moment before going up. From the top of the stairs she could hear Natasha singing Russian nursery rhymes to Charlie in his bath. There was much splashing to be heard from the end of the corridor, a few whoops of childish glee followed by Natasha's booming laugh.

I might have known, she thought as she entered the bedroom, I might have guessed. Well, at least it was something quiet.

Her clothes, all of them, clothes for every occasion and every season, had been piled in a great ugly heap at the foot of the bed. The drawers had been tipped out, her underclothes, handkerchiefs, jewellery, all had been added to the pile. He had swept the top of her dressing table clean. There was face powder everywhere. A bottle of toilet water dripped slowly into the accumulated disorder.

She sat on the side of the bed, conscious of the rising smell of expensive perfume which sickened her to the soul.

He returned to an empty house. There was a note on the hall table telling him that she had taken Charlie to the Head of Chancery's house. They had packed and would be leaving in the morning for London. He was not to try and stop them, not even to come to the airport to say goodbye.

Most of the disorder was still piled at the foot of the bed. She had taken what she wanted and left the rest. On the bed were spread his dinner jacket and his tails. Each arm had been sliced in two at the elbow. Both pairs of trousers were neatly set out, each leg raggedly amputated at the knee. She had ripped the front from crotch to waistband.

'These things happen, Gareth, in places like Moscow. Not everyone can take the strain.'

'I must see her.'

'I fear that might be unwise in the circumstances. We don't want a fuss, do we? We don't want Big Brother to know.'

'No. But Charlie—'

'I have already arranged that you will all go to the airport. Together. Just as soon as we can arrange their exit visas. This will take a little time, but meanwhile you must not see them. You do understand that? Then you will all go to the airport with Elizabeth and me. I will drive as if it were all perfectly normal and straightforward. You will say goodbye to each other as though it were the most natural thing in the world.'

'I see.'

'It's best. You do see that? After all, you'll be home yourself in September and you'll both have had the chance to reflect. Time is a great healer.'

'I see. I have no choice, it seems.'

'No choice. There's a good fellow.'

Patience and Charlie left from Sheremeteyvo where, six months before, they had all three arrived in their different states of foreboding. The militia were, as usual, all too evident: less evident were prying civilian eyes, although no one doubted they were present. All four adults were very pale. Both Gareth and Patience were thin-lipped, hollow-eyed. Only Charlie looked anything like his normal self and his tears could have been those of any child leaving home for school for the first time.

'Goodbye, Charlie,' Gareth said. 'Chin up, what?'

'Goodbye, Daddy,' Charlie replied. 'Oh, Daddy.' He clung to

his father's neck until he could be gently detached by both the parents together. Their fingers touched.

'Goodbye then, Gareth,' she said, kissing him lightly on the cheek. She was wearing rich Russian furs which enveloped him despite herself. He felt the tickle of her fur hat on his face. 'Have a good life,' she whispered in his ear and turned on her heel. He watched them go through into the immigration control, feeling her last contact on his cheek and smelling her expensive perfume. They were gone.

'Come along, Gareth, old fellow. We'll give you a stiff drink before lunch.'

'Thank you,' Gareth said. 'You've both of you been very kind.'

'Keep a grip,' Elizabeth said. 'You're still on show, remember.'

'I remember,' Gareth said. They walked out of the airport as naturally as they could through all the hurrying crowds. Outside it was starting to snow again. Elizabeth said, 'To think we've still got three more months of this. No wonder the Germans got so depressed. During the War.'

'I say,' the Head of Chancery added. 'Why don't we all go to the Praga tonight and cheer ourselves up with a plate of their *osetrina*? Gareth, what d'you say?'

'Eh. What was that?' Gareth said, looking back at the airport. 'That would be very nice. Thank you.'

They had their headlights on all the way into town. It was still only midmorning.

- FÜR ELISE -

There followed months of desperate quiet in the house. And suddenly one morning there was sound. Downstairs in the drawing room a hand at the piano riffled hesitantly through the notes searching for the key. Once found, both hands, emboldened, took up the well-known tune.

From the landing Gareth's first reaction was one of frank disbelief, turning quickly into a sense of outrage. In his house, in his own house without permission. . . . He came quietly down the stairs determined to put a stop to it at once, as unpleasantly as possible, so that it would never happen again. By the time he reached the bottom, however, the sound had already begun its soft work. He paused on the last step, caught in the web of spangled noise, already half aware of subtleties of inflection, minute differentials of pressure in the finger muscles, strumming the music into renewed life. He reluctantly had to admit that whoever the intruder was, he had never heard an instrument sing so convincingly.

He opened the door as quietly as he could. There was a duster draped over the end of the piano. A young girl, by now deep into the argument, sat absorbed at the keyboard. She wore a dust-coat, unbuttoned, over her maid's uniform but no cap. Her head, Baltic blond hair done up in mädchen plaits, was haloed by the sunlight streaming in from behind. Gareth had to squint into the glare through the wall of sound between them.

'Good morning,' he said stiffly in his formal Russian when the music came round to its final resolution. 'I take it you are the summer relief?' She looked up. Gareth caught the movement of her head and the soft swing of her breasts but the face remained invisible against the startling light.

'I am . . . I am . . . sorry, sir,' she said. 'Truly I am sorry. I should not have disturbed.' She rose quickly and took up the duster, the image of penitence.

'No, you should not. Not without permission,' he said, testing the ground. She winced visibly under the rebuff. 'But then,' he said, softening, 'it was very'—he searched for a word—'pleasant. The piano is not played enough.'

'In the Soviet Union the piano is often played.'

'I mean this piano,' he said dryly. 'I am well aware of the high standards attained by Soviet pianists.' Not knowing how to take this, she turned back to resume her dusting. He watched her for an instant, wondering if she was the deliberate plant everyone warned about.

*

Don't trust anyone. Anyone at all. Remember you are constantly watched for the slightest trace of weakness.

A bachelor is an obvious target. Or one of the married temporarily without a wife. Perhaps they're the worst.

Never forget it. Never let your guard down. Never.

*

Later, over breakfast when he was absorbed in the London papers, a new hand slipped the plate in front of him. A young hand, soft-skinned, very cool, with briskly cut nails. He looked up sharply into Scandinavian blue eyes.

'Your breakfast, sir,' she said. He now noticed that her accent was strange, containing little of Moscow.

'What was that piece, the one you were playing?'

'You don't know?' she said, her voice rising in faint surprise.

'I expect the whole Soviet Union knows,' he said wearily. 'Everyone knows the tune. It's so familiar it's impossible to place.'

'"Für Elise,"' she replied. 'Beethoven's "Für Elise."'

'Of course. How stupid of me.'

She smiled and shrugged her shoulders in sympathy with his self-vexation. She went out through the swing doors, the hem of her dress swishing through as they closed behind her. She was bare-legged, her thin ankles giving no evidence of the passing summer. Later she came back with the coffee. She smiled again, this time timidly, knowing he was waiting for her return. She started to pour, a firm muscle in her forearm tensing under the cream-pale skin.

'You are a pianist then?'

She looked pleased at his interest. 'I am at the Conservatoire. Not far from here. Gertsena Street. Third year piano. The violin too, of course.'

'Of course. But surely this is the vacation? Shouldn't you be on holiday?'

'I have to work, sir. Sometimes I go home. Always I am home-sick in Moscow.'

'What? You don't have a scholarship? I thought all Soviet students were paid for. No?'

'Oh yes, a scholarship. But private lessons, musical scores, tickets for recitals. Everything has to be paid for.' She shrugged her delicate shoulders, gesturing with the coffee pot she was still holding. She wore no makeup, emphasizing the modelling of her high cheekbones, the wonderful purity of her skin.

'And your name?'

'I am Anna's niece, sir, your cook. Randpère.' As she reached the door she paused slightly, not turning round. 'Please to call me Elise. I am often called Elise.'

She was gone. Randpère, he thought, of course. An Estonian, not a Russian at all. All that explained—what? The music in her soul, offspring of all those singing generations. The taper-ing of her thin body from the shoulders, the supple elegance of her waist, the long legs of the north.

Elise. I am often called Elise.
Always I am homesick in Moscow.

Who is not? he thought, tucking the papers into his attaché case and taking off down the street towards the Embassy. At the lights at Frunze he found himself staring at the towers and the more purposeful roofs behind the Kremlin wall. Again he con-templated the possibility of a plant. Surely not, surely not this young beauty in her first radiance? With all her simplicity and her astonishing talent?

Everyone. Every time. Suspect everything. In Moscow everything is suspect.

The sun shone into the river while he crossed the bridge. For once the scattered strollers relaxed, even cheerful, enjoying the brightness of a day without dust, one of the elementary Muscovite pleasures beyond ideology, beyond politics. A fat, overoptimistic man was fishing from the river wall, drinking in the warmth. A river boat swept under the bridge, giving Gareth a glimpse of the girls, Russian girls and therefore women, in cheap skirts and no-nonsense blouses. This was the Russia he knew, the drab, puffy, protein-starved Russia of the stodgy diet and the eternal queues.

Please to call me Elise.

She seemed light years away from the Russia before his eyes. He had never met a Balt who was not anti-Russian, a natural dissident. They all seemed totally and permanently immune to the chaotic, generous, soft-centred idealism which gave the system its opportunity in continental Russia. The northern peoples were naturally sceptical, European, ironic. Lovers of plain furniture, unvarnished wood, all the astringencies of the sauna from the charcoal fumes of the chamber to the birch twigs in the snow. Naturally melancholy people looking out across the Baltic to their fellow Finns with prison-hollow eyes.

Everybody. She wouldn't be working for you if she wasn't working for them.

He turned the corner by the old factory. Two militiamen were pacing outside the high Embassy railings. At the gates he looked up at the house where the Ambassador's Rolls-Royce was waiting under the *porte cochère*, an impeccable symbol of the capitalist West, his world and, he could not help feeling, the real world. He walked up to the Chancery building thinking of his calm office, its air of normality, order, restraint.

What nonsense, he thought, crossing the entrance hall, she's just a chit of a girl. A student. A part-time domestic who would be gone before long. The other one would be back, the Russian Natasha built like a bolster. Take a grip, man, he thought, you're beginning to imagine things. He went unseeing up the stairs.

'D'you know?' the British guard behind the reception desk said, turning to his chief with indignation. 'That bugger has passed me every day since I arrived three—no, I tell a lie—four months ago. And not once has he said so much as a good morning.'

'Take no notice, Harry,' said his chief. 'There's always one awkward sod per embassy. You'll get used to it in time.'

'I dunno,' said Harry, still grumbling. 'Even H.E. says hello.'

'Look,' said the chief, 'don't worry. You get paid, don't you? You get your beer and cigs. What does *he* matter? You're a lot better off than he is. Happier than he is—know what I mean?'

'You think so? You really think so?'

'Yah. Just look at the poor gink. All the cares of the world on his shoulders. Just the sort to crack up in the end. You watch.'

Gareth looked for her in the evening but she had gone. In the kitchen Anna looked up, he thought rather slyly, but then he realized that this was only the third time in a year he had crossed the threshold from the dining room. 'Can I help?' she asked. 'Is there something you want?'

'No, Anna. Nothing. I was just looking. Making sure you were here.'

'Ah. I am here, see,' she said, wondering at the softness in his voice.

In the drawing room he went over to the piano, eerie in its mute repose. He tried picking out the tune with one finger but could not even find the first note. If only, he thought, if only I could find the first note the rest would follow.

He wondered what those listening in were making of it.

We've got him. He's thinking.
We all know what he's thinking. But have we got him?
Sure of it.

He persisted, convincing himself at last that he had found the note he was looking for. A black note in the treble register—but no second note quite seemed to fit. Eventually he gave up and banged the lid shut. Time to change for dinner.

The shower gurgled over him, the water trickling over his lean flanks. Für Elise, he was thinking, Elise.

Hooked, I told you. I'm sure of it.
How can you tell?
Hunting about the piano like that for the tune. I told you she was the best. Didn't I tell you?
Didn't sound much like the tune to me.
Never misses, that girl. One hundred percent.

He shivered, wondering whether it might be so. The water continued to pour, striking his chest and streaming down over his long body.

She was waiting for him at the bottom of the steps. Looking down on her flaxen hair his heart turned over. Hearing his step on the staircase she looked up and he saw it was Anna. Despite her fine wrinkles and her chapped hands the family resemblance was there, something he found reassuring. Anna watched him come down, bathed, freshly shaven, and waited to speak. Surely, he thought, it's not that obvious . . .?

'May I have a word, sir?'

'Of course.'

'It's about Elise.' His heart stopped beating for a millisecond until he saw hers was a minor worry.

'Yes? What about Elise?'

'She's never served at table before, sir. Very inexperienced she is, particularly with the drinks. So complicated you all are. And what with twelve for lunch tomorrow you may need someone extra.'

He had forgotten. Surely not, he thought, surely the lunch was next week. But no, there it was, duly noted in the diary on the hall table. There's something the matter with me, he thought, something is going wrong.

Anna's smile, he was now convinced, had an edge to it. Uncertain about what to say next, he leafed through the diary with mounting irritation.

'It's all right,' she said. 'Don't fret. I have just the person. Not expensive and very experienced. She will show Elise how.'

'I am not fretting,' he said, recovering himself. Grudgingly he gave the necessary orders.

From the top of the stairs the following morning there was a heavy inert silence from the drawing room. He went in despite his misgivings. The sun streamed uninterrupted onto the empty keyboard.

She's gone, he thought. Well, it at least proves her innocence.

The same soft hand slid the plate before him at the breakfast table as he scanned the London papers. He stared at it, fascinated by its brisk, efficient nails.

'Good morning,' she said softly in her foreigner's Russian. 'I hope you have slept well, no?'

'Mmm. What's that?' Gareth said with his practised social nonchalance. 'Thank you. I have slept well.' She measured out his rashers of bacon, his two eggs, the hearty breakfast of his Cambridge days. Her chin was rounder than he remembered, less angular, more yielding. Her eyes, too, looked softer, more confiding.

'No music today?' he said. 'I expected to hear music.'

'No music,' she said, a gleam of amused apology in her eye. 'Not today. Yesterday I was very foolish. You must forgive.'

'Not foolish, not foolish at all. You have nothing to apologize for. You play very well.'

'Thank you.' She blushed slightly, someone unused to compliments. She went out for the coffee. He looked at his breakfast with disbelief. It was an insult, he thought, this abundance on display in a country where there was so little.

'You can practise here if you like,' he said as she poured the coffee. 'A piano needs a pianist.' He realized he sounded somewhat grudging and tried again. 'I would like it,' he said simply. 'It would fill the silence.'

'Ah,' she said, 'all noise fills the silence. That is what we mean by noise.'

'I would like it,' he repeated. 'It is a nice noise.'

'Then I will play,' she said. 'One hour every morning.'

He left the house to a torrent of sound from the drawing room. This was something thicker in texture, drawing on deeper

173

resources. It could have been anything. He had no idea what it was but it sounded more confident, as if something in her had been released. At the lunch that day for the Counsellors of the Western Embassies she followed the expert help around, studying each movement with grave concentration. He found this distracting, and he was nettled when he caught the Greek Counsellor looking at him with wry amusement.

'Congratulations,' he said. 'The authorities must hold you in high regard.' Gareth frowned and turned away.

'Aren't you shocked?' he asked the next morning.

'Shocked, sir?' she replied.

'Shocked, outraged, angry? Whatever the word should be.'

'At what, sir?'

'All this . . . this.' He gestured with his fork. 'All this space, light, air? All this food, this furniture? Everything? All for one person, here in Moscow where there is so little?'

'No. Not shocked. Not anything,' she said. 'We know how things are in the West. We are poor. We are not ignorant.' She looked at him fearlessly, solid on her feet, unwilling to be patronized.

'I'm sorry,' he said. 'Of course you're not ignorant. That's just the point. You know how things are with us and how they are here. Doesn't it make you angry? With us? Or with them?' Automatically he made the circular motion with his fork and saw at once a look of puzzlement in her eyes. It was obvious she had no idea what he meant.

'Our own leaders live well,' she objected. 'Everyone knows that leaders live well everywhere. It is we who have nothing.'

'But don't you mind? Don't you think things ought to be different?'

She shrugged her lovely shoulders. 'Here in Moscow?' she said. 'No, I don't mind. It is how things are. In Moscow. I have my music. That is enough.'

She went out leaving him to brood over this. She came back with the coffeepot and started to pour. He watched, fascinated, marvelling at the shape of her forearm tensing under the weight.

'And what about home?' he asked. 'Is it the same at home? Some with everything, most with nothing?'

She looked round to make sure the door to the kitchen was

174

closed so that even Anna could not overhear. 'Ah. There,' she said. 'There, there is music all the time. We try to forget. We have many . . . complaints.'

'Yes?' he said, afraid she had finished.

'Yes,' she said. 'Here it is only the Party. Here they are the Russians at home in their Russia. There we are different, no? Not Russians at all, only ruled by Russians. You have no idea what it is like. We feel so . . . helpless. Any moment there might be catastrophe—you see?'

'No,' he admitted. 'I have no idea what it is like.' She was still standing with the coffeepot in her two hands. She shifted her weight from one foot to the other. 'Sit down,' he said softly. 'Please sit down. We can talk.'

'Oh, no, sir,' she said, blushing, he thought, slightly. 'Anna . . . Anna will wonder what has become of me.' He understood. The spell had been broken, the masks restored.

'I see,' he said, pressing his lips together. 'Then perhaps you would be so good as to pour another cup for me.' She could see he was hurt but could find no way to retrieve the situation. As she poured, he became conscious that his eyes were level with her perfect waist. 'Thank you,' he said in his softer voice. 'And you will go, now, and play something?' She smiled down at him, her blue eyes filming over.

He left the house to the sound of surging arpeggios breaking through the drawing-room door into the hallway. He paused for a moment listening to her calling on the deepest resources of the soul. The cascades thinned out after a while into a thread of simple melody which he carried with him to the corner of the Prospekt and on towards the frowning library.

There was a cloud over the sun, a reminder that the highest of the high summer was over, that now it was mid-August and the beginning of the harvest. The pedestrians along the Prospekt, as if in response, were striding out with a slightly quicker pace. He slipped into the human stream moving down towards the Kremlin wall, finding the rhythm matched the melody still singing in his head. There were tight little knots of people at the crossing with Semasko and then again at Granovsky, obedient Muscovites waiting for the lights to change.

Bloody English, Cold fish.

Give him time. He's struggling but he is hooked, well and truly. Anyone with half an eye can see that. He's bound to weaken with time. Just keep playing him.

I wish I had your confidence. Cold bloody fish.

Gareth felt the flickers of inner rage at the impossibility of it all. Everywhere the microphones. Everywhere ears to hear. One's whole life exposed, every nerve, every blood vessel. Everything down to its smallest parts observed, analyzed, exploited.

It was like living under the eye of God, an implacable, malevolent God seeking to destroy. Destroying his marriage, pathetically ragged through it was already. Destroying it slowly, by degrees, every death throe duly noted in the files, pawed over, instantly retrievable by computer. Every possibility considered. From the corner where the two Prospekts met he looked down over the great walls and towers of the Kremlin nestling in the Aleksander Gardens. He was trembling and had to stop for a moment to mop his brow. In case anyone was watching, he carefully refolded the handkerchief and restored it to his pocket before rejoining the flow moving towards the river.

Why a pianist? he wondered. By what insight into his soul had they hit upon a pianist? He had never shown the slightest interest in music, which had up to now only been an irritation to him, jumbles of meaningless sound grating at his nerve endings. Embarrassing outpourings of sentiment, either wheedling, cloying and soft or posturing, bragging and loud. It was very mysterious, he concluded, their choice of a pianist.

Cold fish. Why not try something new?

Like what, for instance?

I don't know, something unexpected. Let me see, some sort of artist . . . Let me see . . . Got it.

You would. Let's hear it.

A pianist, that's it, a pianist. Some pretty little thing who can play a bit.

Come off it. He hasn't the least interest. That wife of his hadn't either, as I recall. Can you just check that?

You're right. Neither of them play a note. No hi-fi, anything like that. They turn off the BBC whenever there's a music pro-gramme. There's not a note of music anywhere on their files. Tone deaf, it seems, the pair of them.

What did I tell you? Any other bright ideas?

Yes, but don't you see? That's the point. Like I said, something unexpected. You never know, it might just do the trick. Some-thing new anyway.

Got anyone in mind?

And thus pursued by demons he arrived at the Frunze crossing where a large crowd waited at the lights. There were police blowing whistles everywhere, the length of Frunze as far as he could see and in the square in front of the Borovitsky Gate. Every minute or so a black-curtained limousine streaked by, slowing only to pass under the Kremlin ramparts, its progress marked by smart salutes thrown by the police.

At that moment, by the Frunze lights, cloud and sun sud-denly parted, bringing sparkle back into the sullen Kremlin stone-work, which bloomed a soft ochre the great length of the wall. It was then, without warning, that Gareth experienced a surge of unaccountable happiness, as if the floodgates of a lifetime had suddenly given way, drowning him in a new and totally unexpec-ted radiance. Unexpected but also something totally natural, as if he had been waiting for its coming for months, even years. He realized it for what it was, a searing moment when control was no longer possible.

Für Elise. I am often called Elise.

Finally the policemen relented and allowed the crowds to pass. He crossed with everyone else, one among many, trained for his particular part. He looked unchanged. There was as yet no flow to his limbs, the movement remaining as ever uncoordinated, awkward, not quite right. But this time he did not turn onto the bridge. Instead he followed the road down under the Kremlin wall to where it met the river. He continued walking, his eyes not on the towering rampart but fixed on the farther bank of the river.

The militia were, as usual, on guard before the Embassy

gates. The Rolls-Royce, as it so often was, was drawn up under the *porte cochère* of the Ambassador's entrance, the deep lustrous sheen of its metal evident even at this distance. Members of the staff were hurrying to their appointed tasks.

And there, under the wall, his soul danced.

-CARNAVAL-

She hopped, almost weightless, between the sheets. She had taken a bath while waiting for him and her skin had the rubbed quality he associated with the very young. She looked at him frankly, the blue of the irises as startling as ever.

'And so, my Gareth?' she whispered in his ear.

'And so?'

'We have I think one hour before the cocktail, yes?'

'Yes,' he admitted ruefully.

She laughed out loud, displaying a mischievous tongue. 'I love it when you smile,' she said. 'So serious, you are, so English.'

'Are we so serious then?'

'Oh, yes,' she said, rolling her eyes mockingly. 'So serious even when you smile. Especially when you smile. So—dutiful. Always it is the duty. The office, the cocktail, the dinner. Always on parade. All in a row, all in step like your Imperial Guards, no?'

'No,' he said, rolling onto her and opening his mouth to hers. She threw the sheet off to make for freer movement. Again, he caught himself astonished at the frankness of the gesture, her plain physical greed so unlike her virginal appearance. So restrained around the house, so apparently timid she hardly displaced the air. But here, in bed, it was another story: a triumphant assertion of self in all her youth and need. She came quite easily, without effort, without strain, as naturally as a bird singing. There was no restraining her love of the physical act, carried out with deep uterine grunts to the last cries of pleasure satisfied.

She lay on top of him, sweat beading her now tranquil brow. He looked down on her head, all blond disorder. 'Not Imperial Guards,' he said. 'Just the Guards. We call them the Guards.'

'Just the Guards,' she agreed happily. 'Down with Imperialism, yes?'

He laughed, then choked under her restraining weight. 'I'm sorry,' he said, 'but you cannot expect me to agree to that.'

'No?' she said. 'No matter. Here we are taught to fight Imperialism. But what we want to fight is all the regiments. Maybe you like to join us to fight all the regiments?'

'Ah, that, now,' he said, 'I can agree with. One day, soon, I help you to fight all the regiments. But just now, in twenty-five minutes, I have to leave to join mine.'

'*Ta-ra*!' she said, playing an imaginary bugle. 'But first we make love again, yes? Maybe take shower. Afterwards you can join your Guards again, yes?' With her head cocked on one side and her long hair tumbling over one glistening shoulder she was quite irresistible. She slipped over him with a soft, contented sigh.

*

A week before he had walked the length of the sidewalk between the wall and river. He turned up into Red Square, past the long line of those waiting to see the earthly remains of the dead leader entombed in his double casket of crystal and granite. He walked quickly into the Aleksander Gardens, behind the two entrances to the Moscow Underground disgorging the crowds. He had then, simply and naturally, gone home as if this had always been intended.

She was still playing at the piano in the drawing room. He took a chair and sat down opposite to watch the tensions in the sound reflect in the subtle tensions of her face. She continued to the last great climax of tumbling octaves followed by the twelve hammered chords, the last high in the treble register. When this had died away she turned to him, uncertain what he wanted but every inch the free northern European, no trace of the servant pose remaining.

'The March of David's Regiment against the Philistines,' she said. 'Schumann. *Carnaval*. You have come back, no? You left and you have come back? You are ill?'

'Not ill. I have telephoned. I am not expected today.'

'Ah,' she said, as if this was the answer she expected. There was a long silence. Her hands remained on the piano motionless. She looked down at them, puzzled. 'They cannot think what to play,' she said at last, raising the back of one hand to her forehead. 'They are confused. They do not know what to play.'

'It is I who am confused,' he said, 'Elise.'

She got up from the piano, went over to him, and kissed him fully on the mouth. When she had finished she pressed his head between her young breasts. 'Ah, my friend,' she said, 'I fear it is a mistake you are asking.'

'I am asking nothing,' he whispered.

She looked down at him, a smile twitching at the corners of her lips. 'Then it is a mistake I am making,' she said, attempting to break loose. 'I thought there was something you wanted to ask.' He gripped her tighter, allowing his body to speak.

On the way upstairs he imagined every microphone quivering with expectation. The very walls seemed to vibrate with excitement. He gripped her waist tightly, feeling her weight yielding under his arm.

Got 'im. I told you.

He took his time about it. I thought she was losing her grip for a while.

Worth the wait. Wait till Control hears. He won't half laugh.

Turn on the upstairs mikes, will you? Here comes the good bit.

Better try the bathroom first. Tee-hee.

Gareth laughed aloud, remembering the parting of sun and cloud and the re-sparkle of the stone. At the bedroom door he raised a fist to the listening walls.

'What is it?' she whispered. 'I do wrong?'

'Not wrong,' he said. 'I have something to say but I cannot find the words.'

She brought his clenched hand down to kiss. 'There are things only to be said in bed. Yes? The pillow talk?'

'Not these things,' he said, opening the door. 'These are things I mean for the moment to forget.' She looked bewildered but soon had her mind on other things.

Under the shower with her, he paused, holding the soap against her flat stomach. 'That Schumann you played,' he said. 'That was a march, surely? Everyone has to march to something—or don't you believe that?'

'Schumann, he makes jokes. Carnaval, remember? But tomorrow I play you Scarlatti,' she said. 'No parades, no regiments anywhere. Laughter only. Laughter, singing, and making love.'

And the following morning she was at the piano playing something crisp and transparent, like good champagne. She was again the maid, the summer relief, her hair severely drawn into mädchen plaits.

'Who's in uniform now?' he teased against the music.

'Outside the uniform,' she replied, not stopping, 'inside the laughter, the singing, and the making love. Like at home.'

'Like last night?'

'Last night, tonight. Tomorrow if you like.'

'Forever?'

'Ah, my friend,' she said seriously, stopping suddenly in midstride. 'Forever is too long. Already Anna, your cook—she knows.' She saw the startlement in his eyes. 'No worry. She is of the family. But forever?' She shrugged. 'Besides, I am too young for your forever.'

She started on the Scarlatti again, but this time the rhythm was leaden, the two hands scarcely together. She was trembling and her bottom lip quivered. Two tears found their way over her lower eyelids and stained her cheeks. 'No good now,' she said. 'you and your forever.' When he reached for her she grasped him desperately, as to a piece of flotsam after a shipwreck.

'And so Anna knows,' he whispered fiercely. 'And so who else knows?'

'She is my aunt. She is of the family,' she wailed. 'But in this country who knows who else knows? They make it their business to know everything, the leaders.'

'Just remember,' he said out loud, enunciating very clearly, 'I don't care who knows. Do you understand? I don't care.' She drew away to look at him more closely. Searching his eyes she saw at once that this was so. There was no flinching. He looked relieved, liberated, exultant.

'So. Now I will love you,' she said. 'I will truly love you. As long as you like. Only not forever. Never say forever.'

In the street outside he could feel the first suggestion of autumn in the slight edge to the morning breeze. He hurried along the familiar sidewalks, conscious for the first time of the unquestioning uniformity of the crowds. Always the same pace, not quite in step but as if aware of the need to do nothing bizarre, extraordinary. No one smiled, clapped hands, raised a voice. There was a lightness about him so palpable he could have skipped. Ridiculous, he thought, ridiculous. . . . Happiness, yes, but happiness with a recognizable end. Happiness until the moment came when it was decided that enough was enough.

Give it a while longer. The poor bugger deserves a break.
   But we've got enough surely?
   Yeah. A few grunts and stuff. We can surely do better than that. Besides, he doesn't care. It's no good until we can get him to do something he's really ashamed of. Shame's the name of this game.
   Right, chief. Gotcha.

He nodded briskly to Harry behind the desk in the entrance hall. 'Good morning,' he said. 'Autumn's coming on, I think. There's a real nip in the air.'
   'Good morning, sir,' Harry said, wondering. 'It's been a long hot summer. We shouldn't complain.'
   'We will though, we will,' Benton said, moving towards the stairs.
   Harry laughed. 'Too true, sir,' he shouted after him. 'We wouldn't be British otherwise.'

'Someone must have had a word,' Harry said to his chief. 'D'you know? This morning that bugger was actually smiling, even. Sure as I'm standing here.'
   'He must have got used to your face. Takes some getting used to, I admit.'
   'That's what all the girls say,' said Harry with a wink.
   'Tell you what, though,' the chief added. 'Seriously. He's going over the brink. You can always tell.'

*

183

From the bathroom door, completely nude, she saluted, mockingly aware of the perfect lifting of her breasts.

'You can stay the night if you like,' he said from the bed. 'There are no parades tonight.'

'I am so glad,' she replied, lowering her saluting arm. 'But in the diary there is dinner. Always there is dinner. Lunch, cocktails, dinner. Always it is the same.'

'I have cancelled,' he said. 'Supper will be laid downstairs. It is arranged.'

She came slowly towards the bed, her eyes fixed on him. From the foot of the bed she looked down, a faint smile on her lips. 'It is a lot, you ask,' she said, 'of Anna. I know she is family, but it is a lot you ask.'

'I ask nothing of Anna,' he replied. 'She must say what she pleases to whoever she pleases.'

She shivered, crossing her hands over her breasts. 'We are very foolish, no?' she said.

'No,' he said. 'Or rather, yes. But there is nothing I can do about it. Only you are free. Free to go, free to stay.'

'Oh, yes,' she said bitterly. 'I am free. It is guaranteed in the constitution. Our leaders have wished it so.' But it was with the same abandon she fell upon him with low gurgles of pleasure. It was, he decided, impossible to make her out.

He woke up already formulating the questions he needed to ask, but her side of the bed was empty. She was standing in front of the mirror in Patience's best ball dress, pinching it in at the back to make it fit the long line of her waist.

'It has a belt, look,' he said, indicating the hanger. When she had put it on she curtseyed to him mockingly through the mirror. Then, on tiptoe in imitation of high heels, she hung her head on one side and then on the other to judge the off-the-shoulder effect. She twirled to try out the fullness of the skirt. Without makeup and rested after love she looked all of twelve years old.

'She must be beautiful, your wife,' she said to him through the mirror. 'I see her somewhat older than me but very beautiful. Very beautiful and distinguished, no?'

'No,' he said, 'not exactly beautiful. But distinguished certainly. Upright. A lady.'

'An English lady?'

'Of course. An English lady.'

'Ah,' she said. 'I see. An English lady. Very expensive and always on parade also.'

'No.' He laughed. 'Not very expensive and not always on parade. But at her best on parade.'

She slipped out of the dress and hung it carefully back in the rack. She fingered through the other racks until she found a linen suit, a cool pastel Patience had often worn on formal calls in the afternoon. She searched the drawers for a frilly blouse, pouncing on the right one with unerring instinct. When all was ready, she ran long fingers through her long hair and minced up to the bed.

'Sir,' she said, extending her hand, 'I trust I find Your Excellency well. This garden is pleasant, no? Always the sun is shining. You have tasted our English strawberries? Always so good, the strawberries in our England.'

'You have a strange idea of our English manners.'

'You must teach me. I say the wrong things?'

'No,' he said with a sigh. 'The right things, alas. But English manners? I am not sure they can be taught. Perhaps we are born with them.'

'Here there is no need,' she said with a touch of sadness. 'Here we have no garden parties either. No, nor pretty clothes.'

'Take them if you like. Go on, take them. Take them all.'

She was outraged. 'Never,' she said, eyes flashing. 'Take the clothes of another? Never. Besides,' she added, 'they are not yours to give.'

'True,' he admitted. 'I should have remembered.'

'Yes,' she said softening. 'But tonight we play-act, no? I try on here.'

Once started her thirst seemed unquenchable. For the first time Gareth appreciated the full extent of his wife's wardrobe. Thirty pairs of shoes, six hats for various occasions. Dresses for the morning, dresses for lunch, dresses for afternoon calls. Inexhaustible numbers of short cocktail suits, more formal wear for dinner parties, three good ball gowns—each, he now remembered, costing a fortune.

She tried on everything, innocently slipping them by turn over her slim nude body and zipping them into place with a small cry of pleased surprise. His face contorted with the pain of hated memories. The wastes of his past life stretched out around him, grey and featureless. The heartless cocktail parties, dinner parties heavy as corpses. Hours of vacant talk, inert as tombstones. With Patience, always with Patience on parade at his side, waiting for doors to be opened for her, for waiters in white coats to glide into view with empty, practised politeness, for the glassy smiles of her host and hostess conscientiously spending the money provided for the purpose. Looking back, none of it seemed comprehensible, or even possible.

She turned quickly to test the swing of silk from the hips. Her smile froze at his expression. 'What is the matter?' she asked. 'I do wrong?'

'No wrong,' he said, shuddering off his memories. 'No wrong. Come back to bed.'

'No supper then?' she said, displaying a wicked tongue. 'I thought there was supper downstairs?'

'Supper afterwards,' he replied. But by now she had long arms stretched over her shoulders reaching for the zip.

For supper Elise had chosen a quiet little afternoon dress Patience had bought on impulse one rainy Saturday afternoon during their first year together in Berlin. She was still her marriage weight then, with a waist almost as small as Elise's now. It was simple enough for someone as unpractised as Elise to wear with conviction, and the frills at the cuffs emphasized the transparency of her skin. Her eyes danced with candlelight.

She refused a third glass of wine. 'No,' she said. 'Tonight I play for you. No practice tonight. Tonight I really play.'

He was surprised by her first choice. Three soft chords with the right hand, then the whisper of a rising scale on the left, a perfectly balanced response, inevitable, dreamlike. Three soft chords with the reverse tilt and an answering scale, this time descending. From such small beginnings the sound slowly blossomed into full flower, hung on the air for its allotted span, sank to a hushed close, dropped lifeless into the silence. After a second's pause she took up another theme, this one with a quicker lilt, the hands flittering across the keyboard sometimes in the same direction, sometimes in opposition, until they merged in one magisterial chromatic leap to a single booming chord sustained for what seemed an eternity. In the afterglow the three original chords emerged, an echo from far away. The subject again blossomed, again dropped, this time nodding, into silence.

'What is it?' he said, marvelling.

'Beethoven. Who else? But shh. I have not finished.'

Rising chords this time, quickly, in thirds, starting quietly but tumbling shortly into a fierce series of descents, stony, insecure. Her hands were transformed, the fingers moving with steely concentration through the roar of sound. It was as if she hated everything, her rotten life, the bars of her prison, even their few days together. After the final chord banged out with an unrestrained fury, she pulled up like a thoroughbred under the rein, panting, eyes distraught.

'Elise,' he said quietly. 'It's all right. Really, it's all right.'

'You know nothing,' she said with contempt. 'What do you know about this horrible country? And we cannot change it. All we can do is suffer. You speak this, the language of we who suffer, but you know nothing.'

'I know. I'm sorry.'

'Sorry? What is sorry? A word only. You come here, protected, you stay a few years, and you go. For us it is a life sentence. You do not know what it is to suffer.'

'I am sorry,' he said quietly, 'but that is not true. I too have suffered. Not for the same reasons, but does that matter? At heart all suffering is the same.'

She could see at once that he meant it. 'Ah, my friend,' she said. 'It is maybe an injustice I do you.' She shrugged. 'Do you want to know how Beethoven went on? To console us he gave us this.' She paused for a moment to gather concentration. This time her hands seemed to relax as they let solace well up, nobly, from the depths of the sounding-board. At the end she held the three last notes of the dying fall one by one until each attained an almost perfect silence. With the last she murmured, '*Adagio con espressione*. And now *Allegro vivace*' and her fingers skittered away, dazzling, into the playful melodies of a finale. There was a moment before the end when the hands again relaxed to take up the earlier grave sonorities. Three dying notes, a brief burst of activity so quick he could scarcely follow, and she had finished.

Her head was bowed over the piano. 'Beethoven,' she said quietly. 'There is no other.'

Later her hands took up something he vaguely recognized. Towards the end it came to him.

Schumann. Carnaval. You have come back, no?

He had taken a chair and had sat down to watch, not her hands that time but the subtle tensions in her face.

So few days. It felt like eternity, as if things had always been so. As if he had always been happy. Always free. Always certain of the end, certain that it would come, certain that it would be sudden and brutal like death itself. He found he did not care. In that certainty was contained all the reasons for his happiness.

When she had hammered out the last ten great chords, she ran her fingers through her hair and looked up. 'Carnaval,' she said with a wistful smile. 'You remember?'

'I remember. Of course I remember.'

'Such progress,' she said, a long way off. 'In three weeks, such progress you have made.'

- CHANTERELLES -

For her last Sunday they had agreed to have a picnic together. They had chosen to go to Peredelkino because the automatic ticket machine at Kursk station left fewer traces than the usual ticket office. And of course they travelled on separate trains.

He was waiting on the platform when her train drew into the little station. She emerged carrying a large peasant basket covered with a folded tablecloth in red-and-white check. She wore a rough kerchief over her flaxen hair and already there was pink in her cheeks. Afterwards he felt that there had been something not quite right about it all, something theatrical: she could have been a young duchess playing at being a peasant. But she was natural enough, blithe even, when she kissed him warmly on the lips and took his arm as if they had been married for years. Gareth, noticing the envious looks of some of the crowd bunching at the exit, felt a small warm gush of pride about the heart.

'Pouf,' she said. 'I thought I was going to miss you altogether. I had to wait hours for the sausages, so many people had been told, you know? One hour we waited. But in Gorky Street— you have heard of the courtyard in Gorky Street?—there was just arrived wine from the Cypriot comrades, not expensive. And so I reached the station just in time. Today we are lucky, I think.'

'I would have waited,' he said. 'I would have waited all afternoon if necessary.' She smiled secretly to herself as if she had been expecting this and squeezed his arm affectionately. Ahead of them in the crowd, a Russian recognizing their foreign accents turned round to beam benevolently on them. He winked and Elise laughed.

From the station they found their way to the small trail that leads upwards through the stands of birch still in full leaf. There was no chill in the air, only the deep-blooming sunlight and the longer shadows indicating that high summer had passed and autumn was coming on. She would not let him take the basket which, like a housewife out shopping, she carried in front of her with both hands. She moved softly, gracefully, gazelle-like. The going was easy and Gareth too felt attuned, never so much at peace with himself and with his life. Within minutes there was no further trace of the dachas of the great and they appeared to be completely alone. They climbed, breathing the good air and savouring the silence.

'I shall miss you when you are gone,' he said at last.

'Will you?' she replied, her mind evidently elsewhere. 'But I shall return. Only nineteen days in Tallinn with Papa and Mama, and then I can take up the studies again at the Conservatoire. We can meet, no?'

'Well, that might be a little difficult,' he said. 'For you. And for me.'

She sighed. 'Again so many parties,' she said with resignation. 'They start for you again. Summer gone, time again to be on parade. You and me, both on parade.'

'First I go home—' he began.

'Ah,' she interrupted. 'Just so. Your wife and little son. It is to be expected.' There did not seem much to add so the silence was resumed. She hummed a little air which Gareth recognized as a Russian folk song of undying love. They did not look at each other but with a common instinct started to search for a good picnic site at the top of the hill.

'Look,' she said in surprise. 'And so early.' She was pointing to a distant clump of mushrooms growing in the shade of the clearing. 'Chanterelles,' she added. '*Lisichki*. Little darlings. Come here, my pets.' But as she bent down to pick them she turned round in disgust to him. 'Bah,' she said. 'I should have known. They are *poganki*, toadstools. No good. Poison. Bah. The Russians call them *kokoshniki*, the hats of the peasant ladies, you know?'

'How can you tell?' he asked.

She shrugged her shoulders. 'Experience, I suppose,' she said. She laughed. 'Like human beings, no? At first you trust everyone. Then you trust no one.'

'And now?' he asked, curious to know her answer.

'Ah, now you know, you hope you know, the true from the false. But even now we are sometimes deceived. I think it is so. Sometimes we are deceived.' She grinned. 'With people, yes? Never with chanterelles.'

'Now who's been making progress?' he said and she laughed. Later he wondered whether he had not detected an edge in her laughter, as if she could anticipate what was to happen.

When they had found a spot on the edge of a glade sloping towards the south she spread her tablecloth. She had done what she could: some good Russian country sausage and gherkins, black bread, a couple of eggs, and some doubtful tomatoes. Also two good apples, the first of the season. 'From a peasant,' she said. 'There was this peasant at the station. There was just time. Of course I could not bargain.' She rolled her eyes in mock outrage. 'I told him he was wrong to ask so much. A capitalist exploiting the toiling masses.'

'What was his reply?' Gareth asked.

'He merely smiled and shrugged his shoulders. So I paid. He was not surprised.'

'Thank you,' he said simply. 'Can I contribute?'

'Certainly not,' she replied with finality. 'Today is my day. I told you.' It was time to eat. She handed him the bottle of wine and two tumblers. The bottle was corked with a flimsy bit of silver paper, and the stuff inside was barely drinkable. When he grimaced under the impact of the first sip she smiled sadly and patted his hand.

'The best we can do,' she said. 'We like it because it tastes of the Mediterranean. All those islands we shall never see.' And, indeed, after the first glass Gareth too found himself imagining a warm tideless sea with cicadas singing in the carob trees under stunning sunlight: they might have been on a different planet.

She had hitched up her skirt to allow the sun to play on her long legs. She took his hand and let it stroke her thighs while she leaned back to soak in the sun. He watched the slow ebb and flow of her breathing, her long eyelashes in repose. Occasionally her lips twitched in secret amusement but he did not want to disturb their mutual silent contentment by asking for explanations.

'You want we make love in the sunshine?' she said dreamily, as if half asleep. She did not open her eyes. 'You want—yes? Yes?'

'Oh, yes, I want,' he said. Soon they were naked and Gareth fell on her greedily, conscious only of the warm sun on his back and the sweetness of the earth under her pretty head and her face contorted with pleasure.

'All right. That's enough of that. Get up, man, and get dressed.' The voice was resigned, hard-bitten, the voice of the policeman everywhere. Gareth looked up into the sun-dazzle. There were four of them, one armed with a small movie camera. They were dressed like hikers but there was no mistaking what they were. He could scarcely make out their faces in the glare but he could tell they were mightily pleased with themselves, even relieved. 'You too, Lisa,' one of them said. 'Get dressed, girl. We have some business with your friend.'

Benton looked at her with disbelief. She had covered herself with her hands. Her eyes were empty, drained of depth. She might have been stunned; it was impossible to tell what was passing through her mind.

*

Everything. Everyone. Every time. Trust no one.

*

When they were dressed she was led away frozen-faced, perhaps under shock. She was taken away down the hill, and the last he saw of her was a flash of kerchief through the birches. Two of the policemen remained behind with Benton, who stood erect, half a shoulder taller than either. The older of the two was evidently in charge. 'You are aware, I take it,' he said, facing Benton, 'that your actions are an offence against public decency, punishable under the appropriate sections of the Criminal Code?'

'But I am a diplomat,' Benton said icily. 'I claim immunity under Section Thirty-one of the Vienna Convention.'

'Oh, yes, Comrade Benton,' the older man said. 'We know

precisely who you are. I think you had better come with us. We shall need to have a little chat, I think.'

'I refuse.'

'Please, Comrade, please. Do not make this more difficult than it need be. You know that resistance is useless.'

Benton looked around. Uniformed men now ringed the site at a discreet distance. 'You see?' the older man continued, lifting his hiker's arm. 'There are many witnesses. And of course some documentary evidence.' He nodded in the direction of the hiker with the movie camera. 'Do please come. Please.' Gareth shrugged his consent and the older man beamed encouragingly at him. He waved his hand over what was left of the picnic, the red-and-white tablecloth with its crumbs and the two tumblers grubby with wine lees. The man with the camera took the basket, which had fallen over, and started to fill it with the remains.

The small posse soon found the trail and moved down it through the stands of birch. Below, on the road, there was a convoy of grey-green vehicles waiting for them.

'Cigarette?' the oldest hiker asked. He pushed a packet of black-market Marlboros across the deal table.

'I don't smoke,' Gareth said shortly. He looked round the grubby room, bare except for a table and two chairs. There was a five-year-old Aeroflot calendar on the wall displaying the days of a distant December.

'Look,' the old man said confidentially, 'this is, I know, very unpleasant. So embarrassing for a man in your position.'

'You called her Lisa. Is she known to you?'

'It is enough,' the old man said silkily, 'that we have discovered you in what might be called ... delicate, yes, delicate, circumstances. This would not, I take it, be entirely understood by your authorities were we to ... arrange for the details to reach them. Sexual intercourse with a Soviet citizen is I believe as *mal vu* by you as the reverse is to the Soviet authorities. Such a pity. You with your brilliant career so far. Mind if I smoke?'

Benton made a despairing gesture of acceptance over the packet of Marlboros. 'Thank you,' the old man said. 'So much nicer than our Belomor, I always think. Even the packs are better designed. I can't imagine why the Americans are so determined to give them up. But there, human nature. ....' He took an age to open the pack, shaking his head meanwhile over the folly of mankind. Finally he lit up, a deep drag, and cocked his head at Gareth.

'Now then,' he said as if summing up a particularly tricky and difficult legal argument. 'Where were we? Ah, yes. Human nature. Human nature and your career. I mean, you can see the possible consequences? I don't need to spell them out to so able a representative of the profession?'

'No,' said Benton firmly. 'I am afraid that I cannot for the moment foresee them. Perhaps you will be so good as to explain.'

The old man sighed. He lifted his eyes to the ceiling, his head held high, as if trying to recall some half-forgotten quotation, some line of verse learnt in childhood.

'Beethoven,' he said softly, 'something about Beethoven. How does it go on? Ah, yes. "Beethoven. There is no other."'

'I see,' said Benton.

'It was the thirteenth sonata, by the way. E flat, always one of my favourites. I tried to master it when I was young. But then, you know Beethoven. So difficult.'

'No,' said Benton. 'I don't know Beethoven. As a matter of fact I have detested music in all its forms, all my life.'

'Really? Then perhaps you might be more interested in other material we happen to have. Your imagination might perhaps be able to suggest some other incidents in your recent past. Some activities of a more physical, even intimate, nature? Something more resembling the pleasures of this afternoon which it was our melancholy duty to interrupt. Would you like me to play some of it? We have made a little digest to avoid the tedious repetition of daily life.'

'Bastards,' said Benton softly.

The old man turned hard, flinty eyes on him. For the first time Benton realized they were exactly the same blue as Elise's even though the whites had turned yellow, blood-veined. 'Well, I suppose you leave us no choice but to play you some of it—a brief extract, you will understand—and invite you to contemplate how it would sound to your wife, or perhaps to your authorities, were we so minded as to send them a copy.'

'You must do what you think fit,' Benton said. 'But first you must understand. I was prepared for this. I expected it. There is nothing you can do to intimidate me. I have accepted. All along, from the beginning I have accepted it. It was the price, after all.'

The old man opened his eyes wider. 'Ah, the English,' he said, 'how they never cease to surprise. Still, you understand, these are my . . . instructions.'

'We all have our instructions,' Benton said. 'That is what is wrong with us.'

To his amazement the old man looked across the table at him and involuntarily nodded. Benton realized at once that the idea was far from new to him. 'Ah, my friend,' the old man said, 'it is the history of our sad times. In other circumstances I would enjoy the pleasure of a deep discussion of the matter, but time presses. It is perhaps more complicated than you think. Alas, we have but a short time before the regrettable rules of diplomatic immunity will fall between us, cutting short all exchanges of views, however interesting.'

Later, when the tape had been played, there was a long silence. The old man took out another Marlboro and lit it reflectively. 'We shall use it, you know, if necessary,' he said at last. 'It is the procedure. We have the power to destroy you. We shall use it, if necessary.'

'I see,' Benton said. 'You know, of course, I need hardly say it, but you have no hope.' He had sat through the whole thing, his face wooden, revealing nothing. He had listened to the mocking, distorted echo of all that had passed with Elise over the last three weeks, hearing every tender moment being rent, torn up like so much waste paper. It had been excruciating but he had borne it unflinching.

'We have gone to much trouble'—the old man sighed—'to obtain your future cooperation. Nothing immediate, you understand. We simply want you for an asset—that's it, an asset for the future. Somebody to call on when we are needing a little help. It would be truly disappointing to learn that you would be prepared to ruin everything—life, career, everything—in a quite meaningless display of bravado. What do we need to do to persuade you to help us? We have more, much more. There are some particularly delicious little discourses by your wife on the subject of matrimony. Would you like to hear them?'

'I know my wife's views on matrimony.'

'Come on, come on,' the old man coaxed. 'It's not so hard to work with us. Think of the alternative. To be destroyed. Finished. Cast out.'

'Isn't it much the same for you?' Benton replied with a combative smile. 'All this won't look good on your personal record file either. All this expenditure of money and manpower for no result. Your superiors might begin wondering whether you're starting to lose your touch, whether it's not time to put the old boy out to grass.'

'That does it. That does it,' the old man screamed. He came round the table, eyes blazing, and slapped Benton very hard across the face. He stood above him, panting, a bull at bay.

A trickle of blood appeared in the corner of Benton's mouth. 'I see,' he said, his face pale with anger, his jawbone tightening. 'Do you not think it is time the rules of diplomatic immunity were observed? There may be repercussions.'

The old man nodded fiercely, accepting the situation. Benton got up and moved towards the door. When he had his hand over the handle, the old man said, as if to himself, 'The Austrians, the Austrians, you know? They think the thirteenth sonata is a musical joke. Always looking for a joke, the Austrians. Here we are more serious.'

'And Elise?' Benton asked. 'Does she think it was all a joke?'

'And just wouldn't you like to know, comrade,' the old man said quietly. 'Just wouldn't you like to know.'

And they both knew it was so.

HOMEWARDS

-TRUTH-

The Ambassador, trained by life to face disaster calmly, remained impassive behind his large desk. During the long and frequent pauses he tapped his blotter reflectively with a paper cutter, but otherwise he gave no sign of emotion. It was early Sunday evening, the hour when the cavernous rooms of the Residence brooded in the failing light.

The younger man did most of the talking, but clearly it was not easy for him either. In the silences they were both aware of the heavy ticking of the clock, resonant as water dripping on stone.

'I see,' the Ambassador said at last. 'And that's the whole story, is it? There's nothing more?'

'No, sir,' Benton replied. 'Except to say that I am very sorry. So very sorry.'

'I'm sure,' said the Ambassador sympathetically. Gareth was listening very hard but could detect no fleck of irony behind his words. 'You were of course right to come at once. It means instant recall, you do realize?'

'Of course, sir. I'll go just as soon as it can be arranged.'

'I'll telegraph London. They won't be best pleased, having to find a replacement at short notice, but that can't be helped. We can have you out by the week-end.'

'Thank you, sir.'

For the first time the Ambassador warmed to this member of his staff. He had always found Benton unsettling, even though his wife kept telling him how good Gareth was with even the most taciturn Russians at Embassy receptions. But, the Ambassador reflected, in the office who was always the most

199

knowing, always so damned superior? It just went to show. . . .

'You'll have to tell Patience. She must be forewarned in case they try sending her something. Photographs or whatever.'

'Of course. It's unlikely to be a problem, though. Not any more.' Gareth's tone told the whole story.

'Oh, I see,' the Ambassador said. 'I am sorry. But you always looked perfectly happy together. Well suited, that kind of thing. No?'

'No. Not so, sir. Not for a long time. If ever.'

'Any particular reason?'

'No,' Gareth repeated. 'Life perhaps. This life perhaps. Ourselves. Who knows? Perhaps it never really got started. Despite the boy, there were . . . difficulties. Worse here, of course, knowing they might be listening. Anyway, whatever the reason, the marriage is for all practical purposes over. Finished.'

Despite himself, the Ambassador felt only relief. One less thing to worry about, he thought, no trusting little wife to consider, someone who might go to pieces, cause a scene.

'I imagine,' he said after a pause for reflection, 'I imagine it was very disagreeable, the interrogation? They're famous for it. No violence or anything, I hope?'

Gareth shuddered at the recollection. 'Not much,' he said. 'Nothing to speak of. Most of it was very quiet, almost civilized. On the surface, that is. We spoke of Beethoven.'

'Beethoven?' said the Ambassador, incredulous.

'The thirteenth sonata. In E flat. Curious.'

'Very,' replied the Ambassador just a shade dryly.

'Yes,' Gareth continued. 'But it was what was implied that was so shaming. They seemed to know everything. It was as if they had planned—well, you know, everything.'

'You can't claim you didn't know, surely?' the Ambassador said with a slight undertone of irritation. 'You can't say you weren't warned before coming out here? It's the classic case. Set someone up with a girl, still better with a boy, and threaten exposure in the event of non-cooperation. One can spot it a mile off. Lesson One in their training manual, I shouldn't wonder. I must say, Gareth, I'm slightly surprised at you. Couldn't you guess what was happening?'

'Oh, I did, sir,' Gareth said. 'That's the whole point.'

'I see. You let it all happen. You fell into it deliberately?'

'Yes, sir.'

'May I ask why?'

'I have no answer. I fear it's too long a story even if I were sure I understood it myself.'

The silence was unusually long as they both absorbed this. Not for the first time in his life the Ambassador looked into the abysses of the heart, the ultimate chasms where there were no explanations, or none that helped mere human understanding. You had to hand it to the Russians, he thought. To have found these chasms in Benton required genius. It's what came of reading all those novels. Dostoevsky. . . . It was uncanny.

'Yes,' Gareth said after a while as if there were no one else present. 'I expected it. I almost welcomed it when it finally happened. What was unimaginable was how brutal it was when it came. Nothing private, nothing of yourself is left intact, you know? Nothing. There is nothing left.' After another pause he put his head in his hands. 'The waste,' he said, 'the waste.'

The Ambassador had heard more than he wanted to. 'I will send the telegram in the morning,' he said with a touch of his habitual authoritativeness. 'I am sure you will not want to say anything to anybody. It's always easiest to say nothing in such circumstances. I suggest you go home and start packing. We will arrange for an exit visa.'

When he opened the front door he found Anna sitting in the hall. She had obviously heard the news. She was dabbing red eyes with her apron as the tears coursed down her cheeks. As soon as she saw him she went into a paroxysm of grief, rocking backwards and forwards on the chair, sobbing.

'I'm so sorry,' she managed at last. 'I am so sorry.'

'Get up, woman,' Benton said. 'If you want something useful to do, prepare a samovar and give tea to your two friends on plain-clothes duty outside.' He looked down with cold distaste, certain she knew everything. She caught his look and understood at once.

'Oh, no, sir. No, no, no,' she wailed. 'It was not I. I swear. Already the authorities have been here asking why I told them nothing, when it was my duty to tell them. Of course I knew what was happening but what could I do when it involved Lisa, my own child practically? I have been bad, they say, very disloyal.'

'I expect you have,' Gareth said with a short bitter laugh. 'Letting a Soviet citizen sleep with a Western imperialist without informing the authorities. I don't believe a word of it.'

Anna got up and started to run towards the kitchen, holding her hands over her ears. 'I will no longer listen,' she cried amidst her tears. 'You are very wicked. Unfeeling. You think only of yourself. You're as bad as . . . as bad as—them.'

'Oh, yes, you will,' he shouted, shaking her by the shoulders. 'Yes, you will listen. I have something to say to that precious niece of yours, your own child practically. Elise. Lisa. If that is her name.' He raised his hand to strike.

She looked up wild-eyed into his white face. 'But no one has seen Lisa,' she howled. 'She has gone. Disappeared. No one knows where she is.'

It was true. He could see in her face that it was true. No one knew where they had taken her. It could be anywhere. A recreation centre for agents between assignments. A punishment cell in the Lubyanka or worse. She could already be on a train somewhere out along the flat featureless railway pointing interminably east. Exile, a long exile in prospect, among strangers, farther than ever from home.

Anywhere. She could be anywhere. What did it matter, he thought, as long as she is not here?

*

You have no idea what it is like. We feel so helpless.

We have many . . . complaints.

Any moment catastrophe. You see?

*

His hand dropped. Anna saw that his eyes were unfocussed, that his face was by now the colour of chalk. She saw with amazement that he too was beginning to weep. Quietly, containing himself as she imagined all Englishmen did, but unmistakably weeping. She drew close. Like twin outcasts, they held on to each other, letting their tears flow unchecked.

Before leaving and with his baggage already gathered in the hall, he entered the drawing room for the last time. He opened the piano lid to look once more at the keyboard in search of its secret. Dust had already gathered on the keys. He tried picking out the tune, finding to his surprise that after a few false starts the first phrase eventually came, a few simple notes arranged rhythmically to make nine, a springboard for the rest.

Für Elise. I am often called Elise.

He pondered the mystery, his gaunt figure caught head bent in the streaming sunlight among the motes spiralling gently to the floor.

He tried again. This time the nine notes came easily but he could get no further. Again. Again. He looked up into the corners of the room and shook his fist. He closed the lid of the piano with a bang to shut out her memory. Finally he wiped the dust off his fingertips with his handkerchief and refolded it carefully in his pocket. Benton was ready to leave.

Anna was not there to see him off. She had left a note saying that she was returning to Tallinn now that her permit to remain in Moscow had been rescinded. *These times, you know*, she had written. She wished him well from the bottom of her heart. There was a postscript:

No news. The family has made enquiries. There is no news.

Stout-hearted Natasha, with the arms of a market porter, helped the driver stack Gareth's luggage in the car. She gave him a grin and a bearlike hug which he knew better than to resist. 'Big kisses to Charlie' were her final words. 'Tell him his Natasha misses giving him the bath, yes?'

The exit formalities at the airport betrayed no apparent interest in his movements. His visa was checked and stamped by a negligent official in need of a shave. Only the duty officer from the Embassy was there to see him through, and even he seemed a long way off as if part of some dreamlike sequence obeying a logic of its own. Afterwards Gareth could only remember the briefest of handclasps. If either of them said anything he could not recall what it was.

It had been put about the Embassy that he had been recalled to be interviewed for something important in London.

'What did I tell you?' the chief behind the reception desk said. 'Cracked up like I said. Didn't I say he would? Didn't I, Harry?'

'But he's coming back next week,' objected Harry. 'I've been detailed to meet him Monday week with a car.'

'Come on, Harry, you weren't born yesterday. I'll bet you a carton of ciggies.'

Harry was impressed. He whistled softly to himself. 'How d'you know, Bert? Little dickie-bird tell you?'

'Nah,' Bert replied. 'You've only got to look at their faces. Even H.E.'s. Talk about keeping secrets. Don't make me laugh.'

Continental Russia in all its vast immensity lay below, bathed in autumn light. From thirty thousand feet it looked like anywhere else: fertile, prosperous, untroubled by the authorities, tended by a happy people proud of their responsive government. Gareth felt a small gush about the heart as if some pressure long held had been released. He felt his spirits lifting in spite of everything at the sight of a normal British cabin crew going through their well-practised routine in a real world, ordinary citizens going about their business outside the walls of a prison.

*

Everyone. Every time. Suspect everything. Trust no one.

*

He could see her fingers at the keyboard raging against the bars. For us it is a life sentence, she had said. Elise, forever free, forever trapped. It was impossible to say which.

*

Outwardly the uniform. Inside the laughter, the singing, the making love.

*

Yes, he thought, but what did anything she said prove? Not innocence. At most, hatred of her role as a paid seducer acting for the state. Practised words, perhaps every one rehearsed with cunning policemen beforehand.

And then again, perhaps not. She could have been like him, greedily snatching a moment's freedom in a lifetime of captivity.

All along he had been the willing victim. Knowing the end, he had surrendered at the beginning. Perhaps it was the same for her. Perhaps it started for her as an assignment but had turned out otherwise. Perhaps, perhaps. It was impossible to know.

Anything was possible. Every incident, every word, every gesture even, was capable of two explanations at least, perhaps more. He had not cared. But now it was over he needed to know what it all meant and he knew he would never know. Her radiant image would glow for him always, mocking, enigmatic: something giving a meaning to his life, a meaning ultimately unfathomable.

His face grimaced with pain, blinding him to the landscape of continental Russia rolling under him in the autumnal light.

An official car met him at Heathrow. Two civil servants in clerical grey, strangers both, spotted him as he emerged into the immigration hall and led him away. 'This way, sir, if you don't mind,' one said firmly, brooking no protest. Benton did not think to question their credentials. The tone spoke for itself.

As he so often did, Gareth felt a wave of melancholy engulf him at the sight of his country, the cosiness of Chiswick from the fly-over, the unnecessary squalor of the Earl's Court canyon, the drabness of the week-end crowds. They had chosen his hotel, a quiet little place in Edwardian brick behind Victoria Street. The younger official, the silent one, carried his bags and dumped them unceremoniously in the room they had selected for him. It was Saturday afternoon and raining. The rain looked as if it had set in for the week-end, with dreary wastes of Saturday evening and Sunday looming ahead.

'I wouldn't go out, not if I were you,' the senior official delegated to speak said. 'Just report to Personnel on Monday. You have an appointmnent at ten.'

'But what do I do meanwhile? Sit here in my bedroom and do nothing?'

'Oh, no, sir. There is a bookstand in the lobby. Otherwise there's the television, look. You must have missed it where you were.'

'I take it,' Benton said, finally discovering the tone which asserted his rank. 'I take it you will have no objections if I go round to see my wife. She's living off Sloane Square.'

'Just give us the address. We'll see that she calls you.'

They left him with the evening paper, which he idled through when he had finished unpacking. He had reached the end-of-season cricket news at the back before the telephone rang.

'Hello,' he said defensively. 'What took you so long?'

'Gareth? Is that you?' Patience said, not quite believing she had heard his question correctly. 'Are you all right?'

He found her voice oddly soothing, familiar, even matter-of-fact. He had not expected to find her voice so welcome.

'Well, you know,' he said hesitantly, 'what's all right? Yes, perhaps I am all right. Just.'

'What happened? Can you say? The men wouldn't say.'

'Not really, not on the telephone. Are you free for dinner?'

'I don't know.' She paused as if silently questioning someone else, someone in the room with her. Finally she said, 'All right. Where?'

'The hotel. Say eight o'clock.'

'All right. You'd better give me the details. They didn't say where exactly you were.'

When she finally hung up, Gareth found himself staring into the mouthpiece wondering who she was with. He realized with a start that he had not asked about Charlie. It was as if Charlie already belonged to someone else.

She came through the revolving doors a little too fast, as if she had been nervous and wanted to get the first part over as quickly as possible. Her umbrella was loose-folded and very wet. Her hair was windblown and her complexion had recovered its soft English quality, something which he had admired in their early days. They shook hands in the crowded lobby in front of everybody.

'You're late,' he said, to cover over the nervousness he was feeling.

'I know. I'm sorry,' she said crisply, not caring what he thought. She had a greater air of authority than he remembered, a sturdier independence of mind. He looked at her with more respect.

'Your hands are freezing,' he said more kindly. 'Let me relieve you of that umbrella and things.'

'Well, it is September,' she said, 'and you know what

206

London's like even on a Saturday. I had to park miles away.' Her face smiled but there was no true sparkle of intimacy. She had come bringing with her unacknowledged new beginnings, connections he knew nothing about. He recognized, with a pang, that there was the bloom of the sexually satisfied about her mouth. He wondered whether she had not been in bed when she called, nestling against some warm, by now familiar body whose secrets were now her own.

'You're looking well,' he said grudgingly. 'Much better than in Moscow.'

'I'm fine,' she said, putting up fresh defences. 'Is there time for a drink?'

'Of course,' he said. 'I'm sorry.'

They moved on through to the bar, where there was a small hard table for two in the corner. There were dirty glasses on it and a full ashtray. A barman in a red blazer came over and cleared up for them. When he asked her what she would have she said, 'A gin and tonic, please. A large gin and tonic.'

'Gin?' Gareth queried. 'Are you quite sure?'

'Quite sure. Otherwise I shouldn't have asked.'

The barman twinkled at her. After Gareth had ordered whisky, he went away to busy himself at the bar.

'Nervous?' she asked with a hard-edged smile. He recognized she was better balanced on her feet than she used to be, less vulnerable. Their relative positions had changed.

He nodded. 'Yes, decidedly nervous. Aren't you?'

'No. Not especially,' she said, turning from him to look on to the distance. 'Well,' she admitted at last, 'perhaps just a little. Do you want to tell me what happened?'

The barman came with the drinks. He hung around waiting to be paid until Gareth remembered where he was. 'Sorry,' he said, pulling out a five-pound note. He was startled how little change there was. 'I haven't paid for drinks in an English bar for centuries, it seems,' he said with a rueful grin. 'I'd forgotten the routine.'

'So?' she said, raising her glass when the barman had finally left. She looked at him softly, trying to encourage.

'No. I don't want to tell you what happened. But I have to, insofar as I can. I'm advised that I have to.'

'Oh, well,' she said with a sigh. 'Orders always were orders. I had hoped you might want to.'

'Why?'

'It might have helped. I thought it might have helped.'

'The problem is,' he explained, 'I do not think I entirely understand what happened myself.' They fell silent with their own thoughts, unable to connect. Patience thought it tactful to move on to news about Charlie, doing well, so she claimed, at his co-educational vegetarian prep school.

The story came out more easily over coffee, when he began as if at a prearranged signal. Patience listened, stirring her cup from time to time but not drinking it for fear it might break the spell. He found words, somehow, to dignify what had happened, to clothe the more humiliating episodes in tatters of pride. He was aware that she could piece the rest together without any help from him.

'Poor Gareth,' she said at last. 'It's my fault, isn't it? You think it's my fault?'

'Not at all,' he said quite sincerely. 'In all honesty I must say that it is nobody's fault. Either that or it is everybody's fault. Fault scarcely seems the word. Going back as far as Berlin, it all looks inevitable to me.'

'But if I'd stayed?'

'I seem unable to convince anyone that everything that has happened, back to Berlin, even longer, has happened because I wanted it to happen. I willed it to happen. I wanted you to leave. I wanted Elise to happen, and I wanted them to find out. I have chosen. I didn't know I was choosing, but that is the truth.'

She stirred her coffee, thinking about this. 'Perhaps,' she said. 'I used to think that perhaps I too had chosen you. But it isn't true. It was what was . . . expected. I was of an age when it was expected and there you were.'

'And much good it has done both of us,' he said. 'I am very sorry. That is what I will not forgive myself.' There was a long silence while she drank her coffee cold.

'How very clever of them,' she said at last. 'They must have known. And we hardly knew ourselves.'

'Yes, but don't you see?' Gareth said eagerly. 'Elise might have been sincere. She might be what she seemed. That's the unguessable element. I shall never know what it all meant. To have made her suffer so much. To suffer myself so—uselessly.'

Patience looked at him, all wide-eyed innocence. 'But my dear,' she said, 'it hardly matters, does it? The consequences are just the same.'

He had no answer to this. She looked on his bent head with a pang, realizing that, inadvertently, she had given the knife one more twist in the wound.

- CONSEQUENCES -

The Head of Personnel looked over the river to County Hall, heavy with the last illusions of Empire. A couple of pleasure steamers crossed in mid-river both only half full: late tourists taking snapshots. 'I've seen the Ambassador's account,' he said. 'It would be helpful to have yours. Everything you can remember, however small. Don't think we're being prurient, but we simply have to have all the details in case we need to take ... countermeasures. Have you told Patience?'

'Yes. We had dinner together on Saturday evening.'

'Dinner? So it's true, then, that you two are splitting up?'

'We have split up, Dick. Months ago. It's just that we're only now beginning to admit it to others. I wasn't sure myself until Saturday. Completely sure, that is. I always thought there was a chance. Despite everything I thought there was still a chance.'

There was a long pause. The Head of Personnel was obviously waiting for something. Benton raised an eyebrow.

'Your account?' the Head of Personnel reminded him. 'Your own account, down to the tiniest detail?'

'Ah, yes. I've written it all up,' Benton said, reaching into his briefcase. 'There was precious little to do yesterday. It will need to be typed but it should be quite legible.'

'You always did have a neat hand,' the Head of Personnel said, looking over the papers. 'I envied you that from the beginning.' He did not seem to have anything else to say. They had joined the same day, Benton reflected in the painful silence, and their careers had been roughly parallel. Dick Watson had always been the most approachable of men, too approachable, he often thought, too coarse-grained, reckless of speech. What was the difficulty? Why did their eyes not meet?

'Look, Dick,' Benton said at last, 'there's really not a lot to it. In your job you must see it all the time. It's a pity it was in Moscow, I admit, but not a great deal of harm's been done. It could have happened to anyone. You can imagine the pressures once Patience left.'

'Of course, of course,' Watson readily agreed. 'Believe me when I say we do understand. We're all human beings after all, despite what the Service thinks of its Personnel Department.' Watson still did not look very happy. He fingered through Benton's account as though he had a wounding message to deliver and was searching for a way of putting it. 'It must have been a ghastly experience,' he said as his eye came to rest on a particular line towards the end. 'They really play rough, don't they?'

'Ghastly, Dick, ghastly. You've no idea. Words can't express it.' Benton sought unsuccessfully to avoid the pleading tone. 'They're masters of insinuation, at the hidden menace. Masters.'

'So I've heard,' Watson agreed dryly. 'I say, apart from Patience, is there anyone else you should tell? You know, anyone else who might make you—well . . . vulnerable?'

Benton was impressed despite himself. Watson really did understand, he had to admit it. He swallowed hard before committing himself.

'There's not another woman in the case, if that's what you mean,' and Benton could see in Watson's face that that was precisely what he meant. 'But there is my father. He's getting on. He's always been ambitious for me.'

'With some reason, I think,' Watson interjected, causing a warm gush to flow round Benton's heart. 'You must tell him,' Watson ordered crisply. 'He must know.'

'But I can't, Dick. I simply can't. He's over eighty. It would kill him.'

'If you don't they will. Somehow they'll get to him, get at you through him. Best to tell him. I would.'

'Sorry, Dick,' Benton said, his voice breaking. 'It's a risk I'll have to take. I can't tell him. I simply can't.' Watson looked at him sharply. There was no need for words. It was perfectly understood between them, the whole sorry mess. For a second Watson almost relented but then realized that it would be no good; he simply had to stand firm.

'I've told you,' he said quietly, 'what would be in your interests and those of the Service. You will understand how much hangs on this.'

'All right,' Benton said bitterly. 'I will tell him if you insist. But I am not answerable for the consequences.'

Watson looked relieved, almost amiable. 'Tell you what,' he said. 'When you've got that over—and the sooner the better— you might think of taking a month off and go walking somewhere. You were a great walker, I seem to remember. Get away for a bit, get this'—he waved at Benton's account—'all this out of your system.'

Benton thought this through as an awkward silence again descended. Perhaps the Pyrenees,' he ventured. 'I seem to remember Tennyson loved walking in the Pyrenees. I read a description somewhere. It would be something new, at least.'

'Try this country, I would,' Watson said a little too quickly, 'and leave us an address where you can be contacted if we need you.' Benton understood. He was no longer trusted. He found the experience unsettling, not at all what he had expected. He who had conformed, he who had modelled himself into the very image of a British representative abroad. He of the soft tread and the practised tongue, with his reputation for hard work and sound judgement. He felt the ground yawn under his feet and for a moment or two felt giddy.

He decided on the bold line, the one that had stood him in such good stead in the past. Particularly here, he reflected, here in this room over the years as his career was mapped out step by step. 'What happens then?' he asked. 'What will you have for me when I come back? Have you had time to think of something?'

'Well,' Watson said with a rueful smile. 'We're not sure yet. All this was so . . . unexpected. You must give us time. You do see, Gareth, that you've given us a lot to think about, I hope?'

One of his telephones rang. Looking at Benton half apologetically he picked up the receiver. 'Watson. Can I ring you back? . . . Oh, Minister. . . . Yes, I do have a visitor but he's just going.

Can you hang on a minute? . . . Thanks.' He clapped his hand over the mouthpiece. 'Sorry about this, Gareth.' He smiled half apologetically but was not to be gainsaid. 'OK? Leave us an address, all right? And don't forget about your father, eh? Oh. And good luck.'

They shook hands across the table as Watson turned back to matters on hand, all attention.

'Yes, Minister? You were saying?'

Benton picked up his hat from the pile of files on the desk and went out. In the outer office two girls were typing furiously and could spare him only the briefest of nods. On the steps outside he pulled his hat on angrily and savagely buttoned his gloves at the wrist. The wind of the week-end had dropped, leaving room for a faint but distinct autumn chill to seep up from the river. He turned right along the Embankment towards the Houses of Parliament. Big Ben, looming ahead, showed precisely ten thirty. The whole interview had taken less than half an hour. Strange, he thought wistfully, it had felt longer than that. It should have taken longer: he felt he should have been given longer.

There was nothing to do before lunchtime except to return to his hotel. He felt entombed by Watson's civilized reticence, at once gracious and inflexible, deaf to his own implied appeals. Gareth could see that the problem for Watson was a purely organizational one to be handled with as much practised despatch as he could muster. In the best interests of all: naturally, in the best interests of the Service and of himself.

No one else wanted to see him. The Office had fallen silent to let Watson be the spokesman. It was the neatest, most professional way of dealing with an awkward situation. He had to recognize that he would have done the same in their position. It was, after all, the only sensible thing to do.

And thus, with his private sufferings, he crossed Parliament Square under the sprightly statue of Jan Smuts and the brooding figure of the great Churchill, saviour of the nation. The leaves on the plane trees were at last showing signs of turning and the far vistas of the Park dissolved in a slight mist as on the day when, full of hope and ambition, he had joined the Service to which he had devoted half a working life.

He looked up at the flank of the old Abbey, always there,

mostly disregarded except for the tourists. Even the stones looked unforgiving.

Since there was no alternative, he went up to Cambridge to see his father. He walked from the station hoping to derive some inspiration from the genius of the place which would help in the wrenching interview which was to come. He received little help. The university seemed to belong to someone else, a colony of some foreign power. There seemed to be as many young women in the streets as young men, all identically dressed in old jeans and sneakers. In the centre of town there was a fat red car park on top of a fat red shopping centre. All he recognized at first was the crispness of the East Anglian autumn, which left the impression of a region where rain was unthinkable. In due course the colleges began, their stones rather cleaner than in his day, but still in spirit their ancient, settled, corporate selves.

He had tried to explain on the telephone that he would prefer not to lunch in Hall; that he had some news of a private nature he would prefer to give his father at home. 'Can't be good news,' his father had grumbled down the telephone, 'and you can't expect more than a crust of bread and a lump of cheese.' In fact, and rather touchingly, his father had gone to some trouble. There was smoked trout with an excellent hock and the best saddle of lamb Gareth had ever tasted. 'The college chef,' his father explained shortly, seeing his surprise. 'Can't beat them these days. The colleges are the last outpost of English cooking. Miles better than that awful club.' They were served by a fat jolly countrywoman who was, however, too obtrusive to allow of intimate exchanges between them.

After lunch his father had muffled up for his afternoon walk in a fine collection of old standbys which had seen better days. He was stooped and frail-boned particularly over the shoulder blades and at the wrists. His hair, snow-white by now, was worn longer than in his prime and this, together with his blackthorn stick, gave him a dashing look, something between an Old Testament prophet and a Victorian dandy. Age had slowed him and retirement had mellowed him, but walking beside him through the Backs, Gareth recognized that he was the son of a distinguished, even in a small way a historic, figure. He blenched before the task ahead of him.

They found a bench under a pair of chestnut trees, by now

well on into the dying season. Using his walking stick as a support for his chin his father gazed at the magnificent architecture in a sombre, almost elegiac, mood as though cataloguing its splendours for the last time. But his mind was on other things and had lost none of its sharpness. 'You have something to tell me,' he said, 'and I take it there's trouble at home. But is that all there is, or is there more?'

Gareth was startled. 'Much more, I'm afraid, Father,' he replied, 'but so much more I do not know how to begin.'

'We have the afternoon,' said the old man, 'and I have no occupation worth talking about any more.'

So Gareth told him. As he went along he found there was something in his father's attitude, in the position of his body, though he did not once turn to look at him, that made the telling easier than he had imagined. It was no longer as if he were still the schoolboy before the imperious examiner but as if, at one time, they had been friends.

When he had finished his father nodded emphatically as though indicating that the message had gone home. After a pause he said, 'Damn considerate of the Foreign Office. Quite right you should tell me yourself. Painful, I imagine.'

'Yes, Father. Very painful.'

His father thought about this for a moment and then nodded again. 'I could have guessed. I sometimes feared something like this. When I sit here sometimes—I do often, you know—I reflect that we could have made a better go of things, you and I, if I had not been so preoccupied years ago. I thought it was important, what I was doing. Illusion. Illusion.'

'Is it, Father?' Gareth said, amazed.

'Yes, of course it is,' his father said impatiently, as if everybody should have known. 'Voltaire said the role of the doctor is to keep the patient amused while nature takes its course. And all the while we might have had each other. Like other fathers, other sons. That would have been something at least.'

'But you're not shocked?' Gareth asked. 'I confess that looking back on it I am shocked myself. In Moscow—what was I thinking of?'

His father at long last looked sidelong at him over the top of his stick. He grinned, the impish grin of the very old who no longer have responsibilities. 'Ah, well,' he said, 'as to that, you must be the judge. Who knows? Perhaps it was worth it for the experience.'

'But the consequences? Surely you can see I'll never be trusted, fully trusted, again?'

'Probably,' the old man said, twinkling. He turned back to gaze sombrely over the buildings, watching the light fade on mellow brick and stone. He seemed to have lost the thread, but Gareth did not feel he could interrupt his father's chain of thought. 'Yes,' he said after a while. 'I am afraid the next stage of your life is going to be very difficult. I do see that. But then, what does it all matter in the end? We all end up on park benches in the autumn sunlight, wondering whether this will be the last, whether our old bones will survive another winter.'

'That's all very well,' the son said impatiently, 'but I've half a working life ahead of me. How could I throw it all away? I have, you know, just thrown it away, deliberately, even with a kind of joy. I'll fight for it, but I can see already there is no chance.'

'True,' his father replied simply. 'But I think I should like to offer you tea. You can tell me about young Charlie. I shall tell you about the tempests of academic life, taken so seriously here because of their fundamental unimportance.' They got up and moved towards the bridge across the little river. Gareth, supporting his father now, could feel the warmth of his body under his guiding arm. They stopped on the bridge to watch the fading sky in the slow flow of the water. 'Yes,' his father said, 'we shall talk of such trifles over tea. But you must not think that under it all I do not grieve for you, my boy. And you must accept my apologies now for the rotten job I made of being your father.'

They neither of them had anything further to say. Father and son, the son now taller than the father, walked slowly on towards the King's Parade where the street lamps were just coming on.

Brr. Brr. His mouth went dry listening to the signal. He let it ring ten, fifteen times, before hanging up. He tried again at noon. This time she picked up the receiver. She had been running again, her breathing not entirely under control.

'Patience Benton.'

'That sounds encouraging. It's me,' he said, half apologetically.

'Who? Oh. Gareth.' She sounded disappointed, as if she had finally managed to get him out of her life weeks ago. 'How was Snowdonia? Good walking?'

'All right. You seem out of breath.'

'So would you be with all these stairs. I heard the telephone from the front hall. So what's new?'

'Nothing much. I saw Dick Watson again last night in Personnel.'

'And? How did it go? What did he say?'

He told her, not sparing any of his anxieties. There still seemed to be some difficulty about finding him something to do. He had been back from Moscow four weeks and still there was no certainty.

'Poor Gareth. Never mind, it will probably be all right. They just need time to think about it. You've given them a bit of a surprise, that's all. They can't find jobs out of a hat, particularly at your level.'

'That's what they say,' he replied grimly, 'in just those words. But it's the end, I fear. They never did like me much. I've made too many enemies, especially when I've been right. Over that Czechoslovak business, for instance.'

'But that's why they respect you, silly. Anyway, nothing's going to happen for ages. I wouldn't worry. You ought to start thinking about selling the house. Remember we talked about selling the house? Remember?'

'I rather hoped we might think about that again.'

'What?' She could not restrain her incredulity. 'What's that you've just said? Or am I imagining things?'

'I've been thinking it over. All the time I was in Snowdonia I thought it over. Couldn't we? I mean, couldn't we try to make a go of it? Once more? For Charlie? Even for ourselves perhaps?'

There was silence at the other end of the line. He wondered for a second whether they had been cut off. She gave a little giggle, as if sharing some low secret with him.

'Patience? Patience?'

'Oh, but Gareth,' she said at last, as if explaining something to a child. 'You know that's impossible. You know I can't.'

'What do you mean can't?'

'Can't.'

'I see. Any reason?'

'Reason? Reason?' she said with a certain grim humour. 'Do I need a reason? You know the reason.'

'There's someone else, isn't there? Who is she?'

'No,' she said. Then, correcting herself, 'But what if there were? What difference would it make?'

'Could I come to see you?'

'No, Gareth. That would not be a good idea. I'd concentrate on trying to sell the house if I were you.'

'Why?'

'Because,' she said with some exasperation. 'Don't you see? It's over, Gareth. Finished. We're just not the same people, don't you see? We know who we are now. It's not the same.'

'No, I don't see.'

'Ah, well, my dear,' she concluded very calmly, 'then I cannot help you. You will need to adjust to the idea all by yourself.' She rang off. He sat for a while considering his next move. He looked out on the jumble of grey slates glistening in the October rains. It was over. He could see that. He was left with nothing but a single room in an Edwardian hotel. A television set for the evenings and a bookstall in the lobby. And a house to sell in Hampstead so they could share the profits and start again. Alone.

He waited an hour and then went in search of her down in Chelsea. He inspected the panel for her name but there was a blank opposite the number. Perhaps, knowing he would be returning to London after his holiday, she had moved the name in the vain hope of throwing him off. He pressed the bell anyway but there was no answer. He sat in the pub opposite until closing time but no one went in or out and no light appeared in the window. He walked the streets, returning over and over again to the door, a moth to a flame. She had gone. She had somewhere else to go. Anticipating him, she had left quickly, sure of another bed for the night.

He had more luck the next night. From the pub, just at closing time, he had seen her sauntering down the street arm in arm with another woman. They scarcely looked abandoned, he thought, more like two sisters companionably comparing notes. He waited for them to go inside, for the lights to come on in the windows of the third floor. Then he crossed and rang the bell.

There was no answer. He crossed the street again to make sure there was no mistake. Then he went back and leant on the bell, demanding admission.

'If this goes on for another minute, Gareth,' she called from the windows above, 'I shall call the police. Please go away.'

'Patience. Patience.' By now he was crying, the tears on his cheek glistening under the lamplight.

'Go away. You're drunk,' she shouted and closed the window with a bang.

He waited about disconsolately until two o'clock in the morning, when the lights went out and he realized he had no chance. Couples strolling by looked at him curiously, and one or two snickered when they had gone far enough to think they were out of earshot. By the time he returned to the hotel he was thoroughly chilled and sober. He had forgotten a night key and there was no porter. He pressed the bell, but there was no response, not even an audible sound. He blew warm breath onto his hands and shifted his weight from one foot to the other in an effort to keep warm. He pressed the bell again, knowing already there was no possibility of being heard.

He resumed his walking but this time went east and then up a deserted Whitehall, electric-blue under the high street lamps. There was a policeman at the corner of Downing Street who eyed him curiously but, seeing he was an English gent, made no move to stop him. Otherwise the vast avenue, in the daytime thronged from one end to the other, was as silent as a deserted tomb.

Under the arcades of Charing Cross he drank detestable sweet tea from the cabbies' pull-up. There were dozens of derelicts, wrapped in brown paper, asleep on the pavement. Occasionally one stirred, sat up, scratched a puzzled head, and fell back with the rest. Another policeman passed, looking them over, resigned to their presence.

'Missed the last train, have you, guv?' a cabbie asked as they both watched a late tramp settling next to the others for the night. He was arranging his brown paper with pedantic attention to detail. 'Can I take you somewhere? Cost you double, but better than hanging about here all night for the first train.'

'No, thank you,' Gareth said, looking down from his great height. 'I only live round the corner.'

There was something in his eye which told the cabbie all he needed to know. 'Oh, it's like that, sir,' he said with customary kindliness. 'I am sorry. I only asked.'

- ABYSS -

His father, of course, was right: the next stage of his life was very difficult.

The letter, when it did come, was clear and concise but, as intended, gave nothing away. He had whiled away empty days selling the house and consulting lawyers about the divorce. He was alarmed at how little was going to be left over when the two sides had agreed to the terms of the settlement. He put his share of the money into a deposit on a small house on the unfashionable slope of Dulwich, all he could afford. Before he could move, however, the letter had come in and he had spent nearly all of the twenty minute ride on the Underground trying to decipher it. He was thus unnerved for the next interview with Watson, which went as badly as his worst fears.

'Protocol,' Benton said with dull finality. 'I might have known.'

'It's not a bad job when you get used to it,' Watson suggested. Benton could not fail to notice the fat file on the desk—his own, doubtless, complete with all the details. 'I admit it's not the best,' Watson went on, 'but you've left us in a bit of a fix. It's all we could come up with at short notice.'

'I've been waiting about for three months,' Benton reminded him. 'Surely you could find something more—well, relevant?'

'I'm afraid that's out of the question.' Watson's tone was firmer now. 'We're neither of us in much of a position to negotiate. I because you've come to us rather out of the blue. And you because—well, you know . . .'

'No. I don't know. I can't be the first case you've ever had. You must have a drill to cope with it.'

'Yes, we do,' Watson said wearily. 'This is it. You must see that. It sort of follows automatically, don't you see? It's not so difficult to follow the reasoning.'

'I'm not trusted any more,' Benton said with pretended indignation. 'That's it, isn't it, Dick? You none of you trust me any more.'

'Perhaps you'd like to consider your position,' Watson replied, 'and let me have an answer in, say, forty-eight hours?' Benton opened his mouth to protest but Watson had a hand up already. 'Forty-eight hours. All right?' he said. He got up, the interview at an end. He held a hand out and Benton could think of nothing more useful to do than shake it glumly.

'Dick,' he said, meaning to add a lot more.

'Gareth,' Watson said with finality, cutting off further communication. Gareth had the feeling of a door being shut on him, not exactly angrily but certainly with impatience. He could imagine what they had been saying to one another, there behind the doors in the Department.

What? Benton? Gareth Benton? You must be joking.

I only wish I were, old boy.

Lor'. Whatever got into him? Ambitious sod, always was. How did he get himself in such a fix?

Read the file. Seems pretty obvious. At least it was a girl. But he fell right into it. So it seems he was a fool after all. A womanizer and a fool.

So what happens now?

Protocol happens now. Give us time to sort this mess out.

Benton telephoned the next day accepting the job, as Watson knew he would. He could hear Watson's voice positively beaming at the other end of the line and wondered whether, given the evident relief, he should not have held out for something better.

'Thank you,' Watson said. 'I'm sure it's for the best. You'll see. It will be a lot more fun than you think. You have got a uniform, I take it? No? We'll have to kit you out with one, in that case.'

And thus Benton joined the little world of Protocol, the world where everything is just as it seems. He was at once struck by the unimaginable pettiness of the detail, the concern—he had to remind himself—of grown men and women. He still had a good, clear mind however and took some pride in getting it right, whatever it was. The job brought him many contacts in Church and State. He later realized that the officers of Church House must have noticed a firmer hand in the arrangements and had been making enquiries.

It took him longer to master the language, as remote from English as Court Japanese.

'Ah, Mr Benton. I have a slight problem, and as always when I have a slight problem I think of you. Mr Benton, we all say; now that Mr Benton understands.'

'Excellency. How nice to hear from you again so soon. To what do I owe this pleasure?'

'My wife, Mr Benton, my wife.'

'How is the dear lady?'

'Fine, fine. She was asking this morning when we might receive our invitations to the so excellent ceremony on the twenty-ninth? Our invitations, yes? And, of course, our ticket to the car park. It is essential to have the car park ticket here in your so beautiful, but alas so crowded, capital.'

'Your Excellency is of course aware that the event is a Commonwealth one. It is the High Commissioners only that we have troubled on this occasion. We have no desire to disturb the week-end for the Ambassadors.'

'But we are friends, Mr Benton, allies almost. It would be no trouble to attend on Her Majesty, who will, I believe, grace the ceremony with her presence? We feel we should be no less— what shall I say?—no less appreciative of an opportunity to participate in this august occasion as our Commonwealth colleagues.'

'Alas, Excellency, there are many High Commissioners and space is so very limited.'

'If I may mention a personal consideration, a mere trifle but a painful one. It is that my wife's mother, despite her great age, has come over for the Christmas season to be here with her grandchildren. She had hoped to have the indescribable honour of a formal presentation to Her Majesty during her stay.'

'I quite understand, believe me, Excellency. If there were anything, anything at all I could do, I would not hesitate. But as things stand, I fear . . .'

'Ah, well. I shall try to explain at home. The ladies are not always so reasonable as one could wish. You will appreciate my small difficulty.'

'Only too acutely, Your Excellency. When seeking to explain matters to Madame you will not fail, I hope, to express my personal sorrow. You could add that I shall seek an early opportunity to compensate for my regrettable inability to help on this occasion.'

One of the indispensable requirements was the ability to change gear with the least possible evidence of strain.

'Garry? Is that you, Garry?' The voice was unmistakably transatlantic, doing its damnedest to be friendly.

'Yes, Ed. What can I do for you?'

'The Ambassador here is hopping mad, Garry, but hopping. I forgot to order his Cup Final tickets, would you believe it? And his small son is crazy about soccer. They say the kid goes to bed with a soccer ball in place of a teddy bear.

'No problem, Ed. We can take care of that. How many do you want?'

'Three for them and if you could find another for me . . . I can't say I'm nuts about soccer, but I am his Private Secretary and it would sorta look good, y'know?'

'I'll see what we can manage. All right?'

'Thanks, Garry. You're a pal.'

Click. The next call.

'Mr Benton? Good. I have to register a formal protest at the totally inadmissible behaviour of the metropolitan police this morning.'

'I am truly sorry to hear that, Excellency. They have a reputation, I believe, for courtesy and tact.'

'They have, Mr Benton, just removed my wife's car and taken it to the police compound, which I believe to be behind Waterloo Station. Some way behind.'

'I am sorry, Excellency. I shall have a word with the responsible authorities. Where had she parked it?'

'In the bus lane outside Fortnum's.'

The winter passed wearily enough and dragged sluggishly into a wet spring. He detested the house he had bought and the halting train journeys in the scruffy crowded compartments. The whole of London seemed to suffer from an incurable bronchial complaint and the pavements were permanently greasy with moisture. There were strings of Embassy cocktail parties which he had come to loathe but his free evenings were worse: totally empty with something simple enough for him to cook while he watched television. The divorce proceedings seemed interminable despite his agreement with Patience on all the essentials. Even his visits to see Charlie at his boarding school were wearisome: cold bedrooms in the only hotel for miles and long hours cooped up in the hotel lounge on rainy days with neither of them having enough to say. He was by now gentle with the boy, his only real contact with the rest of humanity.

The end came in April. Watson asked to see him and for a wild moment he imagined that he was forgiven, that ways had been found to wipe the slate clean.

'You surely didn't imagine that?' Watson said. 'I only wish we could. No one likes this kind of thing. You've been a good officer and really it's been a quite distinguished career. But there it is. We have no choice.'

'No choice? No choice?' Benton said, his voice rising. 'Of course you have a choice. You surely can't get rid of me, just like that? Without a trial, without an appeal? The idea is ridiculous.'

'Ridiculous or not, those are the rules. It was most carefully gone into. There is a Committee. Believe me, no one is sorrier than we are.'

'But the reason?' Benton shouted. 'The reason?'

'The photographs,' Watson said quietly. 'Some have been intercepted. We have seen the photographs.'

'I see,' Benton replied very quietly, feeling himself go over the edge. 'And to whom were they addressed, if I might be allowed to know?'

'Your son Charles. We knew they could get nothing out of it. But we suspected they might try it just out of spite. We kept a check on his mail, poor little chap.'

'Bastards. The bastards.'

'I know. But don't you see? You will always be vulnerable. Always. Always. We can't keep check permanently. You do understand? Believe me, it's best if you go. You'll come to see this in the end. Just give it a week or two, I would.'

After that, the divorce which came through in May scarcely seemed to hurt at all. He did not attend the court but spent the day instead clearing out his desk, making way for his successor. He started with his neat drawers of private correspondence where everything was arranged by categories: official Christmas cards, for instance, or dinner invitations or the series of short notes he had exchanged with colleagues on promotion or on transfer, an essential lubricant in any close-knit society of itinerants. He found he wanted to remember none of them, piled them into a disused diplomatic bag, and rang for a messenger to take them away. This ancient figure with his lined sympathetic face found him smashing the photograph of Patience against a corner of the desk.

'There. There,' Benton said, throwing it in with the rest, 'that's just about everything, I think.' Patience in her windcheater and Hermès scarf gazed up at them myopically through shattered slivers of glass.

'A shame,' the messenger said. 'I could of found a use for the frame.'

Alone again, he went through his confidential cupboard, sorting out what was to be left for his successor and what was to be destroyed. It was here he came across his ancient copy of the seniority list, something he had forgotten about in all his troubles. He remembered with guilt how he used to note the tiny mistakes, the minor character defects of his contemporaries— Napier, Cross, Watson, and the rest—in an attempt to assess his chances against theirs. It seemed so long ago that he wondered if he had actually been so crass or he had only dreamt of doing so. One glance inside confirmed his worst fears. Reddening, he quickly added it to the pile he was preparing for the shredder.

He paused longer over his collection of his own best pieces, including his analysis of the Czechoslovak crisis, the foundation of his former reputation. He thumbed through them, wondering whether he might not one day need them to remind him of a time when he was, if not happy, at least useful. Finally, he added them neatly to the neat pile, trying to avoid looking down too long into the depths of his own despair.

He was ready. He picked up the pile and went next door where, under the eyes of the silent secretaries, he pushed the documents page by page through the shredder. He knew the girls were staring at him with pity behind his back, but he was determined not to meet their glance.

Afterwards he went back to his room to look out one last time from the window. He stared down on Clive of India dominating his end of the park. Clerical-grey figures were hurrying up the steps, others hurrying down, still others clustering to exchange a few words before separating to go on to their destinations. Mandarins, he thought: those who decide, those who know. Only then did he begin to realize how much his career had meant to him, how much he minded losing it. He turned abruptly and strode out unseeing into the corridor of high doors.

At the end of the corridor he went out through the aptly named hole-in-the-wall into the ceremonial pomp of the main corridor where in effigy along the walls a Victorian Britannia still dispenses the law unto her subject peoples. He passed the well-remembered liftshaft of his first day and outside the Foreign Secretary's suite of rooms turned again down the Grand Staircase, which he imagined he was looking on for the last time. He went down as slowly as he could, inhaling the familiar atmosphere, oblivious to the agency terminals under the stairs chattering out the stories. He was remembering the occasions he had stood with the crowds in the balconies above applauding an outgoing Foreign Secretary descending among the floodlights and the popping of a dozen flash bulbs, one of the hallowed institutions of the house. He smiled inwardly. His own departure was totally unremarked, almost as if he had already become invisible. There were, however, sympathetic faces in the lobby to the Park Door, the private one reserved for the most senior officials.

'Good luck, Mr Benton,' the chief porter said. 'It's a shame.'

'Thank you,' Benton replied, regretting that he had never learned this admirable official's name.

Outside on the green, rain was beginning to bespot the row of government cars awaiting their various ministers. He crossed Horse Guards Parade, threading his way through the ranks of the private cars with official permits. The clock on the old War Office cupola was giving off its traditional formless tinkle for quarter to twelve, soon to be drowned out by the bronze gong of Big Ben, as always a full fifteen seconds behind.

Benton realized, with a start, that for the first time in his life he had nothing whatever to do. He was without employment and without prospects. Ambition had suddenly, just like that, become ridiculous. Behind every window in the wide arc from the Old Admiralty to Birdcage Walk there were people at work, plotting their next move, formulating however subconsciously their ultimate goals. Only he was cast out, useless, without point.

And, he added to himself with a stab of pain, wifeless. By now, once again, unmarried with no one to turn to. The rain was gathering strength. He hurried across the Mall amidst the swishing taxis and up the Duke of York steps to the Club. Surely, he thought, there in the classified columns of *The Times* there would be news of something he could do, something by which he could begin to define himself once more, however humbly, as his father had so proudly defined himself in the past.

- RESCUE -

Rescue came, as it so often does, through the Club. He was seen to come into the morning room, as usual, to read through the vacancies advertised in the newspapers. There, deep in *The Times*, he became aware of someone sitting expectant in the next leather armchair. He looked up surprised to see a vaguely familiar face peering at him owl-like through thick glasses. A twinkling cleric, nattily attired in purple vest and socks, a small crucifix in the lapel of his smart dark suit.

'Good morning,' the figure said cheerfully. 'You're Gareth Benton, I do believe.'

'That's right. And you're . . .?'

'Witherspoon. John Witherspoon. We were up at Jude's together. I was reading Theology. Played rugger for the college. But then the clergy all do that.'

'I remember.'

'Of course I was a bit thinner in those days. You know, your name came up at a meeting I chaired yesterday.'

'Oh?'

'Yes. I'm chairman of several committees over at Church House and we were talking over the need to have a good Protocol Officer, a professional. Liaison with the Government, the World Council of Churches, and whatnot. Somebody, I forget who, said you were first-class but out of a job, sort of. Funny you should be here. Talk of the devil.'

'Yes. As a matter of fact I am. Out of a job. I've resigned from the Foreign Office.'

'Any particular reason?'

'Change of life, perhaps. It coincided with a divorce. It's time to think things through, start again from scratch.'

'Ah. Like to think about Church House?'

'I'm not a churchman.'

'Nothing to do with it, old boy. It's the protocol thing we need. The last chap was a disaster even though he was frightfully pi. And he wore his collar the wrong way round. I say, why don't we have lunch next week, say Thursday? That gives you nearly a week to think about it.'

'All right. How do I get in touch with you?'

'At Church House. I'm the Bishop of Penge. Don't laugh. Someone has to be the Bishop of Penge.'

And thus it was that a month later Benton found himself entering under the steep façade of Church House behind the Abbey to direct the protocol of the General Synod of the Church of England.

He was at once fascinated and appalled. Fascinated by the standard of debate and of the high seriousness with which small problems were discussed in even the most informal of committees, so different from the mocking disrespect of the Foreign Office, where the gravest world issues, perhaps because they were so grave, could be treated with glancing ironies. Appalled by the passions which could be so easily aroused over what seemed to him to be wholly irrational causes.

'Too easy, old boy. The clergy have always been like that. Think of all the nonsense over the date of Easter. You remember, first find the Golden Number, then guide your eye sidewise to the Left Hand in the First Column, and so on?'

'I haven't understood a word.'

'It's all in the Prayer Book. You can find our calculation of Easter Day from the year 2200 to the year 2299 if you're so minded. The Orthodox, of course, won't have any of it. They would die in the last ditch for their version. They're quite mad, most of my brother clergy, bless them.'

'I tell you what, though. One thing's certain. We're moving fast in the direction of Rome. It makes a lot of sense. I know there are some bishops against it and quite a lot of clergy in the parishes. But it makes sense. You watch.'

And sure enough, over the decades the movement had been gathering momentum. In the middle sixties the Archbishop of Canterbury had visited the Pope for the first time since the Reformation, a practice repeated by each of his successors until it became routine.

Also routine was the posse of the lower clergy that regularly greeted the Archbishops at Heathrow with banners proclaiming 'No Popery,' the same posse that turned up in St Peter's Square to sing hymns throughout the encounters.

By the seventies, low mass was celebrated in the side chapels at Canterbury with increasing frequency; the Cardinal Archbishop of Westminster preached in the Abbey to a congregation of his separated brethren and thereafter attended the greatest state functions, the jubilees and the Royal Weddings, as a matter of course. A Royal Wedding was permitted according to the Catholic rite and performed by a Catholic priest even though the children, it was known, were to be brought up in the Anglican tradition. In the early eighties, the diplomatic post at the Vatican was upgraded from Legation to a full Embassy: the pronuncio in London was at the same time upgraded to a full nuncio, and in time the embarrassing holder of the post was replaced by the cardinal who was one day to become Boniface X, Bishop of Rome, the Supreme Pontiff, successor to the Fisherman Apostle.

And then the Pope, the Polish one who made waves, visited Britain in the year of the Lord 1982. Virtually the whole Bench of Bishops expressed the wish to attend his mass at Coventry until it came down from high places that so great a show of enthusiasm might be imprudent in the circumstances.

'Some of the lower clergy wouldn't like it, old boy. It seems that some of them prefer women priests, imagine. And they're the lot that rabbit on about Roman celibacy, for goodness' sake. They need to be jollied along a bit. The bishops are for it to a man, of course.'

The Pope went to Canterbury and there in the glorious Corona beyond the Trinity Chapel, where Becket's head had been kept during all the years of the pilgrimage, he prayed with the Archbishop for church unity. By this time the Corona had become a memorial to all the Christian martyrs of the twentieth century whatever their denomination: the heroic Father Kolbe of Auschwitz as well as the heroic Pastor Bonhoeffer, hanged from a meat hook in reprisal for the July plot.

Describing the ceremony, *The Times*' religious correspondent congratulated the Anglican church on its evident vitality and the authenticity of its traditions even in these awesome circumstances. Witherspoon took a different view.

'Mark my words. It's only a matter of a few years now. We live in the most irreligious country in the world. I sometimes think St Augustine shouldn't have bothered, that it was all a waste of time. It makes no sense, we few Christians quarrelling here in England. The barbarians are already inside the gates, have been for ages. All we've got to do is keep the women out: if we start ordaining women, it'll be the end.'

Throughout the period, then, Benton found enough to do to keep himself occupied. But, as always in such cases, the full extent of his wound only gradually became apparent to him. His reading of the Latest Appointments recording the movement of ambassadors on the court and social page of *The Times* became obsessive: at the appearance of each familiar name the cut went deeper until he could scarcely pick up the paper without wincing. The Church was amiably eccentric, but his heart ached at each remembrance of the powerful, even elegant, machine across the Park which had so conclusively rejected him. From time to time his work took him to the Foreign Office and he again trod the tremendous courtyard and the high-ceilinged corridors, grieving. He shrank from the prospect of running into any of his contemporaries, always so solicitous, none of them daring to ask any of the right questions or indeed to mention their own expectations for fear of embarrassing scenes.

Yet run into them he did, of course, and this invariably when his mind was clouded with fresh regrets. He suffered acute attacks of self-hatred, which had to be restrained lest they become too obvious and make him even more vulnerable to their secret mocking laughter. It was no wonder he was a sight to be feared, someone to avoid unless an encounter was inevitable.

'Hello, Gareth. What brings you here?'

'The Royal Wedding. I've been appointed temporary assistant to the Earl Marshal. Protocol, of course.'

'Ah. Of course. Must be fascinating.'

'Yes it is. Fascinating.'

As a result of his work on that particular Royal Wedding he was awarded the CVO from the hands of the sovereign, and for a moment there was a thin gleam of satisfaction in his heart. And then he saw that Napier had been knighted and sent as Ambassador to Brussels, and the skies darkened again to their habitual grey. In such moods he was impossible and many in Church House came to regret his appointment, despite his evident skills which made him indispensable, almost irreplaceable.

*

Grey certainly, but his life was not constantly and uniformly black.

In the Underground from Victoria to Westminster one foul November day which ruled out his habitual walk through the Park he felt a tap on his shoulder.

'Hello,' said a familiar voice. 'Do you come here often, as we say at the Palais?'

His heart turned over as he turned to look once again on her lovely hair, gold-on-brown. 'Beth,' he said, which was all he needed to say.

She was ten years older, and now in her mid-thirties when women, contrary to the general opinion, reach their full bloom, the maximum realization of younger potentialities. There was a fullness, a roundness in her face which softened the slight angularity of her Berlin days. 'Bastard,' she said, smiling, 'abandoning a girl like that just when we might have got a little thing started.'

'You can understand,' he said. 'It was of course a mistake. But that's all I seem capable of making.'

'Perhaps I should say, poor bastard,' was her reply. 'I can't say I've had much luck in that line either.'

'Married? Divorced?'

'Married and divorced. And back in the office pounding a typewriter again. Only they're electric now. And the telephones are automatic, would you believe?' She smiled at him in the old

233

way and he felt a sudden relief from strain, as if a siege had been lifted. They got out at Westminster and walked up the stairs to the street as old friends. He offered her his arm so that she could huddle under his umbrella and they sauntered in the vile weather to the Foreign Office entrance. He could feel her slender body under his arm. Through all the layers of their clothing, she was as firm as ever.

'Beth,' he said, suddenly awkward.

'Yes?'

'Could you manage lunch today? I must talk to you.'

'Of course, silly man. I thought you'd never ask.'

Her accent had improved, or so he thought, but she still breathed the knowingness, the lack of pretence that things were other than they were, that marked the London girl he had known and had so foolishly turned away from all those years before.

'I love it when you smile,' she said. 'Sort of crooked, you know? Crooked but not dishonest. I never thought you were dishonest, despite everything.'

*

And from the beginning it was a relationship based on total honesty. She made it plain that there was no question of marriage or even of living together. 'Once bitten, twice shy,' she said early on and she thereafter made it absolutely clear she meant it. They would meet in one of the Westminster pubs after work two or three times a week. They would go to a theatre or have dinner somewhere, and she would occasionally give him supper at home. Whatever happened, they would invariably end up in bed, but, however late, she would insist on his returning to his own house on the dreary edge of Dulwich. There were never any exceptions no matter the weather.

'But it's snowing. It's the coldest winter since 'forty-seven.'

'Too bad, big boy. Up you get. See you Thursday.'

'Ah, Beth. This once? Just this once?'

'No. Not this once. We agreed, remember?'

The compensation was that she was quick and funny. No matter how much he had raged inwardly, or even outwardly, during the day, she could disarm him in a moment.

234

'You look as if you've spent the day killing people.'

'Beth, you've no idea. The stupidity. The sheer, crass stupidity.'

She patted his hand. 'I'll buy you a drink,' she said 'and you can tell me all about it. You can sit here and practise unknitting your jaw muscles. Remember, we've got to eat tonight. You can't do that if you've got lockjaw.'

She was also as incapable of pretence about herself as about anything else. Gareth was constantly in amazement when she talked of her past, so different from his own. The life of the streets seemed bawdier than he had ever imagined, even for girls that looked like goddesses.

'The first time? Against the kitchen wall with my mother and father asleep in front of the television next door. I was so frightened I can't remember what happened. If anything.'

'Why did you let him do it? Then, I mean?'

'I didn't want him to go around saying I was a cock-teaser, I suppose. No girl in our neighbourhood would want to have a reputation for that.'

'What had you been doing to him beforehand?'

'More or less what I'm doing now, I imagine.'

'Goodness.'

'We all did it. The girls in the class thought you weren't normal if you hadn't had your knickers off by the time you were sixteen. You just weren't trying. The boys were all risking jail. We could have blackmailed half the neighbourhood.'

'Love? Oh sure, we used to fall in love. Big deal.'

'Why big deal?'

'Most of the girls I knew were married by the time they were nineteen. With, as we used to say, a bun in the oven. Awful expression, don't you think? The poor girls were finished after that, in the same fix as their mothers. The boys too, of course. All in the name of love.'

'And why not you?'

'I was lucky. I was a bit brighter than most and my parents cared. So I went to Secretarial College instead.'

235

'Weren't you tempted?'

'What? By Hackney? You've got to be joking. That's why falling in love was so painful. There was never any future in it for either of us.'

It was in this manner that Gareth first learned something about real people. Beth was very wise and very tolerant, something she had learned to be from her earliest youth. She gave him no pretext for believing she was entirely faithful to him either. She invariably went on holiday alone and would come back from the Greek islands or Spain or wherever, bronzed and fitter than ever, her hair more gold than brown, and smiling a secret smile whenever she glanced away from him. He tried rage the first time but she only looked at him more frankly than ever.

'Come off it, Gareth,' she said, 'you know you're not really jealous. You're only doing it for the form.' And he had to admit to himself, ruefully, that the witch was right. 'I've got a good idea,' she added, half-closing her long lashes at him as she had done so long ago. 'You can take me off to bed and show me how much you missed me.'

And a couple of hours later, when, satisfied, he was fingering her light bones and laying a hand on her long waist, she suddenly gripped him passionately.

'Ah, Gareth, Gareth,' she gasped, 'how nice to be home.'

Later still, when they had finished again, she giggled.

'That's what my mum and dad used to say,' she explained. 'Every time they came back from Margate or whatever they'd look around the old place with its floral wallpaper and the hideous china ornaments on the television in the corner and say, "It's nice being on holiday, yuss, but it's even nicer to be back."'

Her hand held his so affectionately that he knew she was teasing.

Eventually he felt confident enough to tell her the whole story, leaving out none of the more humiliating parts. To his amazement he found the experience soothing, but then that was always her effect on him.

'I knew,' she said simply when he had finished. 'The externals anyway. It's all around the Office. It comes up from time to time. I say nothing, of course, not even that I know you.'

He recognized glumly that this was inevitably the case. No matter how quiet people tried to keep about scandal, it was in the nature of large organizations that someday everybody would know. The externals at least. He just had to endure it, as he endured so many other humiliations.

'Poor Gareth,' she said in the silence. 'It still hurts, doesn't it?'

'Yes. I am afraid it does. As you say, the falling in love was painful enough, knowing there was no future. The fact is I now don't even know if there is a past. The most important thing that ever happened to me, and it's just a great mocking enigma. With consequences.'

'Well,' she objected, 'at least it's made you a better man.'

'I'm not even sure about that. I'm savage with people, I know that. I can't help it. Every day I'm confronted with my blasted hopes. A life in ashes. A failure. Broken.'

'Yes,' she agreed. 'Broken. But better. You do see that?'

'Thank you,' he said simply. 'This may not be love, you know, Beth, but it begins to feel uncommonly like it.'

'Oh, no,' she cried. 'No. No. No. You must go.'

'Must I?'

'Yes,' she concluded firmly and he knew better than to press his objections further.

She made two concessions in the course of this long relationship. She went with him to his father's funeral in 1988 and she allowed him to use the legacy to move closer to her rented flat behind the Kings Road, the unfashionable end.

'Thank you,' he said humbly on both occasions.

The funeral service took place in the College chapel. The old Master, long since retired, gave the address recounting all Sir Robin's academic and scientific triumphs and his many services to the great, proud old College that he had loved so much. As so often on these occasions, Gareth noted, there was only glancing reference to the dead one's prickly, even disagreeable character ('challenging' was Sir Humphrey's word for it) and even less mention of his exiguous, perhaps nonexistent, faith. Despite Gareth's sorrow, which was genuine enough, he was struck by the ludicrous thought that the old Master evidently considered himself a referee for Sir Robin's next appointment. Gareth's mood changed again when he was called upon to read the sombre lesson, taken, as always, from St Paul. From the lectern he looked down on the massed congregation under the canopied roof, almost too moved to speak.

'Now is Christ risen from the dead,' he began and looked up. He caught Beth's look far back in the congregation, and guessed her eyes were blurring with tears. He took a deep breath and plunged on. The magnificent words took on a life of their own. He felt the first lightening at the words, 'Behold, I show you a mystery; We shall not all sleep, but we shall all be changed.' And at the words 'O death, where is thy sting?' he recognized the lightening for what it was. I am free, he thought. I am free at last.

At the crematorium chapel she stood with him, sorrowing, in the first row. There were surprised looks in the pews behind, which Gareth could guess at, even if he could not see them. Too bad, he thought, but what is the point of freedom if one cannot be free? He was following the hymn sheet when they lowered his father's body to the fires. He looked up after one of the verses to find the coffin had simply vanished.

There was a memorial service in the hospital chapel a few days later attended by the greatest in the land; the list in *The Times* account of the service covered several column inches. By this time the will had been read, leaving Gareth a surprisingly small legacy, enough nonetheless to enable him to move closer to Beth.

It was about this time that rumours had begun to circulate about a possible final reconciliation of the Church of England and the Church of Rome. The first plan, it was said, was for this to be brought about by a pilgrimage to Rome of the hierarchy, accompanied by lay members of the Church Assembly representing the faithful.

'It won't wash, old boy,' Witherspoon said. 'It smacks too much of proud Rome placing a heel on our necks. They'll have to come up with something better than that.'

'What, for instance?'

'Search me. We could, I suppose, try Avignon. At least it's

neutral,' Witherspoon said, snickering at his little historical joke.

The process was temporarily interrupted when John Paul II died and the interminable proceedings to find a worthy successor were begun. But a decision was finally reached, as it must be reached, and it seemed too good to be true when the new Pope immediately suggested he return to Britain where he had been nuncio, to effect the reconciliation.

'Of course it's too good to be true. You'll see there'll be strings attached. It's not for the Pontiff to bow the knee. And after a concession like that he can impose any conditions he likes. What marvellous news. Marvellous.' Witherspoon's face was rubicund with joy. It was as if he had had the Beatific Vision.

'From what I can see, there will be much resistance from the nonconformists. Have you seen what the Ulstermen have been saying in Belfast?'

'Some nonconformists, I grant, but by no means all. And anyway there's nothing any of us can do about the Irish. The Church of England has to choose, and it's bound to return to mother. There's no future with the radicals. Still less with the women, of course.'

The conditions caused much heart-searching, but by now expectations on both sides had been raised to a point where there was no going back. High Mass at Canterbury on the Feast of St Thomas of Canterbury, greatest of martyrs in the struggle between king and clergy, honoured for centuries until cast down by the schismatic Henry, first head of the Church of England, he of the six wives.

'A pretty shrewd blow, that,' Witherspoon observed. 'Henry VIII had the shrine despoiled and the bones scattered to the four winds. He had the great ruby, the watchamacallit . . .'

'The Régale de France?'

'That's it, you evidently know the story. Louis VII of France gave it to the shrine. Henry had it made into a thumb ring, which he wore as a symbol of the supremacy of the State over the Church. He also suppressed the feast; there is no mention of it in the Prayer Book.'

'Do you think the Church will accept?'

'Who? Our Church?'

'Yes.'

'Of course we will. It's too late to back down now. In any case, old St Thomas is the genuine article. A real, consecrated English saint.'

'Like Thomas More, you mean?'

'Oh, we'll be saying masses on More's feast day—July ninth—before my time is out,' Witherspoon replied. He added with admiration. 'A clever operator, that Boniface. He may look saintly enough, but like his church he has forgotten nothing, forgiven nothing.'

'You don't sound too happy about it.'

'Radiant, old boy. Delirious. Thank God, we have to submit, we have no other choice. He'll make it easy for us, you see.'

And that is precisely what Boniface did. All the propaganda emerging from the Vatican was directed to the human side of the decision. Tales were told of the former nuncio forming the ambition to effect the reconciliation of the churches during his years in London; of his subsequent fasting and prayers when he was Patriarch of Venice; of his personal devotion to the memory of St Thomas first inspired by a visit to Canterbury with his friend the present Archbishop. None of it untrue, but it somewhat innocently concealed the true symbolism of the event, which would, as all knew it would, echo forever down the ages.

There was thus some grumbling in the press from the evangelicals but with a ceremony to dazzle the entire world, even they could say nothing which could not be neutralized, contained. In Northern Ireland, the irreconcilables raved from their pulpits and threatened to march; but by now the entire British public, for the most part totally agnostic, had had enough of Northern Ireland, and the official hierarchy got warm support from millions who were otherwise indifferent.

Stands to sense, I mean. I don't hold with it, any of it. But you've got to admit they should have got together years ago.

You're right, Syd. I mean, they all believe the same thing, don't they, when you get right down to it? They've no cause to quarrel all the time.

Yes. Too true. I do believe it's my shout. The same again?

Benton played his part in the arrangements, which took nearly a year to perfect. At first this was a minor role since it was properly for Lambeth Palace, the Archbishop's secretariat, to take the lead. But gradually it dawned on the Palace that the protocol was trickier than they had imagined since the Pope, although a spiritual leader, was also a Head of State. Benton was drafted in to reconcile the conflicting elements. This brought him into almost daily contact with the Foreign and Commonwealth Office, summoning up the old demons he had, with Beth's help, succeeded in laying, if only spasmodically, to rest.

There was a Christmas party gathering in the public bar, but the lounge was nearly empty. They had it almost to themselves, but from the first moment she could see something was terribly wrong.

'I saw Charles Napier in the office today.'

'And how was he? Is Rome all that it's cracked up to be?'

'All right. He's got another post. It sounds like Paris. Either that or Washington.'

'Oh, my dear. I'm sorry. It hurts, doesn't it? After all these years, it still hurts.'

She did not need an answer. She could see from his white face, his colourless lips, that he was stricken. There was nothing she could say, she knew that. She sought to distract.

'Your horoscope for this month is terrible. No wonder you're having such a bad time.'

'Is it?' he said listlessly, despair mounting in his eyes.

'Wait a sec and I'll read it to you.' She fished her magazine from her bag under the table. 'Here,' she said brightly. 'It says with Saturn the dominant influence this month, the third week is terrible for you Cancers and the fourth week worse. It apologizes and says things will quickly get better in the New Year.'

'Apologizes?'

'Because of Christmas, silly. You haven't forgotten it's Christmas at the end of the week?'

'I've been so busy I've hardly had time to remember anything outside the office, least of all Christmas.'

'I think,' she said firmly, 'it's time to remember. If you take me home I'll give you your Christmas present.'

'I haven't got one for you yet.'

'Yes, you have. It's the same one you're getting from me.'

'Oh.'

But it wasn't any good. For the first time in years it was a complete washout. 'The sooner this damned Mass is over, the better,' she said grimly. 'It's time for you to retire. I don't think you can take too much more of this. You've got to get it out of your system.'

'When I retire will you come to Marrakesh with me?' he asked, fearful of her response.

'Who? Me?'

'No other.'

'No,' she said and then paused to think about it. She squirmed, naked, under his touch. 'Gareth? Don't do that. I'll think about it.'

'I said I'll think about it. Off you go. Time to sleep. I haven't said yes.'

'But I'm in love with you, Beth. I have been for years.' He felt he was going to cry but knew it would have no effect.

'That's nice,' she said flatly. Then, more kindly, 'Off you go, now. I haven't said no either.'

And thus were all the pieces put into place for the historic day. Nothing was left to chance. The preparations, both Church and State, were meticulous. On the surface there were the minutiae of ecclesiastical precedence to resolve, orders of service to determine, the great church to be got ready, the cameras to install along with miles of cable for the lights. There was also the invisible substructure of security: detectives specially trained to guard Heads of State, ambulances discreetly parked in the quadrangle of the King's School, teams of medical people tucked out of sight in the crypt behind the Martyrdom. The blood groups of the principal participants were known and the building was minutely searched at dawn to ensure there were no intruders and no suspicious-looking parcels left lying about. The Kent constabulary had been mobilized and were in position by nine in the morning. Entrance was by invitation only, and the Friends of the Cathedral were given the privilege of checking the cards and showing the great ones to their seats.

All was in order. Everything had been prepared. Nothing had been left to chance.

And yet there was Welch. Afterwards there was an enquiry, but somehow it was never discovered why he was there and how he got in.

And Benton was also there, heartsore, uncertain, at the end of his tether.

-COMMUNION-

Boniface turned from the Cardinal to take up host and chalice. He raised them both to the full sight of the adoring congregation and the unblinking cameras above.

> *'This is the Lamb of God*
> *Who takes away the sins of the world—'*

He stopped, unable to go on, cup and wafer wavering. He had caught sight of Welch, haggard with protest at the foot of the steps, swaying on his feet as if about to faint. The murmuring began when Boniface turned to the Archbishop, questioning, his dismay visible in close-up to the watching millions.

The pause lengthened. From somewhere deep among the assembled churchmen came an isolated shout of protest, shocking in its reminder of ordinary life, the life without ritual.

A quick-witted cameraman swung quickly to Welch, gazing, mouth agape, at the symbols of sacrifice clutched to Boniface's breast. Welch looked confused, uncertain what to do next. His eyes started to search, turning slowly, inevitably towards Benton, motionless to the left of the altar, one of the crowd by the Bourchier tomb.

A small voice within whispered: not you. Leave it to others. This is not for you. But Welch's eyes told him: you.

They met at the foot of the steps. The murmuring stopped and the silence deepened to a breathless hush. 'Come,' Benton said, too quietly for the microphones to pick up, 'come with me.' With a hand on Welch's sleeve he looked up into the aching eyes, the giant face now corpse white.

'Come,' he said, 'I'll show you the way out. This is no place for you.'

For a moment it looked as if Welch had agreed. He shrugged his shoulders in resignation and turned away. Benton tightened his grip on the sleeve.

A cameraman high above murmured to himself, 'Great television. I should be so lucky.'

Benton was the first to sense the resistance, a millisecond before anyone else. Something snapped; the sleeve was tugged away. Welch bounded up the steps, his face distorted with rage, knife in hand, shouting.

The next few seconds were destined to become a television classic.

Welch's bellow, barely comprehensible in the hollow silence, lost in the echoing vault. One last bound up the two steps to the High Altar. The knife raised, flashing, poised, plunging. Boniface cringing to meet the blow, his face already grimacing.

A figure darting up the altar steps, catching Welch in a flying tackle. The giant figure buckling at the knees under the impact. Both men rolling over and over down the steps under a wave of frantic, shouting detectives.

Welch pulling clear: panting, wild-eyed, the broken butcher's knife still in hand. Benton writhing, face down, the blood slowly spreading outwards from the gash in his morning coat.

Boniface, motionless at the High Altar, host and chalice clutched to his breast.

Great television.

- ABIDING CITY -

Crash of body against body, the scrape of serge along his cheek.
Bruising blows from step to step, interminable as in a nightmare.
One final ringing thud as the giant Welch landed on top of him at
the foot of the altar.

The voice in his ear was whispering fiercely between gritted
teeth. 'No popery. We'll have no popery here.'

The sour whine of Northern Ireland.

Slice. Jar. Snap. Tearing. Burning. Roar of blood, rhythmic in
gathering blackness. Jangling alarm bells of pain.

Nothingness.

*A single albatross steadying in the air. Brown-white wings
embracing blue combers curling blue-white. An empty sea
rocking to its own rhythm, the shadow of the albatross the only
discordance.*

*Twin wing shadows on the water swinging through the ruffling
eye of the wind: obliquely mounting to one crest, skating down-
side into the next hollow.*

White. White walls. Sheet-white walls but glittering. Glittering
in the white light. Blackness gathering in the beat of blood. In it
comes, blackness roaring like the sea.

*A single albatross balancing finely against the wind. Air streams
combing through bright white feathers, fluttering off the trailing
edge, glittering.*

A sun blank-staring at noonday. All horizons empty. Nothing

but the gliding albatross, searching, And always the sea, the rest-
less sea cradling immensities.

One sheet-white wall glittering in the white light. Faces. What?
What? There are faces, serene-browed, the faces of girls over
glittering collars. They are speaking. What? What? Nothing.

The albatross balancing in the air drops stonelike behind a curling
breaker. The albatross rises, a fish in the beak, wriggling, glitter-
ing silver. The neck cranes to gobble.
    Wind shadows resume, flitting over crest, sliding down hollow.

Faces, the faces of girls speaking. There is a cool hand on his
brow, calming. It is a soft hand, compassionate-fingered.
    Elise's hands. At rest, no longer hurrying.
    They cannot think what to play.
    They are confused. They do not know what to play.

No. Not Elise's hand.

Fish in beak wriggling, glittering silver. Gobbled.

Not Elise's hand. Never again Elise's hand.
    Never.

'There, there,' a girl's voice said. 'Don't move, whatever you
do. You're coming along nicely.' She had a soft country voice,
buttery as clotted cream.
    The hand withdrew. Gareth opened his eyes on a white wall,
glittering aseptic in the white light. Of course, he thought, hospital white: it is a hospital. They had placed him on his right side.
He could feel the bandage pressure over his left shoulder and
under the right armpit. Beyond this there was a blank, nothing.
He waited for the searching to begin again.

There was a needle prick in his left buttock. The same voice
said, 'There. That was all right, wasn't it, my dear? You didn't
feel anything, did you?'
    'What was it?' he asked, not really caring what it was.
    'Something to help you sleep, that's all. Good night.'

247

'Good night.'

She fiddled a little, arranging things he could not see. He was falling off the ledge when she stepped out, turning off the lights. He dropped for a while, then floated, soared.

The pain ebbed at last.

The curtains were flung back on weeping clouds. By turning his head cautiously he could watch the raindrops furrow down the glass like tears. The pain throbbed distantly, beyond reach but only just.

'It's morning, look,' a girl's voice said. 'Not a very good morning, I must admit.' It was a different girl but the same country voice, slow but comforting. 'Did you sleep well?'

'Yes, very well,' he whispered, 'but you could hardly call it sleep.'

'What's that? What's that you said?' She was holding his wrist and gazing at her watch.

'I said you could hardly call it sleep. It was more like being dead.'

'Dream then, did you?'

'I dreamt of albatrosses. Or rather, one albatross.' He realized, too late, how foolish this sounded.

'That's nice,' she said vaguely, putting a thermometer in his mouth. A new thought struck her. 'Speaking of being dead,' she said, 'you were very lucky. We only just got you in time. You had almost gone by the time we got you here.'

'Thank you,' he said through his closed lips. He saw she was what would be described as bonny. She had the face of a cheeky child with lips slightly chapped and fresh country skin. She looked into his eyes and grinned.

'Feeling all right?' she asked. 'Not too bad, I hope?'

'I'm all right,' he answered. 'I suppose I'm all right.'

'Having breakfast then? The breakfasts here are famous. More than you can say for the rest of the food.'

'No. No breakfast.'

'A cup of tea then? You'll surely not say no to a cup of tea, will you, darling?' But by now she was at the door. He heard it close behind her before he could reply. It reopened presently, letting the slatternly sound of a tea trolley seep in from the corridor. 'Morning tea,' the same voice said complacently, somewhere out of sight. 'You'll like that, I expect. Nice and sweet, just the thing.'

Her starched white apron approached and a plump country arm came round his neck. She held a blue plastic beaker, the nursery kind, to his lips. Only then did he realize how thirsty he was. He gulped down the revolting liquid, all tannin and sugar, face pressed against the starched, crackly whiteness, and fell back, grateful.

'There, there,' she said letting him down gently. 'There, there. You're going to be all right, darling, honestly you are. Doctor's very pleased. He'll be along shortly. Perhaps you'll feel like breakfast after that.'

The doctor rather resembled Stewart Sherstone, he of Moscow, but the doctor's eyes, with the same shrewdness, were more open and intelligent. He was younger than Gareth expected: younger and more ironic, someone who had seen patients die. He was also brisk: brisk but reassuring. 'You gave us something of a fright' were his first words as he lifted up Gareth's wrist and consulted his watch. 'You were lucky.'

'Yes,' Gareth said wearily. 'I suppose I was. Lucky. What happened?'

'The knife hit your shoulder blade and snapped. A glancing blow, the worst kind. You lost an awful lot of blood. Happily, nothing vital was damaged. You wouldn't be here otherwise. You can thank your lucky stars.'

'My horoscope was terrible this month.'

'Superstitious, are you?'

'No. Someone read it out to me.'

The doctor was cutting away the bandages across his back. Gareth could feel the threads parting. He had to grit his teeth when the final pad was removed, coming away from the damaged skin like pork crackling. There was a slight shifting of weights as the doctor bent down to have a closer look. 'Hmm. Hmm,' the doctor said in an undertone. 'As we hoped. Starting to heal nicely.'

'That's good.'

The doctor caught the note of irony. 'Well,' he said defensively, 'we wouldn't want to lose Britain's latest hero now, would we? Not after all our efforts so far.'

'Is that what I am? A hero?'

'Absolutely. The genuine article. An A-One hero. Picture in all the papers. There are crowds of reporters downstairs, frantic for a story, brandishing cheque-books all over the place. We've half the Kent constabulary downstairs trying to fend them off.'

The doctor began applying fresh dressings himself, a concession to his important patient. Gareth could hear the nurse busying herself with the polythene wrappings.

'It may be healing very nicely,' he said, 'but it is still very sore. I didn't know such pain existed.'

'That's what all my patients say,' replied the doctor. 'There's an awful lot written about mental agony but for intensity it's nothing compared to physical pain.'

'Ah, but you can do something about physical pain.'

'True, true,' the doctor conceded. 'Or at least partly true. Actually, in both cases it is usually time that effects the cure. If there is a cure.'

'That's what my father came to believe. He came to believe that doctors only exist to keep the patients amused.'

'Good Lord, I recognize that. Are you Robin Benton's son?'

Gareth nodded.

'Well, I'll be blessed. I was among his last pupils, you know. Dear, dear. By my time he was very philosophical, almost resigned, you could say. I was expecting a dragon—well, you must know his reputation—but he was very kind. Almost like a father, he was, to his last pupils.'

It was time to apply fresh bandages. The nurse held him up, panting, while the doctor wrapped him over and over. 'Tell me,' Gareth said between gritted teeth. 'Those journalists down there. Have you given them a story yet?'

'I'm playing hard to get,' the doctor answered. 'The price can only rise.'

Gareth felt the nurse rock with silent laughter. The pain was excruciating. 'I'm sorry I asked,' he said.

'Steady on,' the doctor said, 'we're just about finished.'

They laid him down again in the same position and administered an injection. When they had gone Gareth lay helpless on his side, pinned down by the fear of pain, waiting for the drugs to take hold.

Hero, he thought sardonically. If only they knew.

There was a judge, he was sure of it. A judge, perhaps several, sitting somewhere above him, just far enough to be out of sight. They had spoken: cold-toned, passionless, without fault. They had decided, he was certain of it, but pinned helpless as he was, he could not crane far enough to see them. They had just pronounced but he did not know what had been decided.

He waited, an abject figure staring at the rough planks below the judgement table: crudely shellacked, nail-pitted, dark-knotted wherever the grain wavered. Somewhere above, he was sure of it, they were observing, judging. They had judged.

'Come along now,' a voice said just behind him. 'That's it. All over.' It was the official voice, strong, brooking no refusal.

'But the decision. What is the decision?'

'But you know the decision,' the voice said with quiet reasonableness, knowing that he could only agree. 'You took it yourself. That's the system.'

He remembered. He was the judge: he was the judged. Of course, he thought, how stupid of me. And there was no appeal, he knew that too. That was the system. He had been condemned by the system, his own system.

He tried to laugh, but the pain gripped, gripped.

'Come along now,' the voice said crisply. 'That's all. There is no more. You know there is no more.'

Gareth woke with a start, his breath suspended. He breathed in deeply, out-facing the pain. His heart was racing wildly.

'Hello,' Beth said. 'Come here often, do you?' She was smiling uncertainly but there was relief in her eyes. 'You looked as if you were having nightmares.' The room was flooded with light. She was haloed against the window where there were raindrops sparkling, diamonds on the golden glass. The sky beyond was blue-white-blue, with sunlight spreading at each unshredding of the clouds. 'There's someone come to see you,' she said, 'just as soon as you're awake. He had an awful time getting in. All the police downstairs, you see.'

'What does he want? Who is he?'

'I'm not entirely sure. But he comes from the Pope. He says he has an urgent message. I'll go and fetch him if you like.'

When she had gone he watched, fascinated, as the clouds

came finally apart, releasing the blue in all its intensity. He heard the door open, shut again. There was silence, but he knew she had brought someone and that they were standing just inside the door.

'The Pope. You have a message from the Pope?' Gareth said at last in some irritation.

'Yes. He has sent a message.' The voice was deep, a rumbled bass, a foreigner's voice, accentless or nearly so. 'He asks for your forgiveness.'

'Oh, my darling,' said Beth, bursting into tears.